To a great friend
Olga
always
John

Hearts at Home

Hearts at Home

LORI COPELAND
and ANGELA HUNT

Doubleday Large Print Home Library Edition

W PUBLISHING GROUP™

A Division of Thomas Nelson, Inc.

This Large Print Edition, prepared especially for Doubleday Large Print Home Library, contains the complete, unabridged text of the original Publisher's Edition.

**This Large Print Book carries the
Seal of Approval of N.A.V.H.**

Who has not found the heaven below
Will fail of it above.
God's residence is next to mine,
His furniture is love.
　　　　　　　—EMILY DICKINSON, *Poems*

With love and thanks to the
Heavenly Dazees,
Who have become a community
of believers
Just like those who dwell in
Heavenly Daze.

Prologue

"What goes around comes around," the humans on Heavenly Daze tell each other, and I have to smile each time I hear this saying. I've seen the circle of mortal life spin out so many times—a child is born, he grows to maturity, he ignores the wisdom of his elders and learns through painful mistakes. The young man marries a woman, they bear children who grow to maturity, ignore the wisdom of their parents, and learn through painful mistakes. . . .

No wonder the Father is patient with his human creations.

Greetings from Heavenly Daze, where the Creator has blessed us with an unusually mild winter. I am Gavriel, captain of the company of angels who guard this tiny island in accordance with a believer's prayer uttered more than two hundred years ago. Together with Micah, Abner, Elezar, Caleb, Yakov, and Zuriel, I minister to the humans who dwell here, serving them as joyfully as I serve the Master of heaven.

Our people talk about heaven as if it were some distant place . . . but it is within speaking distance to those who belong there. More than they know, heaven's boundaries are but a breath away.

On my last visit to the third heaven I saw the Lord Jesus sitting on a lofty throne before the crystal sea. Hovering around him were mighty seraphim, each with six wings. With two wings they covered their faces, with two they covered their feet, and with the remaining two they flew. In a great chorus they sang, "Holy, holy, holy is the Lord Almighty! The whole earth is filled with his glory!" As the twenty-four elders produced music on their harps, the glorious singing of one hundred million angels shook the Temple to its foundations, and smoke filled the entire sanctuary.

I shall never cease to marvel at the holiness and love of God. Because I have spent thousands of years observing humans, I have learned that any man can fashion a philosophy that supposedly rewards good people with an eternal heaven. Only God, however, could devise a plan through which sinners can enter this blessed and holy place.

I left the highest heaven filled with an urgency of purpose. The things the Lord revealed to me there were too momentous to be lightly received, and I know this coming month will forever change the lives of those who dwell on our little island.

God is faithful. Every heartache he meets with comfort, every tear he repays with joy. Life moves in a spiraling circle, and each created being must tread his path with wisdom, which the Lord freely gives to any who would ask.

As the winter winds chafe our island and hearts huddle around the hearth, I hope you'll join us for another month on the Island of Heavenly Daze.

Chapter One

Annie Cuvier clung to the ferry railing as the sea spat in her face. "Come away from there, Annie girl," Captain Stroble called, his cheeks flaming above the scarf at his neck. "Come inside the cabin before you freeze your nose off."

Annie waited a moment longer—just to prove she was no off-islander who couldn't handle the wind—then tucked the collar of her coat tighter around her throat and ducked inside the warmth of the cabin. She grinned at the stalwart seaman who ran the ferry eleven months of the year. "Thought you and Mazie were heading south for February."

"Ayuh, we are heading to Floridy," Stroble replied, settling one gloved hand on the steering wheel as the boat pushed its way out of Perkins Cove. "Tomorrow morning, if Mazie's feeling better. She's been a mite squamish the last couple of days, and wasn't up to the drive."

Annie took a seat on the bench behind the captain. "Anything the doctor can do?"

"It's just the usual stomach trouble whenever she thinks about leaving the house. No doubt a few days of sunshine will cure her."

Annie smothered a smile as she turned to look out at the gray sea. A psychologist might say Mazie Stroble's legendary attachment to her home bordered on agoraphobia, but with her husband at sea every day and three sons in the navy, Mazie's devotion to the little house on the hill overlooking Perkins Cove seemed downright sensible.

"What brings you home this weekend, Annie?"

She transferred her gaze to the captain. "Nothing special. Aunt Olympia called to say she's planning a little Valentine's party next weekend, so I thought I'd come down to help her get a few things together."

Ostensibly, the statement was true. But something more had drawn Annie home, an urgent feeling she couldn't quite understand. Few of her friends would rush home if even a favorite aunt called with news of a piddling little party, but Olympia had acted as Annie's guardian ever since her parents had died when she was seven years old. So she was coming home out of obligation . . . and concern.

She looked out at the ocean, where the water had turned the color of tarnished silver. Oddly enough, until last October she and Olympia had not been especially close—in fact, they usually yowled like two quarreling cats when they were thrust together. But last October Annie had come home to say farewell to Uncle Edmund, who died the following month, and since that time she had begun to catch glimpses of the island matriarch's softer side. When Aunt Olympia called yesterday, Annie had felt the tug of responsibility.

One of Stroble's bushy white brows rose. "Olympia de Cuvier, feeling sociable? In the dead of winter?"

Annie rushed to her aunt's defense. "It's sort of a thank-you gesture." Because Olympia had been reared to be proper and cultured, outsiders often thought her chilly, but beneath that frail frame and shellacked veneer beat a vulnerable heart. "The island folk were so kind to her after Uncle Edmund passed, so she wanted to do something special for them. But December was too busy with Christmas, and last month was a nightmare—with the sickness and all. She thought the weekend before Valentine's Day might be a fittin' time."

"Ayuh, so it is. Seems to me a Valentine is nothing but a gussied-up thank-you card to the folks who love us."

"I only hope she's okay." Annie frowned out the window. "She was sick last month— along with Pastor Winslow, Floyd, and Stanley Bidderman—all on account of that horrible tomato hybrid I developed. Dr. Marc assured me everyone has recovered, but what if there are lingering side effects?"

Stroble sent a wink and a grin over his shoulder. "Don't fret yourself, Annie. I heard they were right pretty tomatoes."

"But completely indigestible—and, regrettably, digestion is important when it comes to food plants." She sighed and crossed her arms. "Back to the drawing board, I guess. But I'm not sure if I should keep working with tomatoes or move on to another plant. I've been toying with the idea of a winter-hardy zucchini. . . ."

She let her words trail away as the island of Heavenly Daze came into view. Even in the dead of winter, when the winds pushed the waves over the pounding rocks along the southwestern shore, the sight of the church steeple rising from the town center had the power to warm her heart. Seven of the town's structures had been built in 1798, when sea captain Jacques de Cuvier and a few of his cronies had decided to establish a retirement home for pirates who'd seen the light—or decided thievery on the high seas was no longer worth the risk.

As Captain Stroble cut the motor, Annie quirked a brow. Someday she ought to do a little research on old Jacques de Cuvier. As his only direct descendant still living on the island, Aunt Olympia would enjoy learning more about him.

Annie stood, then braced herself for the cushioned impact of the boat against the rubber on the dock. A breath of freezing wind nipped at her nose as the captain flung the cabin door open and stepped outside. Once he had tossed heavy lines around the mooring posts, he turned and tucked his gloved hands beneath his armpits.

"Have yourself a nice bit of neighborin'

then." Stroble smiled her off the boat. "And give your aunt a hello from me and Mazie."

"Have yourself a nice time in Florida," Annie countered, pausing at the railing. "By the way, who's going to run the ferry while you and Mazie are getting suntans?"

Stroble grinned. "The boat's going in for maintenance—time to get the hull scraped and a new coat of paint slapped on. But Crazy Odell will be at your service . . . whenever he's of a mind to take his boat out. Better call his granddaughter before you make plans, just to make sure he's running."

Annie laughed. "And still breathing."

Crazy Odell Butcher, who would take any customer out to Heavenly Daze for the right price, was ninety-two if he was a day. His granddaughter tried to keep him ashore, but he and his boat, the *Sally,* had helped many a desperate traveler cross to Heavenly Daze when the ferry wasn't running. Last Christmas Annie had been grateful for the old daredevil because he got her home in time for Christmas Eve . . . and inadvertently reunited her with A. J. Hayes, the current love of her life.

"Thanks, Captain." She waved goodbye, then crossed the gangplank and hurried down the wooden dock. Across the way, the lights of Frenchman's Fairest gleamed like gold, welcoming her home.

* * *

Dr. Marcus Hayes rapped on the back door of Frenchman's Fairest, startling the old butler who stood at the kitchen counter. Caleb Smith squinted to peer through the lace draperies over the window in the door, then smiled and waved the doctor in.

"Sorry to bother you," Marc said, glad he had stamped the mud from his shoes on the stoop. Caleb's kitchen gleamed as if he expected company.

Marc sniffed the rich aroma of coffee. "That's a good brew."

"You want a cup?" Caleb reached toward the cabinet where he kept the mugs. "We've plenty to spare. Missy had me brew a pot special for Annie, even though I kept telling her the girl prefers my cocoa."

"I'd love a cup." Marc dropped into the chair nearest the door, then peered around the corner that led into the hall. "Olympia around?"

"She's upstairs, sprucin' herself up for

Annie's arrival." The old butler moved slowly, his hands trembling with the palsy of the aged. Noticing the tremor, Marc frowned. During his tenure as Heavenly Daze physician, not once had Caleb Smith been sick . . . in fact, if Marc had not known better, he'd think the Smith name had some value as preventative medicine. Out of the six men surnamed Smith on the island, not one of them had ever visited his clinic. Though Micah rasped occasionally after a full day of singing, Abner worried about his weight, and Elezar professed an allergy to cats, none of them had ever required medical treatment.

He tilted his head as Caleb set a steaming mug of coffee before him. "You feeling okay, friend?"

A gentle curve touched the old man's lips. "I'm fine, Doc, thanks for asking. We're all happy, you know, because Annie's coming home."

"I'm sure you are. That girl is a gem."

Stepping back, Caleb eyed the doctor with an uplifted brow. "How are she and your son getting along? She doesn't talk much about her love life when I speak to her on the phone."

Marc laughed softly. "Alex doesn't volunteer much information, either—I suppose it's not cool for a thirty-two-year-old man to confide in his father about the woman he's seeing. But from what I can tell, they're still dating steadily . . . whenever Alex has free time. Unfortunately, surgeons have a fuller schedule than most doctors."

He felt his smile fade as he stirred a teaspoon of sugar into his coffee. He'd worked hard to get Annie and Alex together, dropping broad hints that at first offended Annie and infuriated Alex. But he'd done it because from the first moment he saw Annie Cuvier, he knew the woman was something special. His son would be a fool to let her slip away.

Yet, if the truth be told, sometimes he worried about Annie dating his son. Life as a doctor's wife wasn't easy. His own wife had been as patient as Job, God rest her soul, but the early days had been hard for her. She'd been busy raising a baby while he was out trying to save the world one patient at a time. Only by the grace of God did they manage to renew their relationship before she died.

He would hate to see Annie endure the

heartache his wife had known. She seemed to crave peace, and as much as he'd love to have her as part of his family, he wasn't sure she could cope with Alex's hectic New York life. As much as he loved his son, he wasn't certain Alex could appreciate the sweet and simple nature of Annie's island-bred soul.

Marc had come to Heavenly Daze to serve his fellow man and find rest for his weary soul. Over the last three years, in the intimacy of a small town and the power of the sea, he had found the reminders he needed to remember that he was only a servant, and God the Lord of all. . . .

Aware that he had dropped his half of the conversation, he gave Caleb a guilty smile. "This is good coffee. Thanks."

A trace of unguarded tenderness lit the older man's eyes. "Are you worried for your son?"

"I'm worried more for Annie." Marc spoke without thinking, then fumbled for words to explain the disloyal comment. "Long-distance relationships are difficult, and with Alex in New York and Annie in Portland, I . . . I just don't want her to get hurt. And I know my son—I know how busy he is, and how detached he can be at times. It's something a doctor has to develop, this detachment, or we'd go a little crazy. Alex is a fine young man, don't get me wrong, but when I think of all the times I begged him to make time for a visit and he never would, I . . . well, I worry for Annie. I don't want her to be hurt."

Uncomfortable with what he'd just shared, he lowered his gaze to his cup, then took a sip. Delicious. Everything Caleb made was wonderful.

"You care deeply for Annie, don't you?"

Marc lowered his mug. "Of course I do. How could anyone not adore a girl like that? I want her to have the wonderful life she deserves. If she can find happiness by marrying my son, I'll be thrilled. I already love her like a daughter. Why wouldn't I be happy to have her as a daughter-in-law?"

The butler's eyes twinkled. "Why not, indeed?"

* * *

Half an hour later Annie sat at Olympia's small kitchen table, her fingers laced around a cup of hot cocoa, her coat tossed across the desk against the wall. Caleb bustled at the counter, mixing a fresh batch of her favorite brownies, while Tallulah, Olympia's terrier, squatted on the floor by Annie's chair, her bright eyes begging for a treat. Olympia sat across from Annie, looking tired, but content.

"Thank you for coming," Olympia said for the third time. "I am simply out of unique ideas for this little party I'm planning, and I *do* want it to be nice. I've had Caleb cutting recipes out of magazines for days."

Annie sipped her cocoa, then smiled around the rim of her cup. Her aunt could teach Martha Stewart a thing or two about the proper way to host a party, and in more prosperous days she had hosted some of the most elegant affairs southeastern Maine had ever seen. Frenchman's Fairest, though now showing its age, was a grand old house, rich in historical lore and stuffed with antiques . . . though every time Annie came home, she noticed one or two pieces were missing.

"EBay," Caleb had confided on her last visit when she had asked about a lovely oil lamp that had once stood in a niche by the stairs. "The best place for quick cash. Mike Klackenbush has been helping Missy sell a few things."

Annie had learned that any mention of missing items was likely to strike a spark. The one thing Olympia would always possess was a sensitive pride.

She set down her cup and peered out the black window of the back door. "Where'd Dr. Marc run off to?"

"Back to his place, I should imagine." Olympia smoothed the lace at her throat, then gave Annie a frayed smile. "Caleb tells me he offered to run out and walk you home from the dock. That was kind—Caleb is getting too old to go out in this cold and windy weather."

"I keep telling her the cold doesn't bother me." Caleb gave Annie a grin. "But you surprised us by coming in unescorted. I think Dr. Marc was looking forward to seeing you."

Annie lowered her gaze as a blush burned her cheekbones. The entire town must be talking about her romance with A.J., otherwise known as Dr. Alex Hayes, son of the town physician. Since October, Dr. Marc had been badgering Annie about meeting his son, and finally, on Christmas Eve, their paths had intersected at the ferry landing in Ogunquit. In the ensuing five weeks they had seen each other several times . . . when they could find time to be together. With Annie living in Maine and A.J. in Manhattan, they weren't together often, but what were cell phones for, if not long-distance dating?

"How is A.J., dear?" Olympia lifted her teacup. "We haven't seen him since Christmas."

"I haven't seen him in two weeks." Annie shrugged. "We try to get together, but, you know, things happen. He has a medical emergency to attend to, his plane is at the mechanic, or something else comes up. But he's fine. We're fine. Everything's fine."

She fell silent as a touch of the old awkwardness crept into the conversation. Not so long ago, she and Aunt Olympia could hardly exchange greetings without venturing onto minefields of sensitive issues, and now she felt the ground begin to shudder beneath her feet. If Aunt Olympia answered with one of her "That's the trouble with young folks these days . . ."

But she didn't. Giving Caleb a smile, Olympia stood, her hair gleaming in the light from the overhead fixture. "Let's adjourn to the parlor." She bent to pick up her teacup. "Caleb, will you serve the brownies when they're ready? Annie, you may bring your cup, of course."

Feeling a little like a lamb on its way to the slaughter, Annie obediently lifted her mug and followed Olympia down the hall.

* * *

Though Olympia usually took the wing chair by the fireplace, tonight she purposely sat on the sofa to be closer to Annie. Her niece followed, a little reluctantly perhaps, but settled into her usual place at the opposite end of the couch. Careful to take a coaster from the stack on the polished coffee table, the girl set her mug on the sandstone, then reached for a velvet pillow and propped it against her side.

Olympia studied the pillow leaning against Annie's arm like a wall. She'd just finished a *Ladies Home Journal* article about body language, and this pillow-propping gesture indicated that Annie still felt less than comfortable with the woman who had sheltered and succored her for all those years. . . .

Olympia closed her eyes in resignation. Sometimes the young were blind to things they would not understand until they had lived through the same situation.

Opening her eyes, she forced a smile. "Did Captain Stroble bring you over, or have we been reduced to traveling with Crazy Odell?"

Annie laughed. "The captain's still in town. He said Mazie is a bit under the weather, probably from nerves. But as soon as she's better, they're heading off to Florida. Then you'll have to wrangle with Odell."

Olympia shuddered slightly. "I'd rather be island-bound an entire month than travel with that nutty old man. He's as reckless as a teenage boy in that boat of his—in fact, sometimes I think he *is* a teenage boy. Between the ages of fourteen and twenty, you know, the logic circuits in a child's brain become disconnected. I think Odell's circuits never got plugged back in again."

Annie snorted. "What psychologist have you been reading?"

Olympia sniffed. "No psychologist, it's just common sense. That's what's wrong with young people today; nobody places any value on plain common sense."

As Annie leaned forward and reached for her cocoa, Olympia saw her roll her eyes.

She sighed. All right, so this visit wasn't

off to a great start. If they couldn't discuss the boyfriend or common sense, what could they talk about? Certainly not Annie's tomatoes—Annie didn't bear failure easily, and that wound was bound to be fresh. They could plan the Valentine's party, but what if they exhausted that topic tonight? Annie wouldn't go back until late tomorrow, so they'd have to bear each other's company through breakfast, lunch, and the afternoon with nothing whatsoever to talk about.

Annie suddenly stiffened and gestured to the vacant spot near the fireplace. "Aunt Olympia, what happened to the beautiful secretary that used to stand over there?"

"Olives." Olympia brought a fingertip to her lips. "I bought five cans last month from the Mercantile, and from what I hear, Vernie Bidderman nearly noodled herself into an early grave wondering what I planned to do with them. I told Caleb not to let on, though, and you need to keep my secret, too. I want my little party to be a surprise. An unexpected gesture of gentility and good will."

Annie narrowed her eyes. "You sold that secretary, didn't you? Why on earth would you sell that lovely piece?"

"The Vienna sausages, on the other hand,

I picked up in Ogunquit." Olympia lifted her saucer, perfectly balancing her teacup so the delicate china wouldn't rattle. "I knew if I bought too many supplies at the Mercantile, Vernie would know something was up and broadcast the news. So I've been buying things on the sly, taking a guilty pleasure in my little mystery—"

"Don't ignore me, Aunt Olympia." Annie pushed the pillow down and leaned toward her, her eyes as direct as headlights. "What did you do with the secretary?"

Pulling back, Olympia blinked. "What does it matter?"

"It matters to me. You loved that piece, so why'd you sell it?"

Olympia shook her head. "It was just another thing for Caleb to dust."

"It belonged to your grandmother!"

"See? A worthless old thing."

"It wasn't worthless, Aunt Olympia, it was probably worth a small fortune. Haven't you ever watched *Antiques Roadshow?*"

"Is that on TV? I don't like TV. Young people these days spend entirely too much time in front of the television watching claptrap and whatnot—"

"Ayuh, it's a show, and it'd do you good

to watch it. People are always bringing in junk from their attics and finding out their stuff is worth thousands of dollars."

Straightening, Olympia smoothed the folds of her dress. "I'd never have figured you for a gold digger, Annie."

"Wh-what?"

"Don't play coy with me. You know I'm not going to be around forever. But if you're concerned about your inheritance, well, you needn't worry. You know the house will be yours, so I can't see why you're worried about me selling a few dusty old pieces riddled with worm holes—"

"Time out." Annie made a T with her arms, then gaped at Olympia. "What do you mean, the house will be mine? I didn't know that—and I certainly would never ask for it! You and Caleb will probably be living here another fifty years, so keep the things you love. If you're determined to be rid of your antiques, call me first. I'll buy them and at least we can keep them in the family."

Olympia snorted. "That meager teacher's salary is barely enough to support you. How are you supposed to afford antiques?"

"I'm a *professor,* Auntie," Annie countered. "I make a decent living."

"You're a twenty-eight-year-old part-time teacher and researcher who's never had a success in her life. When everybody was talking about how wonderful those tomatoes were, I told Caleb it would just be a matter of time before something—"

"Look what I found, ladies."

Distracted, Olympia looked up as Caleb entered the room, a plate of brownies in one hand and a leather-covered album in the other.

"I was cleaning out a chest upstairs the other day and came across this. Since you two gals have nothing pressing to do tonight, I thought you might enjoy a trip down memory lane."

Olympia drew in a breath as he placed the heavy album on her lap. His timing was impeccable, as always, for she'd been about to tell Annie that her dreams were too big. Things never went well when she was honest with the girl. That was the trouble with young folk these days: you had to pussyfoot around them and use nothing but gentle words. In her youth, people said what they meant and meant what they said, and things were a lot simpler.

Annie's hurt expression softened when

Caleb gave her a smile. "Thanks, Caleb," she whispered.

As Annie took a brownie, Olympia opened the first page. On a sheet of heavy black paper someone had mounted a sepia-toned photograph of her mother and father standing tall and proud on the front steps of Frenchman's Fairest. Her mother carried a baby dressed in ribbons and ruffles.

"Look at that!" Annie leaned closer, her face hidden by her swinging hair. "Are you the baby, Auntie?"

"That's my little brother Ferrell—your father." Even after all these years, a lump rose in Olympia's throat at the mention of his name. She and Ferrell had been close as children and even as adults until Ferrell's wife, Ruth Ann, had come between them. Ruth Ann was soft like Annie, preferring insincere nonsense to plain-spoken truth.

"I can't get used to seeing little boys in ruffles." Annie ran her fingertip over the old photograph. "When I have a little boy—I mean, *if* I have a little boy—I'm going to dress him in blue jeans and overalls. No kid of mine is going to be confused about his sexual identity."

Olympia blanched at the word *sexual,* but

Annie didn't seem to notice. That was the trouble with young people these days: They shamelessly tossed around all kinds of private words without regard to who might be listening. Olympia couldn't say the word *womb* without feeling faint.

Quickly, she turned the page. "This one is me." She tapped the photo of a somber-faced girl holding a kitten. "I still remember that cat. I called him Mr. Jingles."

Annie laughed softly but offered no comment, so Olympia continued through the pages, pointing out landmarks on the island and people related to some of the island's current residents.

"Heavenly Daze has changed." Annie nodded at one of the pictures. "I can't imagine the Gallery without the Lobster Pot standing next to it."

"That restaurant is a positive fright." Olympia pointed to a black and white photo of the church and parsonage. "And so is the municipal building they put up next to the minister's house. My parents protested loud and long, but even they couldn't stand against progress." She sniffed. "At least, progress is what they called it. I call it plain ugly."

Sensing a lag in Annie's interest, she turned a few more pages, wondering when Caleb had taken the time to assemble this book. The last time she'd seen these photos, they'd been cluttering up an empty shoe box at the back of her closet.

"Here." She pointed at a picture of another little girl, this one thin and somber, with dark curls trailing down the sides of her face like tangled ivy. "That's you, Annie. Taken during your first week with us on Heavenly Daze."

Annie bent closer, almost low enough for her nose to touch the paper. "That's me? Good grief, what a mess I was!"

Olympia pressed her hand to her heart as a well of pain bubbled up from memories long suppressed. She'd been a mess, too, in those days, grieving over Ferrell and frightened to death at the thought of raising another child—especially one as odd and fanciful as Annie. She'd passed several nights on her knees, begging God for answers, pleading for strength and wisdom.

Somehow, he had supplied both.

Olympia drew a deep breath, then made an effort to lighten her voice. "Don't be too hard on yourself, Annie. You were a mite upset and confused in those days. Wouldn't have been natural if you'd been a sunny little thing."

Silence stretched between them for a moment, then Annie looked up and met Olympia's gaze. "I don't know if I've ever thanked you properly, Auntie, but I'm grateful you took me in back then." Her brown eyes gentled. "I'm sure it wasn't easy."

Olympia swallowed hard. "Worthwhile things generally aren't."

* * *

From the foyer, Caleb leaned forward, unabashedly eavesdropping on his charges. He'd been alarmed earlier when Olympia's tone had gone frosty, and he could almost see Annie's temper rising. But the photograph album had done the trick and reminded them of how far they'd come together . . . and how much they needed each other.

His preparations were nearly complete. Earlier that day Gavriel had appeared in the kitchen to relay a special assignment from on high. The mission had been years in the making, but tonight it would finally be fulfilled.

The butler glanced at the clock. The women still had time to reminisce. And gentle words shared in the next few hours would last, like apples of gold, throughout eternity.

* * *

As the mantel clock struck eleven, Olympia closed the album, the image of the last picture still floating upon her retinas. The photo had been of her and Annie, locked in an embrace at the dock. That frozen moment had taken place during Annie's parting after Christmas, when their hearts had never been fonder or more united.

She didn't want to lose that closeness, yet time and distance would inevitably take its toll. But if she'd learned one thing from watching Annie nurse those spindly tomato plants, it was that growing things needed frequent doses of water and sunlight.

Relationships needed affirmation.

"I love you, girl." Tears stung Olympia's eyes as the words tumbled over her lips, and for an instant she couldn't look at her niece. Annie would never understand how difficult it was to say such things. Such endearments were against Olympia's nature and everything she'd been taught as a child. Properly brought up women did not emote in public, wear their feelings upon their faces, or wallow in sentimentality. But young people today were more open about their feelings, and if Annie could only meet her halfway . . .

"Oh, Olympia!" Annie reached out and drew her into an embrace. Olympia stiffened at first, from surprise and the use of her name without a title. So she was no longer "Aunt," but merely "Olympia," as if they were no longer guardian and child, but two women bound by affection and friendship.

Slowly she relaxed, then rubbed the younger woman's back. "Shh," she whispered, though Annie hadn't said another word. "I'm glad you're home. Tomorrow after church we'll plan the menu for my party and Caleb will make us a nice brunch. You can say hello to all the townsfolk, and I'm sure some of them will come down to the dock when it's time to see you off—"

Annie pulled back, but kept her hands on Olympia's shoulders. "I don't need hellos from the entire town to feel welcome. I only need you."

"Well, now." Olympia forced a smile, then pulled out of Annie's grip and stood. She took a step forward, then hesitated as the room spun slightly before her eyes. If she'd known hugging could make her feel light-headed . . . she'd have done it more often.

She glanced back at her niece. "I'm going to bed. You coming up now?"

Annie shook her head, then pointed to the flickering flames in the fireplace. "It's so cozy here, I think I'll stay awake and read a while. I'm not sleepy, anyway. Too much caffeine on the drive down."

"Tallulah?" Olympia spoke to the dog drowsing on a pillow near the fire. "You coming up?"

The sly old dog opened one eye, then shut it again, pretending to sleep.

"She can stay down here a while," Annie said, turning to rest her legs on the sofa. "I'll let her into your room when I come up."

"That'd be nice. Thank you, dear." Olympia nodded, then made her way to the stairs, noticing how much brighter the house seemed with Annie in it.

* * *

Annie had read only two pages of her book when Caleb tiptoed into the parlor, a serving tray in his hand. "Don't let me bother you," he said, reaching for her empty mug. "I just want to put these things away before I go to bed."

"Let me help you." She picked up Olympia's teacup and saucer and set them on the tray, then caught the older man's eye. "The album was a great idea. Thanks."

Smiling, he dropped his hand to the top of her head. "I thought so."

"Sometimes it's a little hard to talk to Aunt Olympia, you know. She's so opinionated."

"Missy is strong in many things, including her beliefs."

He hesitated, closing his eyes, and Annie saw his lips move. Caleb had always been given to moments of spontaneous prayer, sometimes audible, sometimes not, and she suspected he was praying now . . . for her. But though she strained to listen, she couldn't understand a word he said.

After a moment, he opened his eyes, looked down at her, and smiled. "You'll be fine, Annie."

She watched him shuffle away, his slippers slapping the polished wooden floors, and wondered what he meant.

"That's the problem with older people

these days," she told Tallulah, who had lifted her head at Caleb's departure. She grinned as she picked up her book. "Sometimes they speak a language I just can't comprehend."

* * *

Seated at her dressing table, Olympia pulled the last hairpin from her bun, then ran her fingers through the hank of her hair, setting the strands free. Birdie and Bea and Vernie had taken to wearing their hair short, but she never could stand the thought of having hair as short as a man's.

Her hair was still dark at the ends, followed by inches of steel gray. Around her forehead the hair had gone snowy white, and she liked to think the effect becoming. Edmund had always said lighter colors brightened a woman's face.

Her husband had loved this part of the day. Even when his snoring necessitated that they sleep in separate bedrooms, he had often entered her room to share the last few moments of the evening. He would stretch out on her bed, propping his head on his hand, and watch her reflection in the mirror as she picked up her tortoiseshell brush and began to pull it through her hair.

"My, my," he'd say, a smile tugging at the corners of his lips. "Miracles do happen. Despite my contrariness, somehow I managed to marry the town beauty."

Olympia had always ignored his silly remarks, for no woman of good breeding went around thinking of herself as beautiful. Such an attitude led to pompousness and conceit, while a lady kept herself above those things. As a young woman she had wanted to spend her life giving to the poor, helping orphans, being an example of all a Christian woman should be . . . then she had fallen in love with Edmund Shots, a man twenty years her senior whose ancestors didn't rate even a footnote in the social register. The situation had rocked her family and scandalized the townsfolk, but her sterling reputation had saved her from total disrepute.

Lowering the hairbrush, she looked at the bed reflected in the mirror. "Oh, Edmund, how I miss you."

She had not lived the life of her dreams, but she had lived. And in the living she had hurt some people and helped some others; she had been loved and feared, admired and criticized. As mistress of the largest and most imposing home on the island, she had taken pains to maintain a certain standard of propriety—employing a butler, making a regular habit of afternoon tea, and keeping the horse and buggy long after everyone else had bought golf carts to traverse the island. She had worked hard to maintain the grand and historic legacy of Heavenly Daze, but all the while she knew the other townsfolk were laughing behind her back.

They loved her, she knew that—she'd seen evidence of their affection immediately after Edmund's death and she felt the warm support of her neighbors every time she attended church or the ladies' quilting circle. The gulf between her and the others was of her own making, she knew that as well. But as the only direct descendant of Captain Jacques de Cuvier, the responsibility of maintaining both his legacy and his town fell upon her shoulders. If not for her vigilance, Vernie would have everyone riding noisy motor scooters, Birdie would be trying to open a bakery franchise up at the point, and Charles Graham would be selling Heavenly Daze landscapes down on the dock. . . .

She caught her breath as a sudden

spasm gripped her chest. Nerves, probably. She'd been a little squamish about Annie's visit, nearly sick with worry that a gale would blow up and prevent the ferry from running. With Captain Stroble due for his vacation, transportation to and from the mainland was iffy, and Olympia shuddered at the thought of Annie riding with Crazy Odell Butcher.

Rubbing the painful spot within her chest, she stared into her mirror, studying the image of an aging woman, eyes red-rimmed with weariness and pain. The mirror was lying again, for Olympia felt no kinship with the woman in the looking glass. In her inmost heart she was a mature woman of about Annie's age, with nearly as many dreams and hopes as she'd nurtured in her younger years.

She made a face at the mirror, then moved her hand to her temple. The headache that had come and gone for weeks had welcomed itself back to her brain, and this time it brought chest spasms for company. Fine, then. She'd ask Caleb to brew a pot of chamomile tea . . .

As if he'd read her mind, she heard Caleb's voice. "Missy?"

Adjusting her gaze in the mirror, she saw

Caleb standing behind her—odd, since she had not heard the click of the door—but this was a Caleb she hadn't seen in years. His face was full and unlined, his head framed by thick auburn hair, his eyes bright and energetic. Vigor had erased the stoop from his posture, his skin glowed with health and light, and behind his back two amazing wings flexed with power and strength—

She turned on the bench, her eyes widening to take in the unbelievable sight.

A glow surrounded the man who had served as her butler for over fifty-five years, a tangible, bright light that seemed to pulse with every breath she drew.

Caleb gave her a lovely, warming smile that reached clear to her heart. "It's time."

Her lips whispered, "Time for what?" but her heart knew. The one who had met her needs and watched over her, who had ministered to her and spoken words of Truth nearly all the years of her life . . . he was no butler, he was not even a man.

He was . . . an angel.

The truth came in a dazzling burst of mental illumination, and an instant later she could not understand how she could have been so blind all her life. Seeing him in the center of that unearthly living light, she would have understood his nature even if he were stooped and frail and cocking his head as if his ears were failing.

His mortal body might have weakened over the stretch of years, but the being before her now was clothed in immortality. And as he held his hand out to her, she felt another pain in her chest, sharper this time, but she had no thought for the pain, only joy and gladness that Caleb stood ready to help her pass one more milestone.

"It's time for you to go home, Missy."

Home—the word vibrated with depths of meaning she'd never fathomed before.

Smiling, she took his hand and stood, then felt her soul break free. On the wings of love and compassion she rose with him, her spirit expanding and her senses quickening as the walls of her room and the house seemed to fade into insignificance and the last sound she heard with earthly ears was the sound of her tired body hitting the floor.

* * *

Annie heard the thump and looked up from her reading, her eyes searching the ceiling.

Aunt Olympia's room stood just over the parlor, and she could have fallen . . . or dropped a book. Sounds could be deceiving in a house as old as this one; the smallest object could sound like a boulder hitting the wooden floors overhead.

Tallulah whined softly. Lifting her head, her eyes seemed to focus on something beyond Annie's field of vision.

Annie studied the dog. "What is it, girl? Should we go up and check on Aunt Olympia?"

Barking, the dog sprang to her feet, then spun in a small circle, finally settling back upon the cushion of her doggy bed. She propped her chin on her forepaws, but her eyes kept darting toward the ceiling.

Annie leaned forward, listening. The bump had been followed by silence—she heard no cry for help, no call for Caleb. So Olympia had probably dropped something. Calling attention to her clumsiness would only annoy her, especially if she were trying to sleep.

Annie settled back and picked up her book, but her caffeine rush had worn off. And the hour was late.

"That's it." She snapped the book closed.

"Come on, Tallulah, let's go up to bed. Auntie is probably missing you."

Obediently the terrier sprang to her feet. Together they climbed the stairs, the dog's toenails clicking against the worn wooden steps. Annie smiled in relief when she saw a line of light at the bottom of Olympia's door.

"Here, Tallulah." Annie opened the door a few inches, not wanting to intrude on Olympia's privacy. "Go on in and get some shut eye."

The dog scooted through the opening, but she did not round the corner as if she were going to the spot where her doggie bed lay. Instead, she trotted to the left . . .

"Aunt Olympia?"

With one finger Annie pushed the door. Her aunt would probably squawk if Annie so much as glimpsed her in her nightgown, but perhaps she was reading in bed.

"Auntie?" She opened the door wider. "You asleep?"

No answer, so Annie thrust her head through the opening in the doorway, then felt her heart do a double beat. Olympia lay on the floor, one hand outstretched, the other clutching a tortoiseshell hairbrush. Worst of all, the smell of death filled the room.

* * *

Through some ability she did not yet understand, Olympia looked down and saw Tallulah and Annie kneeling by the side of a woman on the floor. For an instant she wondered who the woman could be, then the truth crashed into her consciousness like surf hurling against a rocky cliff.

"This is death?" She looked at Caleb, who had not left her side.

"It is transition," he answered, his hand firmly wrapped around hers. "From the physical plane to the spiritual. From earth to the highest heaven."

"I don't understand."

His smile softened. "You don't have to."

Soaring, her spirit lifted like an imprisoned bird that had finally been set free. She looked down again, but the bedroom scene had been replaced by the dim outline of the island of Heavenly Daze, recognizable by the streetlights that formed the shape of a cross. Then that image, too, receded into darkness, and she found the courage to look up into a sea of blackness populated by white stars that moved past her at a dizzying rate.

A tingling sensation sparked in her head and flowed along her arms and legs until she looked down and realized she didn't *have* arms or legs—not like she had previously known, anyway. She could see her limbs—and never had they looked stronger or healthier—but they were as ethereal as air.

Caleb must have noticed her glance and her look of puzzlement, for he was smiling when she met his gaze. "You are spirit now," he said simply, his strong arm holding her as they whizzed through the atmosphere. "Your mortal body has worn out, so it is best you leave it behind. You will receive a new one at the Resurrection."

Speechless, Olympia brought her hand up before her eyes and saw the translucent outline of fingers. "If I don't have a body, Caleb, what am I seeing?"

"Memories. Because living on a spirit plane will be new to you, you will relate to others much as you did on earth. I know it seems confusing now, but soon everything will be clear. Your physical body has died, your soul has flown, and your spirit lives in Christ Jesus our Lord. Until the Resurrection you will live in heaven as a spirit being, seeing and hearing with spiritual eyes and ears.

You will recognize others you knew on earth, but they will be spirit, too. Only One possesses a physical body here—the Son of Man, who lives in glorified flesh. You will know him by the scars he bears in his hands and feet."

Olympia fell silent as the significance of those words registered. She would see her Savior . . . the thought left her quivering.

She fell silent as they flew through a space devoid of landmarks, but the air around them vibrated with sound. Words zipped past her spirit ears with the ferocity of bullets, and after a moment of listening she realized she was hearing petitions and praises from people on earth.

Now, too, she noticed they were not alone. Other forms traveled with her and Caleb—bewildered, delighted souls safe in the embrace of angelic escorts, many of whom picked up other angel guardians along the way. The heavens here pulsated with celestial singing, anthems of wonder and praise.

As the sky around them went from violet to black, Caleb tightened his grip upon her. His eyes narrowed in concentration as four other angels appeared at his side, all of them intently focused upon something Olympia could not see. She wondered at their concern and caution. Only when she saw another approaching light, sparkling and bright, did she begin to understand.

"We want her!" A voice, high and reedy, came from the center of the whirling ball of brilliance. "She doubts, she fears, she is not worthy!"

"You cannot have her!" Caleb's voice echoed like thunder through the heavens. "She has been redeemed by the blood of the Lamb, and he has clothed her in his righteousness! Now go, you disobedient and rebellious servant!"

Olympia watched the light quiver before the authority in Caleb's voice, then it fled away into darkness. Her soul thrilled with a sudden rush of emotion.

Oh, how wrong she'd been to think she could do anything to prepare for this journey. For the demonic adversary was right— she did doubt, she did fear, and she was not worthy of heaven. The frail strength she had tried to cultivate shriveled to weakness in the onslaught of that gleaming enemy, but Caleb was strong and the One he served even stronger. . . .

Shivering, she nestled closer to Caleb's strong frame. "How long will it take?"

He chuckled softly. "Time does not exist here, dear one. You are still thinking in terms of human reference."

"But we've been flying for a while, haven't we?" Instinctively, she looked for her watch, then laughed at the sight of her translucent arm.

"In the span of earthly time, we've just left your bedroom. Annie is kneeling by your side. In a moment, she will call for me . . . and I will answer."

Panic surged through her. "You'll leave me?"

"You have nothing to fear, Missy."

Struck dumb by such authority from the butler who had always been so quiet and subservient, Olympia stared upward as they traversed yet another boundary. The skies brightened to the purest aqua in which a million sparks of diamond light twinkled. In the distance she glimpsed the tall verdant canopies of a rich forest, while in the foreground rose a gleaming temple of the purest white stone.

A host of angelic messengers greeted them outside a shimmering gate. As the gates opened, she and her escorts passed through on a tide of song that carried them toward an open area where spotless columns stood upon alabaster stairs she could not feel beneath her feet. An assortment of angelic harpists sat upon these steps, playing instruments unlike any she had ever seen or heard. They looked upward as they played, and she followed their gazes and beheld yet more harpists gathered around a throne. Behind the musicians, four astounding creatures sang, "Holy, holy, holy, Lord God Almighty, who was, and is, and is to come!"

Olympia trembled as she beheld the throne of the Almighty, lifted high behind a crystal sea that shimmered with the light of a thousand suns. Waves of glory shone from the throne, and she felt her spirit tremble before the power of the being who sat upon it. Around the throne, scores of angels waved palm branches, and something in her wanted to fall to her knees with these lovely creatures, waving whatever sprig of greenery or feathering she could happen to find.

"Look," Caleb commanded, and she obeyed. The throne of the Almighty rested upon two pillars, the left bearing inscriptions in many languages, including English. The Creator had carved the word *righteousness* into the left pillar, while the right bore the word *justice*. Above the throne hovered a pair of mighty angels, their wings softly stirring the air.

Suddenly she was transported over the sea, over the harpists, over even the seraphim. She knelt at the foot of the throne, close enough that she could have reached out and touched the all-too-fleshly foot that rested inches from her trembling hands.

Drawn by a force she could not deny, Olympia lifted her eyes to the One who sat in the center of the universe. She expected a being so bright and powerful that one glance would shatter her into a million atoms, each particle too tiny to ever be of use again, but when her gaze lifted she saw . . . Jesus.

She saw holiness reflected in his white robe and his gleaming hair. She saw power in the strength of his hands. But when she looked into his eyes, she saw compassion and love.

The altogether lovely One leaned forward and smiled when she finally met his gaze. "Olympia, my beloved." He spoke in the warm voice of a father who has spent years yearning for a long-lost child. "I have waited so long to welcome you home."

Olympia lowered her arms to the floor, prostrating herself in the presence of Majesty. Hundreds of other human spirits bowed in various places around the throne. For each the Savior had a smile and a personal greeting, but still she felt utterly cherished and adored. The Lord of Glory had chosen her; he had brought her home.

She wasn't sure how long she knelt in adoration and gratitude, but Caleb's gentle touch roused her to movement. "Come," he said, a twinkle in his eye. "Others are waiting to greet you."

An instant later she found herself standing on a large balcony suspended above the azure heavens. Hundreds of people milled about her in transparent forms that had the features and shapes of human bodies without the substance. "They are incorporeal," Caleb said, apparently reading her thoughts, "spirit beings, like you."

Suddenly, Edmund stood before her. Even if she had not seen the outline of his former self, she would have recognized the warmth of his smile, the joy in his heart, and the kindness of his spirit.

"Olympia!" Love warmed his voice. "Welcome to the kingdom of God!"

"Edmund!" She hurried to hug him, then felt an instant's frustration when she realized she could not. But Edmund had mastered life in the spirit realm, and when she closed her eyes his spirit drew near to hers, enveloping her in a way that left no room for doubts or frustration. Breathing in his essence, Olympia realized this was the warmest embrace she had ever experienced. Two spirits united in love and holiness. . . . As close as she and Edmund had been on earth, this was far more thrilling.

Edmund was smiling when she opened her eyes. "Welcome, darling. So many people have been waiting for you."

Speechless with amazed joy, Olympia shifted her gaze in time to see her mother, her father, Ferrell, and Ruth Ann gathered in a small half-circle. She embraced each of them as she had embraced Edmund, and as she drew near to each of them she marveled that such closeness could exist between two human souls.

She smiled after greeting her former sister-in-law, realizing that her feelings of antipathy had completely vanished.

"We have no place for resentment here," Ruth Ann said, a smile lighting her features. "Resentment is a product of competition, and here there is no need to compete. We are all loved by the Savior, all redeemed by his precious blood. We are one in the Lord, and as one, we are equal."

Again, she felt Caleb's touch. "Someone here would like to meet you."

Olympia turned to see another man, tall and white-haired, but full of life. His eyes snapped as he stepped forward to embrace her in love. "Olympia! I've heard many things about you, and I've seen you offer worthy service in the name of the Lord. I am pleased to have you as a descendant."

She gaped at the stranger. "And you are . . ."

He bowed slightly. "On earth I was a humble sea captain. I am the Lord's servant, Jacques de Cuvier."

If she'd had a mortal body, Olympia knew she would have fainted.

"We have so much to tell you."

Dazed, Olympia swiveled as someone else spoke. "Mama?"

Her mother, who'd been in heaven over fifty years, stepped forward, light sparkling in her eyes. "I know it was hard for you to be parted from me when you were so young, but you were never far from my thoughts. I have watched you so many times over the course of your life. I've prayed for you in your struggles, hoping you would lean on the Spirit for understanding rather than fight your way through your trials."

Olympia felt her spirit sink. "You watched . . . everything I did?"

Her father laughed. "Not everything. In his wisdom, the Spirit shields us from certain sights. We are not omniscient, after all. But we saw your tribulations and your victories. Occasionally we saw your failures."

"But we did not despair for you," her mother quickly added. "For we knew the Lord would use your failure to teach you and mature you. And those were the occasions we saw you grow, dear one."

Olympia sighed. "I'm afraid I still have a lot to learn."

Edmund chuckled. "Of course you do, and you will have many opportunities to learn and serve. What do you think we do up here, sit on clouds and play harps?"

As the others threw back their heads and made the heavens ring with laughter,

Olympia shifted her gaze to the glowing temple on the horizon. "There is only one thing I want to do now," she said. "I want to sit at the feet of Jesus and drink in his beauty."

Edmund stepped forward, offering her his shimmering hand. "Come, my love. Let us worship together once again."

* * *

Annie drew Olympia's inert form into her arms, then pressed her fingertips to her aunt's slender throat. She could not find a pulse, but the flesh was warm, so perhaps there was time to save her.

"Caleb!" she screamed, startling the dog. "Come quick!"

A moment later the old man appeared, his eyes wide. "Are you all right?"

"It's Aunt Olympia! She's—I think she's in real trouble. Can you get Dr. Marc? Can we get her to the hospital?"

"Do not fear, Annie. I'll get the doctor."

The man's eerie calm rattled her; she could have sworn he was more concerned for her than for the woman on the floor. Annie bent closer to her aunt, holding her tight as if she could compel the spirit of life to remain in the room, to return to this frail frame.

What on earth could have happened? Olympia hadn't been eating, so she couldn't have choked. If she'd had a stroke, surely she would still be breathing . . .

The swift answer came on the wings of reason, followed by memories of Caleb's constant admonitions: No butter, no red meat, Missy, watch the salt intake, try and get some regular exercise. . . .

Olympia must have had a heart attack.

But now? She'd never heard anything about Olympia having a heart condition. If she'd had a problem, Dr. Marc should have been more vigilant, he should have come into the house and forced Olympia to eat right and take her pills or whatever. She could be so stubborn, and never more than when she wanted to eat as she pleased.

A few minutes later she heard heavy pounding on the stairs, then Dr. Marc appeared in the doorway, his doctor's bag in hand. He had been in bed, for he wore a chenille robe over striped flannel pajamas.

Annie couldn't speak. Thankfully, she didn't have to, for the doctor dropped to his knees and knelt over the body.

Annie scooted back to the wall, then looked up to find Caleb watching her. She turned away, but continued to feel the gentle pressure of his gaze as he began to pray. "Father," his words were a warm whisper in the room, "be with Annie now and comfort her heart. Help her be strong at this time, and let your peace surround her."

Annie lowered her lashes in gratitude, then opened one eye as a thought struck: Why wasn't Caleb praying for Olympia?

Dr. Marc pressed his fingers to Olympia's neck, then laid her flat on the floor. After checking her heart with his stethoscope, he slowly pulled it from his ears.

"I'm sorry, Annie." He glanced at the clock on the bureau, his face grim. "Time of death is eleven-thirty P.M. That's what we'll write on the death certificate, but I'd guess she's been gone fifteen minutes or more."

Annie pressed her hand to her chest, where her own heart was pounding like a trip hammer. "You can't—can't you do CPR or something and bring her back?"

He shook his head. "I'm afraid not." He rubbed a hand across the stubble on his chin. "If, as I suspect, her heart failed, she would have first experienced a sense of confusion, then lost consciousness and fallen. From that point she entered the state of terminal apnea when her breathing stopped, then she passed into the agonal state—at which point we might have been able to revive her if we were in a hospital. Brain death followed within minutes."

"So I could have saved her if I'd rushed up here when I heard her fall?"

He reached out and squeezed her shoulder. "No, honey. A massive heart attack would damage her heart, and nothing short of emergency surgery and a possible heart transplant could make her well again. Olympia and I have talked about this sort of thing, and she didn't want to be resuscitated in a situation like this. She knew she was at risk for heart trouble, and she was ready for whatever came. She missed Edmund, you see."

Tears, hot and angry, spilled over Annie's cheeks. "But that's not fair! Why didn't she watch her diet more closely? I know she missed Edmund, but she still had me. We were just beginning to understand each other."

She fell into his arms, one fist weakly pounding his chest as a torrent of words and emotions poured out. "I needed her. Who else do I have, if not her? I know she missed Edmund, but I needed her, too. I don't have anybody else, Dr. Marc, not anybody."

His gentle hand fell on her head and smoothed her hair. "Shh, Annie, I know it's hard."

"She is home now." Caleb's voice rang with conviction. "She's with Edmund and her loved ones, and together they are rejoicing in the presence of the Lord."

"Oh, Caleb." Straightening, Annie swiped at the tears on her cheeks. "You make it sound so real."

"It *is* real, honey. More real than anything in this room."

Annie sniffed, wishing she could believe him. She wanted to believe, but sometimes heaven seemed like a fairy tale invented to ease children's fears about death and what lies beyond. . . .

She would face the unknown alone now.

"I never knew," she repeated, turning to the doctor, "that her heart condition was so serious."

"She didn't have a serious problem, but unfortunately sometimes these things are unpredictable, particularly in women." The doctor frowned as he glanced at Olympia's still form. "You could request an autopsy."

Annie considered a moment, then shook her head. "No. If you say it was a heart attack, I trust you."

"I'll call her doctor in Ogunquit. And the funeral home, if you want me to handle that part of . . . the arrangements."

Annie leaned her elbow on the stool by Olympia's dressing table. She had never planned a funeral. Uncle Edmund had slipped away after a long illness, and he and Aunt Olympia had preplanned his funeral and everything associated with it.

She suddenly realized she didn't have the faintest idea where to begin what must come next.

"Would you do that?" Her eyes fixed upon the doctor's face. "The same funeral home that took care of Uncle Edmund would know what to do."

Dr. Marc nodded. "They're good people. If they pick up the body tomorrow morning, I'm sure they can return her Monday for a viewing. You can talk to Pastor Winslow about a funeral on Tuesday." He frowned. "Olympia would want to be buried next to Edmund, but I'm pretty sure the ground is too frozen to be broken with shovels. We'll have to get someone to bring in a backhoe, and that might take a while, given that Captain Stroble's on vacation. We'll probably have to send Olympia back to the morgue until the machine can be brought over."

Annie clapped her hand over her mouth, mortified by the thought of her aunt lying in a refrigerated drawer while they tried to track down a backhoe to break through the frozen ground. Olympia would roll over in her grave . . . if they ever managed to get her into one.

"Aunt Olympia, as you know, was very . . . *refined.*" Annie gave the doctor a careful smile, certain he could read between the lines. "She would want everything to be handled in just the right way. The right flowers, the right music, the perfect mix of ceremony and sentiment—"

"She wrote a letter with her wishes, and left it with her will." Caleb scratched his head. "Seems to me she wanted the boys' choir from that Episcopal church in Wells to sing at her funeral."

"Whatever she wanted, we'll have to get." Annie lifted her chin, determined to take charge of the ceremony and her own emotions. "We'll announce her passing tomorrow at church, and then—"

She clutched at the doctor's arm as a sudden thought struck her. "Good grief, Dr. Marc, could my tomatoes have killed her? You said they made her sick, and that happened only a couple of weeks ago. If they weakened her immune system or something—"

"Annie." The doctor placed his hand over hers. "Don't do this. It's normal to blame ourselves when something like this happens, but none of this was your fault. Olympia had a history of high blood pressure and elevated cholesterol. I'm almost certain an autopsy would show that her heart simply gave out. It was her time."

"The Lord called her." A smile lit Caleb's face as he crossed his arms. "She was happy to go home. You should have seen her face when she knelt before the throne."

Annie frowned. The old butler had to be delirious with grief. The bond between him and Olympia had been deep and strong.

"You go on to bed now." Dr. Marc spoke in a firm and final voice. "Caleb and I will take care of Olympia tonight. You need to get your rest."

Nodding slowly, Annie pulled her hand free of Dr. Marc's grasp, then stood and walked toward the door, patting Caleb's shoulder as she passed.

The men were probably right in saying she shouldn't feel guilty. But if she'd gone up to bed with Olympia, or if she'd flown upstairs when she heard that thump—would Olympia be alive now?

"Thank you," she called, turning to glance at the two men in her aunt's bedroom. "Thank you for . . . everything."

She pressed her lips together to stifle a sob, then moved toward her old bedroom, knowing she wouldn't sleep.

Chapter Two

Yawning, Edith Wickam shuffled to the kitchen stove in her housecoat and slippers. The plastic thermometer affixed to the outside of the kitchen window registered a relatively pleasant eighteen degrees, but temperatures would probably reach the low thirties by afternoon. They'd have a nice day for church services once the sun came up.

Sounds of Winslow's gargling trickled from the newly remodeled bathroom, followed by the soft hum of an electric Gillette.

Ambling from the stove to the refrigerator for butter and cream, Edith set Jimmy Dean sausage to sizzling in a skillet, then dropped a couple of frozen waffles into the toaster. She slid the pitcher of maple syrup into the microwave and punched a minute and thirty seconds, then tightened the rope sash on her housecoat as the oven hummed.

Goodness—why wasn't her robe closing? A full half inch of her nightgown peeked from beneath the edges of her robe—a half inch of nightgown she had never noticed before. Had her robe decided to shrink after five years? Didn't seem likely, but still. . . .

She was wondering if her clothes dryer had begun a program of selective shrinkage when Winslow sailed through the kitchen doorway and dropped his usual perfunctory kiss on her forehead. His aim was off this morning; the kiss landed on the bridge of her nose.

"Good morning, my love."

"Morning, Win. Sit down, breakfast is ready."

Winslow dropped into a kitchen chair, his eyes glued to the note cards in his hand. Edith didn't mind—she was used to Winslow's customary practice of studying his sermon notes over Sunday breakfast. The edges of her robe opened wider as she dished up waffles and sausage.

A moment later she sat down and reached for Winslow's free hand. "Bless this food, Lord," Winslow intoned. "Let us ever be mindful of your love and care. Amen."

Edith got up for the syrup still in the microwave as Winslow lathered butter on his waffle, his eyes intent upon the note cards now on his placemat. Edith sighed as she set the syrup on the table. After so many years of marriage to a pastor she'd learned not to expect stimulating breakfast conversation on Sunday, but a few observations would be nice: *Beautiful morning, Edith. Great breakfast, honey!*

She poured two steaming cups of coffee, and then set the glass carafe on the table. She slid into her chair, then stared down at the bright red of her nightgown. Two inches were now showing, two inches of fabric she'd never noticed before this morning.

She turned to peer at her husband. "Do you think I'm getting fat?"

Biting into a piece of sausage, Winslow nodded absently, his eyes trained on his sermon notes. Chewing, he reached for his coffee cup, then took a sip.

Edith pursed her lips. He hadn't heard a word she'd said.

"Win?"

"Hmmm?"

"Do you think I'm getting fat?"

"Of course, hon. Fine idea."

She bit down on the inside of her lip, realizing she'd get no response as long as he was studying. Unless her words had registered and he really *did* think she was packing on the pounds.

Was she? In January alone she'd attended Dana Klackenbush's poetry reception, eaten two healthy hunks of Russell Higgs's birthday cake, and attended three potlucks after Sunday morning services. The huge community meals were taking a toll on her waistline. Edith could eat her weight in fried clams—and this morning that would be no small feat. She investigated her gaping robe again, then shook her head. Why, she must have put on fifteen pounds since Christmas! She'd been meaning to get a new pair of bathroom scales; the old ones weighed ten pounds heavy and she could never bring herself to step on the nuisance. But mercy, she'd gotten lax about watching her diet. She'd eaten everything in sight at Christmas time, and since then she'd enjoyed a bowl of kettle corn every night and a candy bar every afternoon when her energy flagged. . . .

Winslow had eaten right along with her. In fact, half the time *he* brought the bowl of popcorn to bed, where they munched while watching the evening news. Trouble was, he didn't seem to care about the soft paunch at his middle.

Shooting her husband a glare, she nudged his foot with the toe of her slipper. "Winslow!"

He glanced up, a bite of waffle halfway to his mouth. "What did I do?"

"Am I getting fat?"

His gaze flicked away, then he rammed the waffle into his mouth and chewed for an unwarranted length of time, his eyes darting about the room as if the answer might be found on the kitchen cabinet, the cherry-patterned wallpaper, or the two Teflon cake pans sitting on top of the counter.

Guilt assailed Edith as she waited for an answer. She *was* gaining weight and sweet Win was too much of a gentleman to tell her the truth. As tears stung her eyes, she dropped her gaze and stared at a mound of sausage floating in a sea of maple syrup on her plate.

Finally, when she could have heard a mosquito sneeze, her husband cleared his throat and casually shuffled his note cards. "Aren't we all gaining weight? I noticed my trousers were a little tight this morning."

She eyed him sternly. "We're not talking about your trousers. We're talking about me."

Winslow picked up his note cards. "Edith, if you weighed three hundred pounds, I'd love you."

Edith's jaw dropped. She'd noticed a little extra padding around her middle, but she couldn't see herself the way he could. "You think I've gained *that* much?"

Horror filled Winslow's eyes as he reached for her hand. "Of course I don't think you weigh three hundred pounds. You asked if I thought . . . well, I only meant to assure you that I love you no matter what the scales indicate. You will always look lovely to me and, um—"

He was saved by a knock on the back door.

Winslow pushed back from the table and glanced at the clock. "Who could be calling before seven on a Sunday morning?"

Edith pulled the edges of her robe together as a tide of gooseflesh raced up each arm. Good news hardly ever arrived after midnight or before dawn.

Winslow opened the door, flashing a worried smile to Olympia de Cuvier's butler. "Caleb!"

"Sorry to bother you, Pastor, but I saw your light in the window, so I figured it was okay to come."

Winslow stepped back to make way for the older man. "Of course, come in. Edith and I were having breakfast. Can we get you a cup of coffee?"

The man who for years had been Olympia's confidant and companion moved into the house with an unusual grave dignity. Edith rose from the table. Something was seriously wrong.

"Did Annie get home all right?" she asked.

Caleb nodded. "She arrived late yesterday afternoon."

Winslow closed the door, shutting out the frosty air. "I imagine Olympia was glad to see her."

"She was—and now she's gone home."

"Annie's already gone back? What'd they do, have another argument?"

"No argument—and Olympia's the one who's home. She joined the Lord last night, a few minutes after eleven."

Edith brought her hand to her mouth. Though serious, Caleb seemed perfectly at peace, even content. But perhaps the man was still in shock.

"I need to get to the church," the butler said, tightening the scarf around his neck. "I'm meeting with some of the others for prayer before the service begins. But I knew you'd want to know about Olympia as soon as possible."

Edith's hand slipped and clutched the collar of her robe. Dear goodness. What more could go wrong at Frenchman's Fairest? Annie must be suffering terribly. After losing her uncle in October and now, Olympia. . . .

Winslow looked at Edith; Edith could do nothing but nod. A lifetime of pastoral emergencies had taught her to expect the unexpected.

Winslow reached for his Bible and coat, but Caleb's outstretched hand stopped him. "There's no need to come now, Pastor, you have a service to prepare for. Besides, Miss Annie's asleep. But if you'd be so kind as to announce Missy's home going in the service, I'll minister to those at the house until you can come."

"I'll come—" Winslow's voice cracked—"this afternoon, soon as I can."

"That'd be fine." Caleb moved toward the door. "Thank you, Pastor, for shepherding this flock. Your work meant a great deal to Missy."

Edith stood in the middle of the parsonage kitchen, stunned, as Winslow closed the back door.

Olympia, dead?

Surely this was a bad dream from which she would awaken soon.

* * *

For the first time in recent months, Annie woke on a Sunday morning in Heavenly Daze and decided not to go to church. Caleb would inform the townsfolk of Olympia's unexpected passing. Except, knowing Caleb, he wouldn't use those words to describe her death—he'd probably say the morning had brought cause for celebration, because Olympia de Cuvier had been called to heaven, where she was enjoying fellowship with Jesus, her beloved Edmund, and all those who had gone before.

Caleb could paint the darkest night sunshiny yellow.

Sitting on the edge of her bed, Annie braced her arms on the mattress and focused her bleary eyes on an odd object beside her bed. The object proved to be Tallulah, curled in a scruffy ball. The sight of the dog sent guilt surging through Annie's bloodstream. Dr. Marc had ousted the poor pet from Olympia's room, yet her bed and all her doggie toys were in there. . . .

"Tallulah?" The dog woke, her ears twitching as she lifted her head. "You okay, girl?"

In answer, the terrier stood on wobbly legs, then gave her tail a tentative wiggle.

"Come on, sweetie." Annie lowered her feet, shivering as the kiss of the cool wood raised goose bumps on her legs. Despite the clang and hiss of the old radiators, a chill lay upon the floor.

After pulling on a pair of thick wool socks, she wrapped herself in the old chenille robe hanging from an iron hook on the back of the door. Whistling for Tallulah, she moved carefully down the slippery wooden stairs and went into the kitchen. Evidence of Caleb's ministrations abounded—a plate of Danish lay under a glass dome on the counter, and a pot of coffee steamed beneath the gurgling coffee maker.

Her eyes moved to a note on the refrigerator: *Am going early to speak to the pastor, then to pray with my brothers. Will tell the church of Olympia's glorious home going. Love and prayers, Caleb.*

Stumping forward on legs that felt heavy, Annie moved to the pantry, then sprinkled a handful of diet dog kibble in Tallulah's dish. The dog sniffed at it, took one bite, then looked at Annie and purposefully spat it out.

Annie snorted. "I don't blame you, girl, but there's no way I'm giving you one of these pastries. Olympia would kill me."

Tallulah cocked her head as if to say, *Never mind, I'm not hungry either.* Annie moved to the coffee pot, pulled a mug from the cabinet, and poured herself a cup. She had no appetite—who could eat with a shell-shocked heart, a dead woman upstairs, and a houseful of worries to consider?—but the coffee might jumpstart her addled brain.

After a few slow sips of the fragrant liquid, she moved to the little desk in the kitchen and pulled the old rotary phone closer. Calls, she had to make calls. People needed to know what had happened, and she ought to be the one to tell them. Edmund Junior, Olympia's only child, lived in Boston. Annie had few fond feelings for her cousin, for though he was a celebrated trial lawyer, and Olympia had always praised him, the man had barely made it home for his own father's funeral. He had come to Heavenly Daze only a few minutes before the ceremony and left ten minutes later, with scarcely more than a hug for his grieving mother.

Still, she needed to call him. And Effie, Edmund's 103-year-old mother, who lived in a nursing home in Ogunquit. And A.J., of course.

She made the most difficult call first, waking Edmund Junior from a sound Sunday morning sleep with the news that his mother had passed away. "When's the funeral?" he asked, his voice gravelly.

"Some time Tuesday, I think. We're still confirming arrangements."

"Call my secretary with the exact time, and I'll be there. I expect I'm the executor of the will?"

"I—I have no idea," Annie stammered. "I'll have to ask Caleb. I don't know anything about Aunt Olympia's business affairs."

"Okay. Thanks." Edmund Junior grunted softly, then mumbled goodbye and hung up.

Annie left a message for Effie with the supervisor at the nursing home. "I expect Mrs. Shots will be both sad and relieved," the nurse said dryly. "She complained about Mrs. de Cuvier something fierce, but I think she looked forward to Olympia's visits because each one gave her something new to complain about."

"We don't expect her to come to the funeral," Annie hastened to add, knowing the old woman couldn't handle the trip in February's frigid weather. "Just let her know, okay?"

Finally, she called A.J. He answered on the third ring, his voice low and heavy, but she could hear a smile in it when he said her name. "Annie. I was beginning to think you'd fallen off the face of the planet."

"Sorry for not checking in last night. I was going to call you after I went up to bed, but then I found Aunt Olympia—" She bit her lip as fresh tears stung her eyes. "Oh, A.J., Aunt Olympia died, and it was awful! Your dad came as quick as he could, but he couldn't do anything to help."

"Where is Dad now?"

"He's either upstairs or in the guest house, but I expect him to walk in any minute. The funeral home is sending a boat this morning to pick her up, and he said he'd handle all that for me."

He sighed into the phone. "That island—I don't know how those people can stand to be so far removed from everything and everyone. If she'd had access to a proper hospital—"

"No—your dad said even a hospital wouldn't have helped. He thinks there was too much damage to her heart."

"We'll never know, will we?"

Annie grimaced, wishing A.J. were here. If he were, he'd know from the look on her face that he'd hit a sore spot. Guilt still roared within her, so debating the manner of Olympia's death wasn't going to help.

"The funeral will be Tuesday," she said, changing the subject. "Can you come?"

"I'll check my surgery schedule." Warmth flooded back into his voice. "Dad would be happy if I could buzz up there."

"Sure, take the plane. I'll get Odell to bring you over from the landing."

He laughed. "The crazy old coot in the

rattletrap boat? I'm not sure I want to risk a winter crossing with him."

Annie wrapped the phone cord around her hand and studied the ceiling. A.J. hadn't minded risking a winter crossing with Odell at Christmas . . . but maybe that particular visit had frightened him more than he wanted to admit.

She sighed. "That crazy old coot is all we have right now. Captain Stroble's on vacation and his boat's in dry dock for maintenance."

He laughed. "All right, then. You take care of yourself and I'll try my best to see you Tuesday."

Annie nodded wordlessly, then slowly dropped the heavy receiver onto the phone. Leaning forward, she propped her elbows on the desk and pressed her hands to her face as old feelings of abandonment surfaced, threatening to drag her down into a chasm of memory and loss, the remnants of her childhood.

Why did A.J.'s hesitation bother her so much? He was a doctor and in great demand. She'd be foolish and unrealistic to think he'd be able to drop everything to comfort her in her time of distress. Besides, she was a strong and modern woman; why should she *need* comforting? She had always taken great pains to let her friends know she didn't need a man to make her life complete, nor did she want to be coddled. Her relationships were two-way streets; she expected to give and take, then take and give.

Still . . . something in her yearned to curl up in a man's strong arms, feel his lips brush against her hair. She would give anything to know someone was supporting her as she tried to make good decisions about the funeral, but instead it seemed as though every aspect of this undertaking was destined to fall upon her shoulders.

She heard a creak from the back porch steps, then hurried to swipe a tear from her cheek. A moment later Dr. Marc came into the kitchen, rubbing his bare hands together. He hesitated when he saw her sitting by the phone.

"Sorry, Annie. I should have knocked. But I saw Caleb on his way to the church—"

She shook her head. "You don't have to knock. You're like family."

His dark blue eyes searched her face. "Sleep well?"

She released a bitter laugh. "Did you?"

He gave her a rueful smile as he moved toward the coffee pot. "I've had better nights."

He took down a mug and poured a cup of coffee, then leaned against the counter and took a sip. His brow lifted when he spied Olympia's open address book.

"Did you call the off-islanders?"

"Ayuh." She cleared her throat. "Edmund Junior, Effie Shots, and A.J., of course. He said he'll try to make it Tuesday."

An unusually blank expression settled onto the doctor's face. "Pastor Winslow will tell the townspeople at church. Better brace yourself—I have the feeling they'll come storming over here as soon as he dismisses the service."

"I know they will." Annie pushed back her chair and stood, then raked a hand through her hair and forced a laugh. "I'd better take a shower and get dressed. If I don't clean up Birdie will be declaring I look a mite streak-ed, and Cleta will be asking me to spend the night at the B&B so she can keep me under observation."

Dr. Marc chuckled, but his eyes were serious above his smile. "Before you go up, Annie, I have something I need to show you."

Hearing the somber tone in his voice,

Annie slowly sat back down. The doctor walked to the desk, then opened a drawer and lifted out the Ogunquit telephone directory. Beneath the phone book's faded plastic cover, she glimpsed an envelope.

Dr. Marc pulled out the letter, which bore Annie's name, and tapped it against his open palm. "Olympia wrote this just after Edmund died, when she filed a revised copy of her will. She told me about it and said I should give it to you . . . whenever the need should arise."

Everything went silent within Annie as she accepted the envelope. "Did she know . . . this would happen?"

Dr. Marc leaned against the wall. "She had no idea when the end would come, but no one lives forever. She believed in being prepared."

With trembling fingers, Annie ripped off the end of the envelope and pulled out the folded page. Inside was a note written in Olympia's refined, spidery script:

My dearest Annie:
I know we have not always seen eye-to-eye, my girl, but you should know this—heaven knows I never wished

Ruth Ann and Ferrell any harm, but God brought good from grief when he brought you to us so many years ago. You have been the daughter I was never able to have, and you have brought me more joy than a dozen sons.

Edmund Junior does not need anything from me—indeed, I suspect he wants nothing from me, nothing I would value, anyway. That's the trouble with young folk today—they yearn more for money than things that matter. Edmund cares only for cold cash, so that's what he'll receive as the beneficiary of my life insurance policy. He doesn't need the money, but if he gets it, he will feel less inclined to contest my will, in which I have declared that my home and everything in it belongs to you.

I don't know why you care so much for the old stuff in this house, but I'm glad you do. What's left is yours, dear, every last bit of it.

Frenchman's Fairest is more than an old house—it is a heritage and a home. I leave it to you, Annie, in the full hope that you will fill it with as much love as I have known within its walls. May the Lord, who has always watched over Heavenly Daze with special care, hold you in the palm of his hand until we are reunited in eternity.

> *With all my love,*
> *Olympia*

"I never cared for the stuff—I cared about her." Lowering the page, Annie met the doctor's gaze. "She told me she planned to leave the house to me, but I thought she was just rambling. I mean, it's not like we could agree on anything for more than fifteen minutes, so I was sure she'd change her mind."

"She didn't. And it suddenly occurs to me that I should treat you with more respect—you're my new landlady."

Annie brought her hand to her cheek. In her younger years she had dreamed of being a thousand things, but never a property owner.

The doctor arched his brows into twin triangles. "Her letter may sound strange to you, but Olympia shared her reasoning with me. As much as she loved Edmund Junior, she knew he had made a life in Boston. Since leaving Heavenly Daze, he has never looked back. You, on the other hand, have begun to turn your heart toward home. Olympia thought you had begun to understand how deeply you are connected to the island."

Annie stared at him as a tumble of confused thoughts and feelings assailed her. "But I *don't* belong to the island! I live in Portland! I don't have time to maintain this house and give tours like Aunt Olympia did."

Dr. Marc dropped his hand to her shoulder. "Calm down, hon; don't get yourself worked up. Take a few days, get past the funeral, and settle things with Edmund Junior. Tourist season doesn't begin until late April, so you have a few months to decide if you want to stay."

"If I don't stay . . . what on earth am I supposed to do with the house? The heating bill alone would drain my bank account. I know it was draining Aunt Olympia's. But Caleb still lives here, and you—"

"You could always sell."

"Sell . . . the house?" Annie blinked. "I couldn't. Aunt Olympia would die if I even—" She caught herself. "I mean, Aunt Olympia wouldn't want me to sell. What did she say? It's my heritage."

Sighing, the doctor sank into a chair at the kitchen table. "Olympia made her wishes clear, but there are no stipulations attached to the will, Annie. The house is yours to do with as you think best. If you really don't think you can handle it—well, Olympia might not have approved, but in the end she would agree that you shouldn't keep an obligation that will strangle you financially." He gave her a small smile. "I only hope the new owner will allow me to continue using the guest cottage for a medical clinic."

Annie stared down into her coffee cup, where the brew had gone cold. "Maybe I could rent the house to someone, but sell it? Who on earth would want it?"

"I think you'd be surprised at the market for older, well-kept homes. I also think you'll be surprised at how expensive a house like this would be to spruce up for selling. Your instincts about the heating bill were right, and you've probably noticed that the exterior is sorely in need of painting and caulking. The windows leak, so do the sinks, and the electrical system needs updating."

Annie closed her eyes. "Why would

Olympia leave me a house I can't afford? Her decision makes no sense at all. Edmund Junior has money. He could fix up the house and spend his summers here, then go back to Boston after the tourist season."

"Olympia wanted you to have everything she owned. The furniture, the bank account—it's all yours."

She shot him a quick glance. "And Edmund Junior is the executor of the will?"

Dr. Marc shook his head. "I am. I know where every cent of your aunt's money is, and I know where it's supposed to go. That's the good news. The bad news is there's less than two hundred dollars in her bank account. Olympia was living on Social Security and Edmund's pension. Now both of those will stop."

"But I thought she was okay. I thought Uncle Edmund's life insurance was covering her expenses—"

"The proceeds of your uncle's life insurance went to cover his medical bills and funeral expenses." Dr. Marc's lips thinned. "I'm sure Olympia was too proud to tell you. She didn't want you to worry about her."

Breathing deeply, Annie lowered her head into her hand. This was too much to absorb in one sitting. She loved Heavenly Daze, but in her teenage years the island had seemed hopelessly isolated and outdated. She'd fled Frenchman's Fairest after her high school graduation, and until a few months ago she had tried to avoid the place whenever possible.

But last October life had begun to teach her that maturity meant taking time to appreciate those who had opened their hearts and home to you . . . even when you didn't appreciate them.

Now she would own that home, a lovely, antique house that was—

"An albatross," she murmured.

Dr. Marc frowned. "What?"

"That poem—the one about the sailor with the bad luck bird around his neck. I wonder if this is how he felt."

Leaving the doctor in the kitchen, Annie stood and moved wearily toward the stairs.

* * *

Edith wasn't certain how, but news of Olympia's passing had spread over the island like a grassfire. The parsonage phone had her on the run even before church.

Vernie Bidderman called—could she do anything? Wasn't it awful? Who would be next?

Cheerful thought. Edith sighed as she hung up the receiver.

Cleta Lansdown called a minute later, beside herself with grief: "I just talked to Olympia after supper last night. She wanted to know if I had a certain fat quarter she favored. I told her that I did have the fabric and I'd drop it by after church this afternoon." Edith listened as emotion choked the woman's throat. "I've said such hateful things about Olympia—"

"Olympia wasn't an easy woman to love," Edith said, taking pains to keep her voice low and soothing. "We have all had unkind thoughts, but Olympia is at peace with us now, and I know she'd want us to rest easy about her."

"I don't know—I wish I had apologized for some of the things I've said over the years. Now it's too late. Micah always says we should live each day as if it were our last one, but I never realized how right he was till now." Cleta's voice dissolved into sobs.

Hanging up a moment later, Edith realized that she had not been voicing meaningless platitudes. Olympia had been both friend and foe to every woman on the island at some point. She'd had a tongue sharper than a serpent's fang and a will as stubborn as stone. But her absence would leave a gaping hole in every islander's heart.

Edith wandered into the bedroom and opened her closet door. The full-cut corduroy dress she'd planned to wear to church lay on the bed, but what would she wear to the funeral? Undoubtedly there'd be a few off-islanders present, maybe even some folk who had never met her. Olympia's son was a hotshot Boston lawyer, and maybe he'd bring his wife. Edith would need to look good for Winslow's sake.

She stood before the rack of dresses, her gaze flitting over them until her eyes fell upon a black size eight—the stuff of distant memories. She'd paid more for that one garment than her monthly food budget at the time, but Winslow had insisted she buy the dress for a pastor's banquet they had attended. She had looked nice that night, thin and svelte, and Winslow hadn't been able to take his eyes off her.

But she'd ingested buckets of clam chowder since then, and nothing but her shapeless winter dresses and stretch pants seemed to fit anymore. However, there was a nice dark blue suit in the back, a fuzzy wool coat and skirt that might do for the funeral. . . .

She took the suit off the hanger, then shrugged her way out of her robe and nightgown. A moment later she eyed her image in the mirror and frowned in frustration. The button on the waistband wouldn't fasten, and the fabric formed horizontal pleats across her abdomen. Tugging the skirt from her hips, she reached for another outfit.

And another.

The third, a skirt with an elastic waistband and a boxy jacket, ended up in a pile on the floor.

Standing amid a heap of discarded clothing, Edith realized she didn't have a single dressy outfit that fit. If she couldn't find something to wear to Olympia's funeral, what in the world was she supposed to do about Salt's and Birdie's wedding? The social event of the year was still eight weeks away, but the lovely peach dress she had wanted to wear was form-fitted and two sizes smaller than what she wore now. Worn only once to a teahouse in Boston, the

Leslie Faye designer dress had silver-edged peach lace at the bodice, a tulip hemline, and a delicate rhinestone-studded bow at the hip. . . .

If she tried to wear that dress now, that bow would look like decoration atop a sack of lumpy potatoes.

Defeated and dejected, she sank to the side of the bed and bawled.

* * *

Caleb stood on the porch, carefully playing the part of dignified butler as guests flooded into Frenchman's Fairest. Maintaining a somber expression on this victorious occasion was one of the most difficult tasks he'd ever performed; fortunately, the sad faces of the islanders reminded him to be gentle and sympathetic. Though the reality of Olympia's home going made Caleb want to crow with delight, he'd be less than loving if he allowed his joy to splash out on the shocked mourners around him.

He had risen early to clean the house and prepare finger foods for the crowd he knew would descend that afternoon. Olympia's silver gleamed from the sideboard, candles glowed on the dining room table, and the aromatic scents of pumpkin bread and coffee wafted from the kitchen.

Olympia would be pleased.

A motorboat from the funeral home had arrived at eleven to pick up Olympia's mortal shell, so Annie was truthfully able to refuse the ladies who wanted to go up to Olympia's room and weep over the woman who had been both the thorn in their flesh and the keeper of social order for so many years.

Caleb had never been able to understand the human attachment to fleshly vessels, but after living inside a mortal body for many years, he had begun to understand the reason for their limited perspective.

Inside the parlor, a group of women had gathered around Annie. "Alst I know," Birdie said, her eyes red from weeping, "is Olympia de Cuvier always spoke plainly. If she hated your outfit, she'd come out and say so."

"Course she'd say so *nicely,*" Bea added. "In that cultured way of hers. But she never left you wondering what side of the fence she stood on."

"She had a heart the size of Texas," Vernie said, coming into the room with a plate of sausage balls. "Too bad her purse was the size of Rhode Island. The woman was as close as the bark on a tree with her money—a right admirable thing, in my opinion."

"She wasn't just tight," Cleta said, lifting a knowing brow. "She'd been seein' snow in the woodbox for a few years."

"Annie, honey." Babette Graham drew Annie into an embrace. "We want to help. Charles says he'll do a portrait of Olympia for the funeral if you want one. You can set it on an easel down front, right by the casket."

"We'll help provide food for the wake," Birdie added, taking a sausage ball from Vernie's plate. "Cookies, rolls, finger sandwiches—whatever you want, sweetie." She caught Caleb's eye. "You won't have to lift a finger, Caleb. Abner has already fired up the ovens."

Caleb felt the corner of his mouth twist as he watched the women nibble from the refreshments he had placed on the dining room table: sausages, crackers, olives, nuts, thin slices of cold cuts—all the things Olympia had bought for her surprise party to thank the town for their kindness.

He looked toward heaven and smiled. *You're thanking them now, Missy.*

As he lowered his gaze, his eyes fell upon

Annie, who was struggling to be brave. His young charge nodded to this woman and that and smiled through her tears as she accepted hugs and condolences. Edith Wickam stood by her side, one arm firmly hooked around Annie's waist. "Winslow will do a beautiful service," she was saying. "Olympia would be right proud. We understand she was fond of high church ceremony, and we'll honor her wishes. I think I might even be able to dig up some candles in the basement. We have a wedding candelabra somewhere." She pressed her fingertip to her chin. "I think."

Annie squinched her face into a look that made Caleb wonder if candles were proper decorations for a funeral, but surely the pastor's wife knew what she was doing.

Drawing a deep breath, he moved toward the knot of men who had gathered around the kitchen coffee pot. Once again, Dr. Marc was explaining the events of last evening. "By the time Annie found her, Olympia was gone," he said, one hand wrapping around a ceramic mug. "There was nothing we could do. You know Olympia— for years Dr. Merritt and I have been telling her to watch her diet, but the lady was set in her ways."

"Stubborn as a mule, you mean," Floyd interjected, winking. "I don't mean no disrespect, 'cause Olympia's heard me call her that many a time. But she was stubborn, and no two ways about it."

Leaving the humans to their discussions, Caleb moved to the back porch where his angel brothers had gathered. Zuriel, Abner, Micah, Yakov, and Elezar silently made room for him as he joined their circle, and an instant later he realized why none of them were speaking. Gavriel stood in spirit form at the center of the group, invisible to all but angelic eyes.

"Caleb." The angel captain's voice rang with authority. "Congratulations on a job well done. The Lord commends you for your excellent service to Olympia. She is celebrating in heaven with her loved ones, patiently awaiting the Resurrection."

Caleb lowered his head. "It is my joy to serve the Father."

"He knows." Gavriel's eyes burned brighter. "And it is nearly time for you to move to another place of service. By the end of this month your replacement will arrive to serve whoever is living in this house."

Caleb lifted his head. "Will it be Annie?"

Gavriel smiled. "It is not for me to know. Annie must exercise her free will, though I trust you will do all you can to encourage her to be obedient to the Father's leading."

Zuriel clapped Caleb's back. "Well done, faithful servant."

The other Smith men murmured in agreement, then fell silent when Gavriel raised a hand. "There will be time for congratulations when all our work is done." He lifted his gaze toward the heavens. "Until then, we have much to do, and Caleb still serves Annie."

His gaze melted into the butler's. "Remain close to her side during the coming days, my brother. She is young and easily confused, and her heart is vulnerable from bearing so much pain in so short a time. Minister to her as best you can, and guide her with tender love."

Moved to the core of his spirit, Caleb nodded. "You know I will."

* * *

Edith returned home at 1:30; Winslow didn't arrive until nearly three o'clock. When she heard his tread creak the front porch steps, she set her cross-stitch aside and stood to greet him. Her heart sank at the sight of weariness in his eyes. Usually a persistently happy man, today her husband looked drained.

She gave him a hug, then stepped back to look up at him. "How is Annie holding up?"

"Fine, I suppose." He glanced toward the kitchen. "Do we have anything to eat? I feel like I'm about to fall over."

"Didn't you eat anything at Frenchman's Folly? Caleb had food everywhere."

"I had no appetite."

"Follow me, then." She led the way into the kitchen, then opened the refrigerator and brought out the egg salad sandwiches she'd prepared before church. "I've spent the last hour trying on clothes. I can't find a thing to wear to the funeral."

He sat down, massaging the back of his neck. "You have a closet full of dresses."

"All too tight." She set a plate before him, then paused to gently knead the tight knots along his shoulder blades. He bowed his head for a moment of silent prayer, then picked up a sandwich.

Leaving him to eat in peace, Edith returned to the counter and eyed the remaining two sandwiches. She wasn't hungry; she had eaten her fill at Olympia's house. But, just to keep Winslow company, she could eat again. She could eat a sandwich, garnished with a helping of potato chips . . . or she could eat lettuce and do something practical about her poundage problem.

Pulling a handful of lettuce from a plastic container, she tore the leaves into pieces, then dropped them into a bowl. A moment later she had found a half-empty bottle of low-fat dressing wedged in the back of the refrigerator. Uncapping the bottle, she smelled the contents, then drizzled a little over the shredded lettuce.

After taking her place at the table, she picked up her fork and picked out the pieces of lettuce with the most dressing. Salad had never been her favorite food. Roughage put her colon in an uproar.

Winslow stopped chewing long enough to speak. "Annie wants Olympia's viewing tomorrow."

"So soon?"

Winslow nodded. "The service will be Tuesday. Annie wants to keep it small since most of Olympia's friends are here on the island. She made a few calls to family on the mainland, though."

Edith tilted her head. "What's going to happen to the house?"

Winslow chewed thoughtfully for a moment, then swallowed. "Annie's inherited the estate, and it's too soon for her to be making important decisions. I've counseled her to move slowly, take her time, and be sure of what she wants."

Edith frowned at her tasteless lunch. "Would you like cookies for dessert?"

"Do we have Oreos?"

Dark chocolate, creamy middle, just the right amount of crunch. . . .

Edith stuck a forkful of green into her mouth, then spoke around it. "I think so."

She *knew* so; she'd eaten three with a glass of milk twenty minutes before he got home and she was *still* hungry enough to eat the legs off the table.

Emotional stress gave her the munchies, but the next few hours wouldn't be any easier than the last. Tomorrow she'd have to cope with the stress of attending Olympia's viewing.

Chapter Three

The old grandfather clock was chiming ten on Monday morning when Edith heard Bea's golf cart rattling over the graveled road. Eager to catch the postmistress, Edith hurried through the living room, her head bent as she tightened the back of a loose earring.

She opened the front door just as the bell rang. Bea stood there, her eyes narrow and watery, a stack of mail in her hand. Edith opened the storm door to accept delivery, then smiled at the woebegone woman.

"You look like you could use a hot cup of coffee."

Bea's face crumpled. "I know the mail must go out, but my heart isn't in it this morning."

Edith snorted as she tossed the stack of letters onto the foyer table. "I never get anything but bills and credit card offers, anyway."

Drawing Bea into the warmth of the house, Edith closed the door and led her into the cozy kitchen. She knew how Bea felt; she'd gone on her own crying jag an hour earlier. The close-knit town had lost two residents in a short time, and each death served to remind the islanders of their own mortality.

She turned toward the coffeepot, then heard Bea sigh. "I haven't come empty-handed—Birdie sent this with me, probably hoping I'd find someone to share it with."

Edith turned in time to see the postmistress pull a white pastry box from the depths of her mailbag. She groaned as Bea lifted the lid and the warm scent of cherry chocolate coffeecake washed over her.

"Ohhhhhh." Edith concentrated on the coffee mugs. "That smells good."

"It *is* good. Abner's cakes are downright sinful."

Edith lifted the coffee cups and turned, then stared at the gleaming chocolate cake. Why not eat some? After all, this was a unique occasion . . . and she wouldn't be eating, she'd be *ministering*. Maybe the sugar would lift their spirits. Besides, she hadn't actually started an official diet plan yet, so this could be her day of "last suppers." Like a condemned man who splurges on his last meal, she could eat everything she wanted today and begin her diet tomorrow. She'd wear one of her tentlike corduroy dresses to the funeral and still have nearly two full months to diet for the wedding. Plenty of time to lose a few pounds and fit into her peach dress.

She'd be good . . . tomorrow. After the funeral, she wouldn't feel like eating, anyway.

Bea dropped into a kitchen chair as Edith pulled two plates out of the cabinet, then sliced thick wedges of dense chocolate, her mind momentarily flashing back to the sausage and waffles she'd eaten a little over an hour ago.

This food was okay. It was part of the Last Breakfast.

She'd be disciplined tomorrow.

Bea sighed. "I can't believe Olympia's gone."

Edith set a plate before her guest, then handed Bea a fork. "I've always said I hope the good Lord takes me quick like that. Alive one minute, with the Lord the next."

Bea nodded, cutting into the coffeecake. "Sudden death is hard, though, on the ones left behind. Especially since Olympia went so soon after Edmund's passing."

Edith stirred sugar into her cup. Two teaspoons; she wouldn't deprive herself today.

She cut a piece of cake with her fork. "Olympia and Edmund are together now. I know she must be some happy."

With tears in her voice, Bea lifted a forkful of chocolate coffee-cake. "I suppose Winslow will be doing the service."

Edith closed her eyes as the rich chocolate melted on her tongue, then swallowed. "Ayuh. He will."

"I don't suppose this crisis will interfere with Salt's and Birdie's wedding next month," Bea said, slowly portioning off another bite. "I asked Birdie if she wanted to postpone the ceremony, but she said no. She and Salt don't want to wait another minute."

A sudden realization struck Edith as she studied the postmistress—why, Bea wasn't grieving only for Olympia! She had the look of a woman who had just lost her best friend, but Bea's best friend wasn't Olympia . . . it was Birdie.

Beatrice Coughlin had moved to Heavenly Daze after her husband's death to live with Birdie, her only sister. Edith knew Bea had considered the move permanent, never dreaming that Birdie would fall in love in the winter of her life. Salt Gribbon was a good man, and he'd make Birdie a devoted husband, but what would Bea do when Birdie moved out to the lighthouse? She'd be sitting by the fireplace in the bakery's living quarters all by herself.

Bea dragged the tines of her fork through the rich frosting on the cake. "I'm a third wheel now."

"Oh, Bea." Edith leaned over to pat her hand. "You and Birdie will still be close. She'll be coming to the bakery every day to run the business, won't she?"

"And I'll be out making the mail run." Bea's eyes clouded. "Or selling stamps. Or answering angel mail. Birdie and I always had our special time together at night, after work."

Edith finished Bea's thought. "But after the wedding, she'll be up at the lighthouse with Salt and the kids."

Bea nodded, her chin quivering. Edith remained silent for a moment, giving the woman a chance to rein in her flighty emotions.

"I'll get used to it, I suppose," Bea finally said, lowering her gaze to her plate. "A body can get used to anything, if they try hard enough. Changes are coming, I know, and I'll just have to brace for them. Olympia's gone, Annie will probably sell the house, and Birdie's moving up to the cove. Who knows?" She let out a hollow laugh. "Maybe some nice-looking rich fellow will buy Frenchman's Folly and fall for me. I could find myself serving tea in Olympia's parlor."

Edith made a face at that comment, but Bea didn't see it. Just as well—Bea was only blowing off steam.

Smiling, she tried to steer the conversation into another channel. "Do you really think Annie will sell the house?"

Bea sighed. "I don't think she wants to live here—never has. Olympia always said Annie couldn't wait to graduate and leave the island. She's got her own life now, a new boyfriend, a good job—why would she want to come back here?"

Edith shook her head. Tragedy had touched them all in the last few months, but Annie had been the hardest hit. Would she sell the house and wash her hands of Heavenly Daze altogether? Edith hoped not. Annie was family, and the family had lost too many members lately.

* * *

With her arms crossed and her heart heavy, Annie stood in the dcorway of her aunt's bedroom. The white counterpane lay smooth upon the bed, with only a slight indentation to mark the place Olympia had lain for so many years. An arrangement of silk lilacs on the nightstand cast soft shadows on the worn Bible her aunt had read every evening before falling asleep. The words gave her comfort, she always said, when the worries of life threatened to keep her awake.

Feeling like a trespasser, Annie crossed the threshold and moved to the cedar chest at the end of the bed. To prepare for his funeral address, Pastor Winslow had asked for a few clippings or something that might provide insight into Olympia's youth. Annie knew very little about her aunt's younger days, for the woman had been well into her forties when Annie had arrived at Frenchman's Fairest. Edmund Junior had been a senior in college at the time, so Edmund, Olympia, and Caleb alone had faced dealing with a frightened, grieving seven-year-old. . . .

Shoving the sad memories away, Annie lifted the lid of the chest and breathed in the scents of cedar, mothballs, and wool. A stack of sweaters lay uppermost in the trunk, but after setting them on the bed she saw a green scrapbook. Relieved, she lifted it out, then sat cross-legged on the floor and began to turn the yellowed pages.

A firm, younger hand had written *My Life* on the front page with blue ink—a fountain pen, from the looks of it. Amused by the thought of Olympia as a young girl, Annie turned the page and found black and white snapshots much like those she'd seen in the photograph album Caleb had brought down Saturday night. But these weren't photos of a baby—they were pictures of a young and pretty Olympia on the arm of a tall, handsome, and much older man—Edmund Shots in younger days.

Annie whistled with a new appreciation for the family history. Olympia had always said her marriage caused a scandal in the family, and now Annie could understand why. The age difference was noticeable.

The scrapbook held other pictures—the young couple with their new baby boy, that same boy in a baseball uniform, then in a cap, gown, and honors regalia, graduating from Yale Law School. Sprinkled among the boy pictures, Annie found photos of a skinny little girl peering around the corner of the house, one arm wrapped around a scrawny kitten, the other clinging tight to Caleb's hand. Several pictures featured Olympia standing or sitting beside the little girl, but never touching her.

Annie felt her heart contract as grief rose within her, black and cold. In every picture of her and Olympia, concern and care were etched into the older woman's face, while the little girl just looked . . . lost.

"You shouldn't blame yourself, Annie."

She jumped when Caleb's voice broke the silence. Turning, she saw him standing in the doorway, a look of compassion on his face.

"I just—I was looking for something to help the pastor."

"I know. But I saw your expression just now. You must never feel guilty for coming into Olympia's and Edmund's life. They loved you, dear heart, even if your arrival was a surprise."

As Caleb came into the room, Annie turned another page and found herself staring at several faded real estate brochures. "Live in Sunny Bradenton," one of them proclaimed, while another advertised a development on Captiva Island.

"What are these?" She picked one up and smiled at the dated drawing of a little girl in pigtails on the beach. "I never knew Aunt Olympia liked Florida."

Caleb sat on the edge of the bed. "In the fall of '80 or '81, when Edmund Junior went away to school, Olympia and Edmund toyed with the idea of selling the house and moving south. Edmund was going to work in a bank down there, and Olympia was looking forward to the sunshine. If I remember correctly, they even put Frenchman's Fairest on the market. The place was in better shape then—they would have made a tidy profit. They were all set to move."

"What happened?"

Before the words finished echoing in the room, Annie knew the answer. Her parents had died in '82, killed in a plane crash as her father attempted to land on the Ogunquit airstrip. Shortly after the accident, she had arrived at Frenchman's Fairest.

Caleb's eyes warmed slightly, and the hint of a smile acknowledged the success of her reasoning. "Your mother and father were coming to pay Olympia and Edmund a farewell visit when the plane went down. After that, Olympia said she couldn't leave. She always said Heavenly Daze was the best place on earth to raise a child, and she didn't want to raise Ferrell's daughter in Floridy. She said you'd be freckled as a guinea hen if you grew up down there."

Annie lifted the brochure again, regarding it in a new light. "They gave up their dream . . . for me?"

"They were happy to do it, especially when they fell in love with you. So you shouldn't feel at all guilty about it."

Annie closed her eyes as a fresh on-slaught of tears threatened to destroy her makeup. Seems all she'd done over the last twenty-four hours was cry. The island women had done their best to comfort her, but they'd wept, too, all of them boo-hooing over things they wished they'd told Olympia and things they regretted having said.

Edith Wickam had been the most helpful. With Annie's input, she'd outlined a dignified procedure for the funeral. Knowing Olympia's fondness for history and her place in the Heavenly Daze lineage, Edith planned to summon all the townspeople to the ferry dock at 3 P.M., just as the sun would begin to dip toward the western horizon. A special boat would bring Olympia's casket (a nice oak model, lined with white satin) from Ogunquit, then a team of pallbearers would guide the casket onto a trolley and roll it to Frenchman's Fairest. Olympia would lie in her own parlor while the townsfolk paid their respects, then she'd ride to the church for the funeral service. After the service, when everyone in town had had another chance to say their farewells, the pallbearers would wheel her back down to the dock for another trip to Ogunquit.

Annie knew Olympia had probably wanted to ride to church in her horse-drawn carriage, but Blaze, the old horse, had died right after Thanksgiving. Even if they'd had a horse, the carriage was a two-seater and couldn't handle a casket.

"I can just hear Olympia complaining about us putting too many miles on her coffin," Edith had whispered, the corners of her eyes crinkling with gentle humor. "Truth is, I think she'd like the idea of riding in a procession around town. As long as it doesn't get tacky, we'll be fine."

A conversation with the director of the funeral home had convinced Annie that Olympia would have to travel back to Ogunquit Tuesday evening. Though she had a space reserved by Edmund's side in the cemetery behind the Heavenly Daze Community Church, nothing short of an early spring thaw would permit the men to dig in the frozen earth. "Backhoes aren't all that expensive to rent, but transporting one to Heavenly Daze might be costly with the ferry not running," the funeral director had told Annie. "And I don't think you want Mrs. de Cuvier lying in your parlor until April. So we'll bring her back here until warmer weather permits a proper burial."

After a quick glance at Olympia's checkbook, Annie had decided that the more dignified option was also the more economical one. Neither she nor Olympia had money enough to transport and rent a backhoe, and the mortician assured her he wouldn't charge extra to hold the body until springtime. "We do it all the time," he told Annie. "We just add a discreet line to the funeral program to let folks know that interment will occur in the spring."

And so the last details were finalized. After the funeral, Olympia's pallbearers—Floyd Lansdown, Abner Smith, Charles Graham, Buddy Franklin, Russell Higgs, and Zuriel Smith—would wheel her back down to the dock, return the casket to the funeral home boat, and send her back to the mainland. Edith had thought it would be nice if the women carried flowers to toss into the sea as the boat sped away, so Annie had ordered three dozen red roses from the Ogunquit florist. They would arrive on the same boat bringing Olympia this afternoon.

"Red roses in February," Annie murmured, thinking of her depleted checkbook. "They cost a fortune this close to Valentine's Day."

But she'd paid for the flowers in advance, counting them as a necessary part of the funeral expenses. She'd tried to book the Wells Episcopal Boys' Choir to sing at the service, but their director flatly told her that no parent in his or her right mind would pull a boy out of school, place him on Crazy

Odell Butcher's boat, and send him out to sea in February to sing at a stranger's funeral. "I don't care if the lady was descended from George Washington," he snapped. "We're not coming."

So Annie had borrowed a CD of the Vienna Boys' Choir music from Micah. Perhaps the simple purity of their voices would make up for the missing musicians . . . because they were the best Annie could do. She just hoped she'd done enough.

She couldn't shake the feeling that even now Olympia was looking down from heaven and judging her efforts.

* * *

Olympia walked across a shimmering gold-green meadow with her spirit-hand in her grandfather's. Though many things were still new to her, in some ways she felt as though she had resided in the wonderful place for years. She still found herself reaching up to scratch an incorporeal nose that did not actually itch, or reaching out to smooth insubstantial hair, but somehow she was adjusting to the fact that spiritual things were completely real, though intangible.

Now, for instance, she knew that she held Jean Luc de Cuvier's hand even though neither of them possessed fleshly fingers. To her spirit eyes her grandfather was young and strong, though if she had met him on the streets of Heavenly Daze she would have had a hard time guessing his age. Time meant nothing here, for eternity stretched before them.

She smiled in the warmth of her grandfather's love. "It's so beautiful here." She lifted her gaze to the meadow. The grass moved with the breath of a warm breeze, and a gentle chime tinkled through the air with each movement of the golden leaves.

"How could it be anything else?" Jean Luc lifted his hand, where a graceful eagle circled overhead, then veered out of the way of a speeding angel. "The Creator makes everything beautiful, and heaven has never been corrupted by sin. But this is nothing compared to the new heaven and new earth we shall one day explore. All of creation, above and below us, is waiting for the time when God will redeem the planet. The old, corrupt things will pass away, and all things will be made new." His smile brightened in intensity. "Then I shall once again hold your hand, and when I squeeze it, I'll be holding flesh that will never grow old, never disease, never suffer the debilitating effects of time."

Olympia shook her head. "It boggles my brain just to think of it. I know God has a plan for the future, but Pastor Winslow always lost me when he started talking about Revelations and such. I had a hard enough time following him when he preached on the Minor Prophets."

Her grandfather laughed. "Those prophets, I understand, have a bit of a bone to pick with your Pastor Winslow. After he arrives, I hear Obadiah, Nahum, and Haggai plan to sit him down to clear up a few misconceptions."

Olympia chuckled, then gasped as a beautiful white stallion galloped into the meadow, then paused. His nostrils flared as he studied them, then the majestic creature whickered and cantered gracefully toward the trees at the edge of the grass.

"I didn't know there were animals here."

"Of course there are. All good, created things have a place in heaven. The prophets told us that the Lord would return to earth upon a white horse. If I'm not mistaken, you've just seen the honored animal himself."

From out of the woods at their right, an angel fluttered from the trees, his wings softly beating the air as he hovered a few feet away. He greeted them in the name of the Lord, then casually popped what looked like a snack cake into his mouth before moving on.

"Grandfather, was that—no! They can't have Little Debbies in heaven!"

Jean Luc chortled. "Oh, Olympia, I'd forgotten what a charming child you are! No, my dear, the angels eat manna. It is the food of heaven, and they tell me it's quite wonderful." His voice grew wistful. "I look forward to eating it at the marriage supper of the Lamb, when we meet our heavenly bridegroom in our perfect resurrected bodies. There, my dear, we shall feast as never before!"

They walked farther, saying nothing, but enjoying the fellowship of each other's company. Olympia had no memories of her grandfather on earth; he had passed over when she was only two years old. She had never realized she'd be able to meet and know him . . . another unexpected benefit of heaven.

They crested a small hill, then halted at

the top. Below them, the grass stirred with more movement than usual. Though the babbling, happy sound of children's voices tickled Olympia's ear, she could see nothing.

She squinted, trying to see what moved the rustling grasses. "What is that?".

Her grandfather chuckled. "The children. Heaven is filled with them, and they're hard to see because they're so active. But if we move a little closer . . ."

He lifted her then, apparently by the power of his thoughts, and within a moment Olympia found herself floating beside the flowing grasses. Her lips parted when her spirit eyes adjusted to the speed with which the children moved. There were a least a dozen playing here—beautiful youngsters whose spirits shone with life.

"Some of them lived only a short time on earth," Jean Luc explained, "and some never even drew a breath. But the Creator, in love, brought them all home."

If she'd had physical eyes, Olympia knew she would have wept in a simple outpouring of emotion. She pressed her hand to her chest and swallowed hard—an old reflex that had not yet died—and met her grandfather's gaze. "They are so sweet."

"Innocent," he answered. "And millions of them dwell in this place. They come from every part of earth, from every country. No matter what their situation on earth, here they are tenderly welcomed and guarded by the Father's angels."

Olympia halted in midstep, her hand slipping from her grandfather's as the breeze ruffled the hem of her long white robe. "I can't believe I was ever afraid to come here." Her eyes met Jean Luc's. "Why is that? I knew heaven was a wonderful place, but I was in no hurry to die."

"Perhaps that is why the Scriptures are silent about so many aspects of this place. Tell me, dear one—if you could push a button and transport all your loved ones to this place, would you do it?"

"In a heartbeat." She looked around. "Is there a button like that?"

Her grandfather laughed. "No. Every human above the age of understanding still has to make his or her own reservation. And God has a plan for his people on earth—the world below is sort of like kindergarten, the place where we learn the basics of life and gain a smattering of wisdom. Living on earth is like riding a bike with training wheels—it's here, in heaven, that we really learn how to live, and think, and explore." He shrugged. "Heaven is the greatest adventure mankind will ever know, and this is just the beginning. There is so much more to come."

"I should have listened better," Olympia whispered, addressing the Spirit of God. He was so close she could see the shimmer of his glory with every movement of the wind. He had been close on earth, too, dwelling in her frail frame, but most of the time her mind had been too clouded by earthly concerns to be aware of his presence.

Speechless with wonder, Olympia wrapped her translucent fingers around Jean Luc's shimmering arm. "Tell me more," she said. "We have time, don't we?"

"My dear Olympia, we have an eternity to share."

* * *

By 2:45, a decent crowd had gathered at the dock, though Annie had to peer through layers of winter wrappings to see who was who. Birdie and Bea were encased in scarves and matching wool coats; Vernie wore a navy blue ski mask through which her reddened eyes shone like weak flashlights. Stanley Bidderman stood loyally behind Vernie, probably the only man of Annie's acquaintance who would allow his wife to wear such a getup to such a dignified occasion, but, then again, not many island men were trying to make up for twenty years of neglect.

Charles and Babette stood beside the tiny clapboard ferry office, sheltering their son, Georgie, from the frigid wind, while Mike and Dana Klackenbush huddled with Buddy Franklin and Russell Higgs. Barbara, Russell's wife, was tucked into bed at the bed and breakfast, still recovering from last month's surgery.

Floyd Lansdown stood at the end of the dock, and from where she waited Annie could hear him telling Micah that the town needed its own ferry so they wouldn't have to depend upon Stroble or Crazy Odell. "Course, we need new rubber for the fire engine first," he yelled, his voice carried by the wind. "But after that, a ferry should be our next priority."

At three o'clock, with no sign yet of the boat, Annie peered at the faces around her. Though the wind was brisk, no one was grumbling about having to stand out in the cold. The bright sun had brought the temperature up to thirty degrees, but as it inched toward the horizon the air would become frosty.

Still she heard no complaints. Perhaps they were all thinking that stoic Olympia would have been the last to complain if she were waiting on one of them.

Winslow and Edith stood with Cleta, all three of them wearing expressions of profound regret, while Annie waited with Caleb and Dr. Marc. She kept her face turned toward the restless sea, for every few minutes her chin quivered uncontrollably. To stanch the unpredictable geyser of tears, she forced herself to focus on trivial things—had she remembered to feed Tallulah? At the funeral tomorrow, would Micah think to plug in the CD player behind the church piano? The piano would hide the CD player so maybe no one would realize those pure boyish voices were not spilling down from an angel choir. . . .

She was *not,* she assured herself, weeping out of sadness or guilt. Dr. Marc had persuaded her she was not to blame for Olympia's death, and Caleb had convinced her that Olympia was happy in heaven. So her tears could not spring from grief, but must be rising from the fervent, sincere hope that A.J. would be aboard the boat coming from the funeral home.

He knew about this dockside ceremony. She'd called last night to share every detail. She'd wanted to hear him say she was doing a good job and holding up well under the stress. Most of all she had wanted to hear him promise he'd move heaven and earth to be with her during this difficult time, but though she had given him several opportunities, he had not made those assurances.

But he was a busy man. And perhaps he meant to surprise her.

As Floyd cried out that a vessel had appeared on the horizon, with everything in her heart Annie hoped A.J. was aboard.

"That ain't no funeral home cruiser," Floyd called, shielding his eyes with his hand. "That looks like Odell's boat."

Annie closed her eyes as a tremor shot through her.

"Ayuh." Russell Higgs, a lobsterman who knew every boat within miles by the cut of her prow, stepped closer to Annie. "That's definitely the *Sally*. I'm thinking the man from the funeral home didn't want to risk his nice cruiser in this chop. The sea's downright gormy today."

Annie opened her eyes to a squint, imagining what Olympia would say if she knew she was being ferried to her funeral on the cluttered deck of an aging boat piloted by a daredevil seasoned citizen.

She stood on tiptoe, scanning the *Sally*'s deck for some sign of a tall, handsome doctor. Odell was easy to spot at the helm—a skinny man wearing a fluorescent orange life preserver over his oilskins.

Russell laughed. "Look at 'im. His granddaughter makes him wear that ridiculous vest. I hear she ties him into it before she'll let him out of the house."

"He looks like a pumpkin." Floyd turned to wink at Annie. "But never you fear, sweetheart, he'll have your Aunt Olympia safe on the dock in another five minutes."

Edith moved closer, her gloved hands twisting the end of her scarf. "I do hope he remembered the roses, Annie. If he forgot, it's a sure bet he won't want to go back to the florist to fetch them. Men don't set much store by such things."

"Where do they get roses in winter?" Winslow asked, his eyes searching his wife's face. "I've always wondered."

"I think they fly them in from Argentina, or maybe California." Teetering from side to side, Edith peered at the approaching boat. "If Odell remembered, I do hope he put the roses down in the hold. I don't want the boxes to get all wet from the sea spray."

"I think I see flowers." Winslow slipped his hands into his pockets and nodded at the approaching boat. "Aren't those roses on the casket?"

Annie turned toward the ocean, where the wind was sending showers of spray over the *Sally*. Her mittened hand rose to her lips as she realized that Pastor Winslow spoke the truth—now she could see the casket on the deck, its surface covered by a blanket of roses.

She held her breath as the boat came closer. Olympia had always said Odell was one brick short of a full load, and today he seemed bent on either proving her point or taking some kind of revenge. Annie could see him grinning as he steered toward the Heavenly Daze dock. The bow dipped in a swell and rose again, sending a cool splash of spray over Olympia's polished casket. He had just passed the anchored *Barbara Jean,* Russell Higgs's lobster boat, when—

"Ohmigoodness!" Winslow cried. "Where'd that come from?"

The assembled crowd gasped in concert as a rogue wave rolled in from the sea. Odell cut the wheel sharply, trying to turn and ride the monster, but his response was too little, too late. Lifting the *Sally* from the water as easily as if she were a toy, the surge carried the boat for a moment, her mast tilting at a dangerous angle, then crashed over the *Sally* in a roar that left Annie gasping for breath. The boat rolled onto its side, and everything on the deck— seaman, lobster traps, lines, and casket— went into the sea.

Edith Wickam screamed, Bea collapsed into Birdie's arms, and Vernie released a most unladylike exclamation. While Pastor Winslow moved his lips in silent prayer, Salt Gribbon and Russell Higgs raced toward the dory tied to the dock.

Annie staggered forward. "I should go with you," she told Russell as he jumped down into the boat.

"You stay here, Annie." He settled onto

the thwart as Charles Graham cast off the line. "We'll do what we can."

After a moment woven of eternity, Odell surfaced in the foaming water, his fluorescent orange jacket signaling like a beacon. A few feet away, Olympia's casket trailed in Odell's wake, still covered by its blanket of roses.

"Godfrey mighty!" Cleta Lansdown shook her finger at Russell and Salt, who were rowing like dervishes. "You gotta get Odell outta that water quick! The old man is liable to freeze clear down to his long-handles!"

"And Aunt Olympia!" Annie pointed toward the brown box rocking on the waves. "Get her, too!"

The sound of creaking wood sent horror snaking down her backbone. Out on the sea, the *Sally* groaned, her mast tilting starboard until it touched the water. In front of the vessel, floating amid the feather-white water and several painted buoys, Odell bobbed in his orange life preserver . . . only yards from Aunt Olympia's casket.

A shocked silence fell over the group on the dock as the dory reached Odell. Russell and Salt hauled the old man into the boat, then the three of them sat in silence as the

Sally righted herself, then tipped and slipped beneath the waves, stern first.

"Just like *Titanic*," Dana Klackenbush whispered, one hand pressed to her cheek. "That old boat went down just like the ship in the movie."

Annie stood transfixed, her eyes trained on the flower-strewn box. Olympia's casket floated toward the vortex where the ship had disappeared, spun twice, then caught another wave that pushed it eastward, toward the open sea.

She couldn't speak. She lifted her hand and pointed to the oblong container moving steadily away from Heavenly Daze.

The rescuers had no time for the dead; they were working to save a life still hanging in the balance. Bending and flexing in rhythm, they rowed Odell to shore.

"We'd better get a fire going." Edith tugged on her husband's sleeve. "Odell's going to require warming up."

"I'll get my medicine bag," Dr. Marc announced. He glanced at the pastor. "Shall I meet you at the parsonage?"

"Frenchman's Fairest is closer," Caleb interjected. "And our fire is already blazing. I put on a new log just before leaving the house."

Like marionettes on a unified string, the three men turned to Annie. "That okay with you, dear?" Pastor Winslow asked, softening his tone. "We'll need to get Odell defrosted as soon as possible."

With an effort, Annie hauled her gaze from the sea and returned her attention to the people on the dock. "What about Aunt Olympia?" She met the doctor's gaze. "How are we going to get her?"

The doctor's eyes gentled. "Caskets are airtight, dear. Unless damaged in some way, they'll float forever. We'll send Russell out to search once we get Odell settled in a warm place."

"Okay." Pressing her hand to the side of her face, she forced herself to concentrate on the emergency at hand. "Take the front room of the house; put Odell on the sofa. You can push it closer to the fireplace if you like."

We have plenty of room, since the casket's obviously not coming any time soon.

She glanced back toward the water, where a handful of long-stemmed roses marked the spot where the *Sally* had gone down. Was no one worried about the boat?

As the dory pulled up to the dock, Charles

Graham and Buddy Franklin reached down to grab Odell Butcher. The old sailor kept yelling that he was fine, he could walk by himself, but even from across the dock Annie could see that his lips were blue.

"He's a gormy old cuss," Charles called, grinning at the wide-eyed women as he half-carried, half-dragged Odell across the dock. "But with spirit like this, he'll be fine."

"All the same, hypothermia isn't something we can take lightly," Dr. Marc called, turning toward the house. "I'll meet you inside."

Following the doctor, Annie set out for Frenchman's Fairest. She'd check the fire herself, then set a pot of water on the stove for tea. In anticipation of the guests who would come for the viewing, Caleb had already arranged a few finger foods on the dining room table, so it wouldn't take much to turn the parlor into an emergency room. . . .

With one last glance at Odell's gray skin, she broke into a jog. It wasn't until she reached the door that she realized Odell had been the only living soul aboard the *Sally*.

A.J. hadn't come.

Chapter Four

Annie woke to the sound of voices, wondered for an instant how her apartment had come to be filled with strangers, then remembered she was not in Portland. She was on Heavenly Daze, in her aunt's house, and this was Tuesday, the day for which they had scheduled Olympia's funeral. But so far absolutely nothing had gone according to her carefully laid plans, so who knew what sort of calamity the next twenty-four hours would bring?

Groaning, she sat up and blinked away the last fragments of her dreams, then tilted her head at the sound of voices approaching on the stairs outside her door. She recognized the calm tones of Pastor Winslow, Caleb's soft murmur, and the high-pitched, slightly nasal whine belonging to Odell Butcher.

The old codger had wanted to return to

Ogunquit last night, but Dr. Marc had refused to give him any clothes. Though the old man might have been daffy, he was not immodest. After placing a call to his granddaughter to assure her of his safety, he spent the rest of the night muttering under Olympia's electric blanket.

Only when the old man had been safely tucked in did Dr. Marc come into the kitchen for coffee and conversation. Upon seeing Annie's troubled gaze, he had dropped his hand over hers. "I'm sorry." He squeezed her knotted fist. "I know it must have been a shock, seeing your aunt float away like that."

Annie shook her head. Russell had taken the *Barbara Jean* out just after Odell's rescue, but Olympia had drifted out to sea with the current, and the encroaching darkness had made a search impossible.

"I'm sorry, Annie," Russell had said, shifting uneasily on the porch after his return. "But I can't see anything on a cloudy night like this. We'd best wait until morning, then call the Coast Guard. Or maybe one of the other lobstermen will spot her when they head out in the morning."

Annie had returned to the kitchen to give Dr. Marc and Caleb the bad news. "What am I supposed to do now? I can't just forget about her—what would people think? But how on earth are we supposed to find her? The currents could have carried her anywhere. And if the casket hits the rocks up on the coast, it could sink. Then we'll *never* find her."

"Shh, dear, don't fret yourself." Dr. Marc had stepped closer, pressing her head to his shoulder, and Annie had closed her eyes, relishing the comfort of a kind touch. Dr. Marc was a godsend; she would have lost her head if not for his clear thinking. He had known how to care for Odell; he had sent the other townspeople home to spare Annie from a barrage of comments, and by asking her to help him care for Odell, he had kept her from brooding about Olympia . . . and A.J.

But even he hadn't been able to keep sad reality at bay forever.

"A doctor's life is busy," he had said when she lifted her head. "I'm sure Alex had a good reason for not coming."

"He always does." She had forced a smile. "But though he promised to come for the funeral, I don't know how he's going to get here. Without Odell's boat—"

"Alex is resourceful; he always has been. I'm sure he'll think of something, Annie."

She had drifted off to sleep with that promise ringing in her ears, but those words seemed unrealistic in the gray morning light seeping beneath her window shade. Heavenly Daze had been blessed with an unseasonably warm winter, but a cloudbank had moved in to cover the morning sun, and the wind rattling the window held the promise of snow in its breath.

Quickly dressing in jeans, wool socks, and a sweater, she padded down the stairs and into the kitchen. Caleb, Dr. Marc, and Odell were sitting at the table, and Odell had the telephone pressed to his ear. When Caleb caught Annie's eye, he pointed to the empty place at his right hand, then gestured toward the big bowl of oatmeal steaming in the center of the table.

"I thought you'd be down soon," Caleb whispered, placing a clean bowl and spoon on her placemat. "Eat up, dear one. You'll need your strength today."

Nodding gratefully, she sank into the chair, then scooped up a dipperful of the hot oatmeal and plopped it into her bowl.

Lifting a brow, she nodded toward Odell. "Who's he talking to?"

Dr. Marc grinned. "His granddaughter. We

called her after the accident, of course, and she was relieved to hear he was okay. Now it sounds like her relief has passed into anger."

Annie shook her head.

Across the table, Odell averted his eyes and held the phone an inch from his ear. Every once in a while he'd open his mouth as if to argue a point, then his mouth would close as his granddaughter squawked from the receiver. Annie looked down at her bowl and tried not to laugh. It was comical, the way his mouth opened and closed like a hooked fish . . . but there was nothing funny about Aunt Olympia floating to France.

She dropped her head to her hand as a somber thought slammed into her. "Dr. Marc?"

"Um?"

Not wanting to upset Caleb, she lowered her voice. "There's no way we're going to find Aunt Olympia in time for the funeral, is there?"

His lips smiled, but his eyes did not. "Short of an absolute miracle, I don't think so. But you can still have the memorial service. You don't need a body to celebrate someone's life."

She leaned closer. "There's a good

chance I'm not even going to find her for a springtime interment, isn't there?"

He coughed into his hand and stared down at his coffee cup, then whispered, "You're probably right. Sea people tend to let things rest. I doubt, for instance, if anyone will bother to raise the *Sally*. From what I've gathered from Odell, the little bit of insurance he carried on the boat won't cover the salvage expenses. His granddaughter wants him to let the boat lie."

"On the bottom?"

"Ayuh. It'll make a nice artificial reef. If no one spots the casket in a day or two, you might want to consider it a burial at sea."

Annie leaned back in her chair, then slowly lifted a spoonful of oatmeal to her mouth. Pretending Olympia had gone down with the *Sally* would be the easiest thing to do, but her conscience wouldn't allow it. What would Edmund Junior think? He'd be horrified when he heard what had happened to his mother's remains. She'd be lucky if he didn't threaten to sue her for dereliction of duty or something.

And what of Olympia herself? She had carefully planned her funeral, reserved her plot next to Edmund, requested the boys' choir. Annie couldn't put her aunt to rest without fulfilling at least *one* of the woman's wishes. . . .

She leaned toward the doctor again. "Dr. Marc?"

"Um?"

"I've got to find her."

He took a sip of his coffee, smiled at Caleb, then bent his head to whisper in her ear. "We'll talk about it later, dear. You have a big day ahead of you."

"But—"

"Don't worry, Annie. Caleb called the Coast Guard, and they've promised to call us if anyone reports an offshore casket. At this point, there's nothing more we can do."

* * *

Fat, wet flakes of snow began to fall from the soft gray sky on Tuesday afternoon. Marc brushed the snowflakes from the shoulders of his dark coat, then shifted uneasily as he entered the church behind Floyd Lansdown. Six pallbearers, all shivering in their black suits with no overcoats, had lined up in the churchyard without a casket between them. Edith had insisted they behave as if the dearly departed were present, so the six men pasted on grave expressions and moved down the church aisle carrying nothing. To the right of the communion table, a hastily painted portrait of Olympia de Cuvier stared out at them with a slightly accusing expression.

Marc breathed a sigh of relief when they reached the front, then he slipped into the family pew with Annie. A.J. sat next to her (thank the Lord, he had found a lobsterman in Wells who had agreed to bring him over), while Edmund Junior, clad in an expensive cashmere topcoat, sat at the end of the pew with Caleb. Whisked in by helicopter, he had arrived barely fifteen minutes before the service was scheduled to begin. Bobby Gribbon and Georgie Graham had nearly swooned with excitement to see the chopper landing at the northern end of the island, but the noise had frightened little Brittany. Now she sat in the pew with Salt, barricading herself behind her grandfather's burly forearm as if she feared the helicopter visitor might sweep her up and carry her away.

Marc glanced down the pew to peek at Olympia's son. Edmund Junior seemed calm, but he kept swiping at his red nose with his handkerchief. Marc privately believed the man was suffering more from the cold weather than from any remorse about his mother's passing. If the man had cared for Olympia so much, why hadn't he taken the time to write, call, or visit? Upon arriving at the house, he had scarcely said two words to Annie before asking to see his mother's will and personal papers. He now carried a copy of the will in the pocket of his topcoat.

Marc settled back in the pew and drew a deep breath. However cold-hearted Edmund Junior might be, he didn't appear to be ill-mannered enough to open the will and peer at its pages during the memorial service. After the service, of course, he might harass Annie.

Marc made a mental note to stay close enough to help, should Annie need a hand.

Music by the Vienna Boys' Choir had filled the church during the processional; now Beatrice Coughlin sat at the piano, a small microphone on a stand next to her. At a nod from Edith, acting as funeral director, Bea tapped the microphone twice, then ran her fingers over the keys in a rippling arpeggio.

"O think of the home over there," she sang, her voice warbling over the sound system,

"By the side of the river of light,
Where the saints, all immortal and fair,
Are robed in their garments of white."

"Mama," Georgie Graham's voice rang out, "why are the saints wearing their bath-robes?"

Ignoring him, Bea sang on.

"O think of the friends over there,
Who before us the journey have trod,
Of the songs that they breathe on the air,
In their home in the palace of God."

Marc glanced at Georgie, but Babette had anticipated the break in the song. In perfect time to the music, she clapped her hand over his mouth until Bea began the final verse.

"My Savior is now over there,
There my kin and friends are at rest,
Then away from my sorrow and care,
Let me fly to the land of the blest."

Marc drew a deep breath, taking comfort from the lyrics of the old hymn. His dear wife, Alex's mother, had been dwelling in the palace of God for nearly ten years. He still missed her, particularly when he worried about Alex . . . but now that Alex had found Annie, he would worry less.

Annie Cuvier was a fine young woman, the best of Olympia and Edmund combined into one lovely personality. Like Edmund, she loved to give, devoting herself completely to causes ranging from tomatoes to homeless animals. Olympia had spent many hours telling Marc about Annie's childhood—how the girl befriended wounded birds she found on the beach; how one summer she had adopted a puffin family and wept for hours when one of the babies died. Olympia could not understand that part of Annie—the mistress of Frenchman's Fairest had been a fine person, but she'd definitely been more of a cold prickly than a warm fuzzy. Yet Annie had brought warmth and happiness to Olympia in the last few months, and the place wouldn't be the same without her youthful enthusiasm.

He felt his heart sink. He would miss Olympia because she had been a generous landlady and a faithful friend. He would also miss her because her passing meant Annie had no more reasons to visit the island. With no tomatoes, aunt, or uncle to draw her home, Annie would most likely remain in Portland with her work.

There remained, however, the matter of Olympia's bequest. He wasn't sure what the woman was thinking when she left Frenchman's Fairest to Annie; despite what she said in her letter, she may have intended to snub her son rather than endow her niece. But one thing was certain—Annie had no use for a house. As a young woman, she would want a home of her own with a husband like A.J. as its master. Together they would have strong, intelligent children. The prospect of having Annie as a daughter-in-law should have filled Marc's heart with joy . . .

So why didn't it?

* * *

With A.J.'s firm hand on her elbow, Annie dabbed at her eyes and watched as Beatrice ripped out one final arpeggio.

When Bea had finished, Caleb stood. Annie felt the room grow quiet as movement and sniffling ceased. Everyone wondered what the old butler would say, for he had known Olympia better than anyone except Edmund.

The man's bright eyes swept the room. "Now, dear brothers and sisters, I want you to know what has happened to Olympia so you will not be full of sorrow like people who have no hope." His soft brown eyes crinkled as he smiled. "For since you believe that Jesus died and was raised to life again, you also believe that when the Lord comes, God will bring back with Him all the Christians who have died, including Olympia. I can tell you this directly from the Lord: You who are still living when the Lord returns will not rise to meet him ahead of those who are in their graves. For the Lord himself will come down from heaven with a commanding shout, with the call of the archangel, and with the trumpet call of God. First, all the Christians who have died will rise from their graves. Then, together with them, you who are still alive and remain on the earth will be caught up in the clouds to meet the Lord in the air and remain with Him forever. So comfort and encourage each other with these words."

A murmur of "ayuhs" and "amens" rippled through the room as Caleb took his seat. Then Pastor Wickam stood and walked to the pulpit.

"I do not think I can add anything to the words of comfort Caleb Smith has shared with us," he said, gripping the edges of the pulpit. "But perhaps some of you would like to share a *brief*"—he glanced at Floyd Lansdown, who had a tendency to be long-winded in community meetings—"tribute to our dear friend Olympia."

The women on the other side of the church looked at each other, then Dana Klackenbush stood. "Alst I know," she said, holding tight to the back of the pew in front of her, "is whenever I wanted to know what a lady should do in any given situation, I would ask myself, 'What would Olympia do?' And then I had my answer. She was the classiest lady on the island, and I was honored to call her my friend."

Floyd waved his hand. "Hear, hear!"

Ignoring Floyd, the pastor nodded at Birdie Wester.

"Thank you, Pastor." Pulling herself from the space beneath Salt Gribbon's arm, Birdie rose to her full height of five feet and a few centimeters, then drew a deep breath.

"Olympia had her share of struggles, but she bore them like a stalwart Christian. I never heard her complain about personal things, not even when her only son couldn't seem to find the time to pay her a visit—"

"Sister!"

Birdie halted in midsentence, then looked down at her hissing sibling. She squared her shoulders as if she planned to continue her diatribe against Edmund Junior, then apparently thought the better of it when Salt Gribbon reached out and gripped her elbow.

"Well," she said, the touch of her man's hand obviously settling her down, "Olympia was a class act, true. And when I see her in heaven, I'll be sure to tell her so. I'm only sorry we didn't get to do more neighborin' here on the island."

As Birdie settled back in the crook of Salt's arm, Vernie Bidderman rose and clomped up the aisle in man-sized boots. Annie pressed her hand over her face as Vernie turned by the portrait on the easel, then draped an arm over it as if she were good-naturedly resting her arm on Aunt Olympia's genteel shoulders.

"You all know Olympia," Vernie said, "and you know me. We are two different kinds of people, and about as likely to mix as oil and water. If not for the Lord and this island throwin' us together, I guess we'd never have mixed at all. But Olympia did bring a little culture into my life, and I'd like to think I brought a little grit into hers. But I'm especially happy to think the Lord gave her an honor we never would have thought to offer her."

Vernie paused, lifting a brow, and Babette Graham rose to the bait. "What did the Lord give her, Vernie?"

As serious as a philosopher, Vernie thumped her chest. "A burial at sea."

For an instant no one spoke, then Birdie chirped: "I kinda thought it was fittin', seeing as how she was descended from that sea captain."

A flutter of smiles appeared on Birdie's and Bea's pew. Charles Graham leaned forward, his chin quivering. "All we were missing was the twenty-one gun salute."

"I could start up the siren on the fire truck," Floyd called. "If I let it wail twenty-one minutes, would that count?"

Annie pressed her hand to her chest as Russell Higgs rose from his seat. "She had an honor guard escort—and Crazy Odell Butcher darn nearly had a burial at sea himself."

Vernie thumped her chest again. "Olympia would love that—she dearly *hated* to ride with that man. Said she wouldn't ride with him if he were the last captain on earth!"

Floyd slapped his knee. "Well, I guess she didn't! Bailed out on him, didn't she?"

The remarks continued flying, thick and fast, and through the rising din Annie felt Edith Wickam's gaze meet hers. A moment later Edith was shooting daggers at Winslow. "Win! Stop them! This is disgraceful!"

Pastor Winslow, who had been gamely smiling at the spontaneous comments, now blushed crimson and gripped the pulpit with both hands. "Um, quiet," he called, knocking on the pulpit for emphasis. "This is, ah, a time of reverence and respect. We should not be laughing at the, um, unfortunate cruise—I mean *news*—that no one has found dear Olympia's casket."

A wave of giggles followed his slip, with outright whooping from Vernie and Stanley Bidderman. Dana Klackenbush, who was Annie's age and hadn't known Olympia as long as the others, was trying to hold her face in composed lines, though her cheeks and forehead had gone as red as a woman strangling on a fried clam.

Tears of dismay flooded Annie's eyes. This wasn't what Aunt Olympia would have wanted for her funeral *at all*. The people who knew and loved her better than anyone on earth were howling at the final little joke life had played on the mistress of Frenchman's Fairest—

Dr. Marc stood and whirled to face the crowd. "Hush, now, all of you! Can't you see you're upsetting Annie?"

Annie lowered her eyes as her cheeks burned. While it had been thoughtful of him to notice her discomfort, she wished he hadn't singled her out.

"We're sorry, Annie," Vernie called, wiping tears of mirth from her eyes, "but you have to admit the thought of Olympia being buried at sea is downright comical."

"She was always so proud of being related to that captain," Cleta added. "So it's purely fittin' that things *went down* the way they did."

Another wave of laughter rolled across the sanctuary as Annie hunched lower in the pew.

Without fanfare, Caleb stood and walked to the front of the room, then climbed the steps to the platform. Pastor Wickam stepped aside, vacating the pulpit, but Caleb merely turned, closed his eyes, and lifted his hands.

The noise in the church subsided; after a few last whoops, the sound of laughter ceased.

When every cackle and giggle had faded away, Caleb looked up and smiled. "Thank you, Father, for laughter. I thank you that my dear friend Olympia is now experiencing joy unlike anything she knew on earth. I rejoice in knowing you have reunited her with her dear husband Edmund, her brother Ferrell, her sister-in-law Ruth Ann, and her beloved parents. Many are the souls she knows in your house, and they care for her with a love surpassing earthly affection. But most of all, loving Savior, we are grateful that you are there laughing with our Olympia, sharing your joy so her time of waiting will be full and rich. Thank you, Lord, for your goodness and bountiful grace. Thank you for the laughter and love in this room. Please let Olympia know how much we miss her, and that we honor her with our laughter in her name."

* * *

With Edmund by her side, Olympia peered over the balcony of heaven and witnessed the funeral gathering. She saw her friends seated in the pews, she saw her son stand

and slip his arm around Caleb's frail shoulders, guiding him back into his seat.

She laughed. If only Edmund Junior knew the *true* strength in that frame.

Her soul warmed at the thought that everyone in Heavenly Daze had come to pay his or her respects. "That does my heart good, Edmund," she said, bending to rest her arms on the balcony railing. "And doesn't the church look lovely! Vernie has brought some of those nice candles from the Mercantile, and it looks like Babette has dusted off the silk flowers. That girl always did have a passion for cleanliness."

"The setting is beautiful," Edmund agreed. "But no more beautiful than the smiles on their faces. You will be missed, Olympia, until we are reunited at the Resurrection."

"May it come soon." Olympia fell silent as Pastor Winslow stepped forward to close the meeting in prayer, then she frowned. "Edmund?"

"Yes, my dear?"

"There's no casket at the church. Do you think Annie had me cremated? I didn't want to be cremated; ovens are for cherry pies."

"Annie would never do anything but honor your wishes."

"Then what do you suppose they did with me?"

A smile flitted over his glowing face. "You're here, aren't you?"

"That's not what I meant." If she'd been mortal, she would have blushed. "Where'd they put my body?"

He laughed. "I'm not sure you want to know."

"Why in heaven not?"

"Because sometimes the best-laid plans go awry."

She stared at him, trying to make sense of what she was hearing. "I don't see how anyone could be confused about my plans. I gave specific instructions in a letter I left with my will. I wanted to have a quiet closed-casket ceremony, and I wanted to be buried next to you in the Heavenly Daze cemetery. I picked out lovely plots for both of us, only a stone's throw from Jacques de Cuvier's monument—"

"Your casket went into the drink when Crazy Odell Butcher's boat went down. Annie's got the Coast Guard out looking for it."

For a moment Olympia could not speak, but something in her shriveled in horror.

Olympia de Cuvier, riding aboard the *Sally?* Why, she'd not been willing to board that rust bucket when she was alive, so why in heaven's name had she been traveling in it after death?

"The entire town watched you drift out to sea," Edmund continued, relentless in his needling. "Vernie Bidderman tactfully refers to the accident as your 'last cruise.'"

Olympia snorted. "Vernie Bidderman doesn't have a tactful bone in her body, Edmund, and furthermore—" She paused, seeking the indignation to fire her words, and found . . . nothing.

Edmund was right. Her worn-out physical body was not important now that she lived in heaven, and neither was her pride.

Looking at the man who had known her best on earth, Olympia began to laugh.

Chapter Five

The scents of yeast rolls and coffee filled the church basement as Annie moved down the impromptu buffet line. Every woman in town had brought a covered dish or two, and the folding tables groaned beneath the weight of their generosity.

She smiled as she filled a Styrofoam bowl with a ladleful of Vernie's clam chowder. According to the mistress of the Mercantile, there was no heartache a warm bowl of chowder couldn't mend.

Annie's heart *was* aching. Not only with the loss of her aunt, but with the knowledge that two men who should have accompanied her down the church stairs had fled right after Pastor Wickam said "amen." Edmund Junior had given her a quick hug and run for his helicopter while A.J. had headed for the boat he'd hired to bring him to the island. The first defection didn't surprise her, the latter astounded and hurt her.

After a death in the family, shouldn't a man stick around to comfort the woman he loved? She considered the question as she scooped up a serving of Dana Klackenbush's green bean casserole, and had her answer before the beans and onions hit her paper plate: Olympia would say a hasty exit was not proper behavior for a young man in love.

Because Annie had lingered in the sanctuary, seeking a few moments of silence, she was the last to go through the serving line. By the time she filled her plate, all the other townspeople were already seated and eating, though their conversation seemed unusually subdued. Annie slipped into the empty seat next to Dr. Marc.

Before she could sip from her glass, she felt Pastor Wickam look her way. "Annie? I don't mean to interrupt your lunch, but you didn't speak during the service. We were wondering if you had a word or two you wanted to share."

Inwardly, she grimaced, though she took pains to keep a pleasant expression on her face. She hadn't been able to speak at the funeral; she'd been petrified that she'd break down and bawl. But the others obviously wanted to know how she was coping, so perhaps this was the best time and place to tell them.

Drawing a deep breath, she stood. "Thank you all for coming and furnishing this wonderful meal." She looked down the table, smiling her thanks to Babette Graham, Cleta, Edith, Dana, Vernie, Birdie, and Bea. "Aunt Olympia would be so pleased to know you cared enough to honor her this way. I'm certain she's in a better place now, and I know she's with Uncle Edmund. I only hope I can please her by carrying out her final wishes."

"I heard she left Frenchman's Fairest to you," Vernie said, propping her elbows on the table. "What are you going to do with the house?"

Annie shrugged. "I haven't decided. Since I live in Portland, I'm not sure what good a house on Heavenly Daze will do me."

"You *can't* sell it." This came from Birdie, whose bright blue eyes were like twin laser beams at the end of the table. "Not as long as Caleb's living. He's like family, and you can't evict family from the house."

Annie lifted her chin and glanced toward the end of the table, where Caleb was eating with the other Smith men. Fortunately, he seemed oblivious to their conversation.

"I wasn't thinking of evicting Caleb. I guess I was thinking he'd stay with the house."

"Like a pair of draperies?" Vernie shook her head. "Honey, you can't treat people that way."

Annie felt herself flush. "I wasn't going to leave him with the house. I thought I'd— well, I haven't really thought it through. I don't know what I'm thinking."

Glancing down, she caught Dr. Marc's gaze. He sent her a reassuring smile that gave her the courage to meet Vernie head on. "I don't know what I'm going to do. I want to be sure I honor Aunt Olympia and Uncle Edmund, but I'm not sure that means I should keep the house. If I keep it, I don't think I can afford to maintain it. But if I sell it, the house moves out of my control."

"No telling what kind of riffraff might move in if you sell it," Birdie said. "Best keep the house in the family."

Color flooded Babette Graham's cheeks.

"It's a good thing the people who sold us our house didn't have that kind of attitude!"

Bea leaned over to pat Babette's hand. "You're not riffraff, honey. You fit right in."

"Anybody could fit in if they tried," Bea said, reaching for a buttered roll. "But it takes a special kind of person to live here. Not everybody can do without a car and quick access to a Wal-Mart."

Vernie stiffened. "The Mercantile has everything a regular person needs."

"That's right, sweetums," Stanley loyally replied. "Hear, hear."

"I think," Edith Wickam broke in, sweeping the group with her peaceful smile, "Annie needs to take some time to think and pray about what she needs to do. She's a young woman with her entire life ahead of her. Who knows what the Lord has planned for her future?"

Annie stared down at her plate, hoping the others wouldn't see the confusion raging in her eyes. She was nearly twenty-nine, a far cry from young, yet she had no idea what her future held. Her teaching job was only part-time, her research project had bombed, and her man had just fled in a powerboat. She lived in a rented apartment, had just lost her closest living relative, and had inherited a house that might fall down if a nor'easter roared out of the Atlantic.

Her future was about as stable as the waves of the sea.

Nevertheless, Edith was right about one thing—she needed time to think and pray. Trouble was, Aunt Olympia was still floating around somewhere on the Atlantic, and Annie couldn't think about anything until she'd given her aunt a proper burial.

She didn't believe in ghosts, but her conscience would haunt her day and night until she settled the matter.

* * *

Sitting quietly beside her husband, Edith watched Abner carry a tray of oatmeal raisin cookies from the kitchen to the dessert table. The jolly baker didn't seem so jolly this afternoon. The Smith men had been moving throughout the crowded fellowship hall, shaking hands and quietly consoling the island residents. Micah had pulled Annie aside and was speaking to her in soothing tones.

Edith sometimes wondered if the Smith

men didn't share more than a last name. When trouble arose, as it inevitably did, the gardener, the baker, the shopkeeper, the potter, the handyman, and the butler hovered over the townsfolk as though they were precious and irreplaceable pieces of Dresden china.

True saints, Edith had decided. The Smith men were as saintly as anyone she'd ever known. And right now she could use a bit of saintliness to help with her diet.

Yesterday had been a breeze. After her delicious Last Breakfast, she had enjoyed a Last Lunch of all her favorites—cheesecake from the freezer, leftovers from the fridge, plus three slices of a chocolate chess pie she whipped up between Bea's visit and Olympia's voyage.

After going with Winslow to make sure Odell was safe and sound at Frenchman's Fairest, she couldn't help but notice the delicious finger foods Caleb had arranged on the dining room table . . . so she'd indulged every whim, figuring that she'd count this meal as her Last Afternoon Snack. And last night at dinner, though she felt so stuffed she could barely breathe, she had served a pizza loaded with every topping imaginable and topped off the meal with the rest of the chocolate chess pie.

Sick and bloated, in bed that night she had held her stomach and resolved that the Diet had begun. Tomorrow, Tuesday, would be the beginning of the rest of her life as a thinner person.

She'd done fairly well at breakfast. Still full from the night before, she had downed a cup of black coffee and nibbled on a single remaining crust from the chocolate chess pie. For lunch she had forced herself to eat a salad, no dressing at all, and consoled herself with the thought that evening would bring a smorgasbord of foods after Olympia's funeral. With so much food available, she'd certainly be able to find some low-calorie goodies.

She'd found goodies, all right—but hardly any were low-calorie. She had ignored Birdie's high-calorie meatloaves, Babette's pot roast swimming in brown gravy, and Vernie's crispy fried clams, choosing instead a small green salad with vinegar and oil dressing. But while everyone around her talked and ate and ate and talked, Edith still felt unsatisfied . . . downright hungry. She'd thought she'd feel too sad to eat today, but apparently her appetite didn't feel the least bit melancholy.

Slipping away from Winslow and the table conversation, she sauntered up to the dessert table and spied one of Abner's coconut cream cakes. No one had cut it yet, and since she had nothing else to do with her hands . . .

Gingerly, she picked up a knife and sliced the cake into thick wedges. It felt good to help, and as the pastor's wife, it was her *duty* to do these things. Just like it was her duty to clean that glop of icing off the blade before it fell and made a mess on the floor.

Tracing the stainless steel with her fingertip, she swiped away the offending icing and, with no trash can handy, disposed of the mess by eating it. She closed her eyes as droplets of powered sugar and vanilla exploded in a taste sensation on her tongue. *Oh my.* Abner had used cream of coconut again. . . .

After a surreptitious glance to make sure no one was looking, she scooped another glob of icing off the rim of the plate. She savored the sweetness on her tongue, then licked her fingertip. No harm done. This was only a taste—a wee bit. It wasn't like she was eating a slice. Not that a slice would hurt her, either, after all she'd done without today.

Wielding the cake cutter like an expert swordsman, she lifted out a slice of the cake and dropped it on a plate. She was just about to reach for a fork when Floyd approached, a plate of long neck clams, roast beef, and green bean casserole in his hands.

A wave of guilt assailed her. Cheeks burning, she offered the cake to the mayor. "Dessert, Floyd?"

"Ayuh—that coconut looks wicked."

"It is."

She shoved it at him.

He caught the offering against his best suit, trying to balance the plate in his left hand with the dessert she'd just thrust upon him. Grabbing for napkins, Edith dropped a fistful on top of his cake, then apologized. "Sorry, Floyd. I'm a little distracted today."

He gave her a puzzled look, then moved toward the table where most of the men were discussing the weather. Edith leaned against the plaster wall and forced herself to take a deep breath. She had to focus. To concentrate. Anybody could diet, all you had to do was put mind over matter.

But not everybody was dumb enough to begin a starvation diet on the day of a good friend's funeral and a churchwide buffet. And her cheeks and neck were flaming, which might mean she was about to have a hot flash in the middle of all this—

She broke into a sweat, her hand groping for a folding chair.

Birdie stopped before her, a steaming dish of macaroni and cheese in her hand. "Edith, dear—" her high voice shot through the assorted conversations like an arrow— "you look like you're feeling squamish. Are you coming down with a bug?"

All eyes turned in Edith's direction.

"I'm fine," she stammered, clumsily opening the folding chair. "I just need to sit a spell."

Winslow stood and threaded his way through the chairs. "You okay, Edith? What's wrong?"

Embarrassed, she brushed his concern aside. "I got a little too warm, Win—it's so hot in here. Could you adjust the thermostat?"

"Sure." He grinned at Floyd, flashing a silent message—*you gotta tolerate these women and their hot flashes*—then he paused by Babette Graham, who was wearing a sweater and didn't seem at all warm.

"You comfortable, Babette?" Winslow asked. "How does the temperature feel to you?"

Babette Graham was nibbling on a plate loaded with food, including three desserts and a biscuit dripping with honey butter. Babette Graham had never spent an hour worrying about her weight, her cholesterol, or her blood pressure, and she was far too young to be entering menopause.

So why in the world was Winslow asking *her* about the temperature?

Edith opened her mouth and screeched before her mind knew what her tongue was doing: "Just *check* the dad blame thermostat, will you, Mr. Man?"

A silence, thick as molasses, enveloped the room.

Winslow's eyes bulged as he slowly backed toward the thermostat. "I'll check it right away."

Edith lowered her gaze in horror. Nausea roiled in her stomach as her head swam. What had she done? She had never spoken like that to Winslow even in private, yet she had just flipped a breaker right here in front of the entire town!

Dropping her face in her hands, she ardently wished that the ground would open up and swallow her like it did the grumbling Israelites in the wilderness.

Birdie flitted back to her side, waving for assistance. "Abner! Edith's not herself, she needs help. Let's get her home and put her to bed. Poor thing, all this stress and everything . . ."

Flaming with shame, Edith allowed the baker to take her arm and lift her from her chair. Walking toward the stairs, she kept her eyes downcast. No one spoke, not a single fork rattled. If she stayed to eat she'd probably feel better in five minutes, but she couldn't let these people know she was faint and grumpy because of a *diet*.

At the parsonage, she smiled and thanked Abner. "Go lie down," he said, his fingertips brushing the small of her back as he guided her into the house. "I'll make you something to eat." He cocked his head. "Perhaps a nice chicken broth? Something light."

She sent him a grateful smile. "That'd be nice, Abner. Thank you."

While he went to the kitchen, she walked

into her bedroom and dropped to the mattress, pulling a crocheted afghan over her shoulders. She was trembling now, her muscles complaining about a lack of fuel.

A bowl of chicken broth wouldn't satisfy her body for long, but after Abner had gone home, perhaps she could find a cookie in the kitchen.

* * *

Darkness stole over the island with a chilly peace, turning the new-fallen snow deep blue. Floyd and Cleta Lansdown sat in the keeping room of the Bed and Breakfast, enjoying the rare silence of a house without guests or children. Barbara and Russell had gone to the Klackenbush's to watch a video.

Floyd sank into his favorite chair and folded his hands across his belly, his eyes on the dancing flames in the woodstove. After a good dinner and a solemn occasion like a funeral, a man valued peace and the security of his home.

"Nice service," Cleta said, her knitting needles clicking to the rhythm of the Perry Como record playing on the stereo. "Olympia would have loved it."

Floyd grunted. "Ayuh, it was some nice. But nearly a disaster."

Cleta dropped her knitting. "I *do* hope you're not going to say you wanted to pull her through town on the fire truck."

"No—but firing up the siren in her honor would have been a grand gesture."

"Forget it, Floyd." She resumed her knitting. "So—what was the near-disaster?"

"No public transportation." Floyd propped his feet on the ottoman and nodded at his toes. "I tell you, Cleta, this town needs to operate its own ferry boat. Why, just look at what happened. The doctor's son barely made it, and Olympia's own boy had to hire a helicopter."

"We can't afford a ferry, Floyd. With so few families on the island, how are we supposed to buy a boat? Besides, there's no one to run it. We're all busy with other things."

Floyd shrugged and stretched his toes closer to the stove. Cleta wouldn't like what he was about to propose, but he wasn't so henpecked that he couldn't venture an idea she didn't like every once in a while.

"I'm not too busy. You and Barbara handle the B&B just fine."

"Noooooo. Barbara's going to move as

soon as she gets pregnant, so I'll be here alone. No way am I going to let you spend all your time on the water."

"But what are we supposed to do? Look at us now—Captain Stroble's off on vacation for a month and the *Sally's* gone down. How are we supposed to get around?"

"I don't know, dear." Cleta turned the knitting in her lap. "But I'm not going to worry about it. We can always call in a chopper if there's a medical emergency."

"Who's talking about medical emergencies? What about things like grocery shopping?"

"You can shop at the mercantile."

"But Vernie refuses to carry my brand of potato chips. Am I expected to live the next four weeks without Chive and Cheddar Kettle-Cooked, double-salted chips?" He shook his head, worrying the tip of his pipe between his teeth. "I'll row to Ogunquit in Russell's dory before that happens."

Cleta snorted. "Right. The day you row to Ogunquit is the day I sprout wings and fly. Besides, all that salt is bad for your blood pressure. Maybe you're not supposed to have Chive and Cheddar Kettle-Cooked, double-salted chips."

Grunting, Floyd returned his gaze to the flames. "We need our own ferry; don't need to be dependent on Stroble. He's reliable, but what if he was to get laid up for a spell? That would leave us in a real bind now that Odell's out of commission." He scratched his head. "Wonder who's using Stroble's boat now?"

"I heard it was at some marina for painting and hull-scraping."

"Still . . . does that take four weeks?"

Cleta shrugged. "You're asking the wrong person. Russell might know."

Floyd fingered the stubble at his neck. Careful now, this would be a critical point . . .

"I think I'll give the cap'n a call."

"In Floridy? Why, that's a long-distance call; it'd cost a fortune. And why would you want to bother the poor man while he and Mazie are trying to relax a little?"

"I'm calling." Pushing himself out of the easy chair, Floyd set his feet on the floor. "Now where did Stroble say they were staying?"

"I declare." Cleta dropped her knitting again. "Can't this wait until we go to Wal-Mart and get one of those long-distance calling cards? You can buy cards that'll let you talk for four cents a minute—"

"I don't want to wait for Wal-Mart. This here is important town business. Where was Stroble staying?"

She sent him a glare that would have frosted a lesser man's toenails. "Well, I never."

"That's the truth—never without giving me grief."

Cleta heaved a sigh. "He was staying at the Sand-something Inn on Captiva Island."

"Sand what?"

"I don't know. Sandpiper, Sand Dollar, Sandman. Sand-dingle-fuzzie, for all I know."

Half an hour later Floyd had located the captain and his wife at the Sand and Surf Inn. He grinned when the captain came on the line. "STROBLE?"

"Ayuh—is that you, Lansdown?"

"AYUH. CAN'T TALK BUT A MINUTE 'CAUSE IT'S LONG DISTANCE, YOU KNOW." He shot Cleta a smug look.

"Why are you yelling, Floyd? You having trouble with your ears?"

"NO—BUT IT'S LONG DISTANCE."

"I can hear you fine. Is there a problem at home?"

Floyd blew out his cheeks. Seemed unnatural to speak regular to somebody at the other end of the country.

"We have a little problem. Odell sank the *Sally* yesterday—it's a long story and I can't take the time to repeat it—but I was wondering if you'd give Odell permission to operate the ferry once it's done bein' overhauled?"

"Odell Butcher? Are you *nuts?*"

Floyd had always thought of himself as persuasive, but few men were as stubborn as Captain Stroble. "Now don't be hard-nosed about this," he said, injecting a smile into his voice. "With the *Sally* sinking we're stranded here. Russell's lobsterin' most every day now, and he's not available to ferry us back and forth. Odell's a little strange, but he's dependable."

"He sank his boat, didn't he? Besides, my insurance wouldn't put Crazy Odell on as a driver. He's too old."

"But we need the ferry. Those fellers at the post office in Ogunquit don't always have time to bring our mail, and Bea's already having a fit about not being able to make timely deliveries."

"I'm sorry, Floyd, but I can't let Odell drive my boat. I don't trust him."

Floyd rolled his eyes to the ceiling, searching for inspiration. He had an idea, but the sheer audacity of it spooked him a little. He didn't like to verbalize his dreams too often, lest the speaking somehow dilute them, but if the town needed him—

Gathering his courage, he took a deep breath and plunged ahead. "How about giving me permission to operate the ferry? I'm responsible. If this town can entrust me with the municipal fire truck, I shouldn't think you'd have any problem trusting me with one old boat."

"My ferry isn't municipal property, Floyd. It's my livelihood, and if it goes down I'll have no way to support my family."

"You'll have insurance, won't you? Come on, Stroble, show your patriotism."

"What does my ferry have to do with patriotism?"

"I don't know, but I'm sure there's a link. Why, if you needed the fire truck at the dock, I'd have her there in record time. So—what do you say? Can I run the ferry 'til you get back?"

The captain hemmed and hawed, so Floyd took advantage of his hesitation. "It might help if you remember that Cleta is

Mazie's third cousin by marriage. So we're practically family."

He looked across the room. Cleta had been steadfastly pretending to ignore him, but her left eyebrow arched at the mention of her name.

"You'll have to pick the boat up in York when it's ready," Stroble said.

"No trouble at all."

"Well . . . okay. But you won't have her long—probably just a couple of weeks. That means you'll have to find some other way to get to the mainland while my boat's in dry dock."

"We'll manage somehow."

A minute later Floyd hung up and shot Cleta a triumphant grin. "He gave me permission."

Both brows arched this time. "I don't know who's crazier, him, you, or people who want to go out in February. Folks ought to be tucked up inside their houses where it's warm. Just keep this in mind, Floyd—if you let anything happen to that boat, we'll never hear the end of it."

He rubbed his hands together. "You tend to your knittin' and let me worry about the ferry. Ain't never sunk a boat yet—and you tell the town that anytime they want to go to the mainland, just give me the word." He crossed his arms and leaned back in his chair, content to gaze upon the crackling fire and dream of the days ahead. "This ought to be fun."

"Only a fool hen would want to drive a ferry in February." With that pronouncement, Cleta stood and left the room.

Chapter Six

Sitting in the warm kitchen of Frenchman's Fairest, Annie wrapped her hands around a mug of fragrant tea and wondered when she would stop thinking of the room as Olympia's kitchen. By all rights it should belong to Caleb, for he'd done all the cooking for as long as Annie could remember.

The aging butler stood at the sink now, washing up the last of the breakfast dishes.

"It's not like I live here," she said, launching into yet another recap of her situation. Somehow it helped to verbalize her options aloud. "I've lived in Portland for the last five years. And if things develop with A.J., I might be living in New York within a few months. Heavenly Daze will seem a world away."

"Ayuh." Caleb cast a grin over his shoulder. "But sometimes we miss the places we aren't able to visit. We grow homesick."

Annie bit her lip, considering his comment. Would she ever be homesick for Heavenly Daze? Maybe in fall, when the island glowed with autumnal colors and the scent of wood smoke filled the air. Most of the tourists had departed by Columbus Day, and from October on Heavenly Daze was pure delight.

Then again, the tourists weren't totally terrible. They descended upon the island in the spring and livened things up so much it was sometimes hard to remember that only twenty-five year-round residents lived on the island—twenty-*seven,* now that Salt had gained custody of his two grandchildren. And summer on Heavenly Daze was wonderful, sunny and boisterous by day and blessedly cool and quiet at night. Growing up on the island, Annie had always thought the wind rocked everyone to sleep, for no matter how many people crowded into the bed and breakfast guest rooms, the island and everything on it seemed to whisper at sundown and murmur into the night.

Even winter on Heavenly Daze held its charms. Where else could you stand by the frozen shore and feel like nothing but thousands of diamond stars stood between you and God?

If she sold the house and left Heavenly Daze, she'd probably never come back except for funerals. After all, Caleb wouldn't live forever. Neither would Vernie, Birdie and Bea, or Cleta and Floyd. The Grahams and the Klackenbushes were younger, but they hadn't lived here during Annie's childhood, so they weren't as close to her as the others.

She sipped her tea, grateful for Caleb's silence. He was allowing her to figure this one out for herself, and she appreciated him trusting her judgment enough not to give unwanted advice. Yet . . . though she'd usually resented Olympia's unsolicited comments, the woman had always painted things in black and white.

Annie lowered her mug, then propped her chin in her hand. A little black-and-white advice would be welcome about now. Things were too gray for her taste.

Selling the house would enable her to finance a decent burial for her aunt. Hiring a ship to search for the casket would cost a fair amount of mitten money, but the house would need to be repaired and spruced up before she could sell it. The roof needed replacing, the floors needed supporting, and the entire exterior needed caulking and a couple of coats of paint.

Then again, how could she sell the house and leave Caleb to face new owners? Worse yet, what if the new owners didn't want to employ an aged butler who shuffled around in twenty-year-old slippers?

"Caleb," she shifted her gaze to the old man, "have you been happy on Heavenly Daze?"

He looked at her, his eyes widening. "Of course, Annie. I'm always happy doing the Lord's will."

"But how did you know you were following the Lord's will? I mean, it's not like he writes things on the wall these days."

Caleb laughed softly. "He told me to come here."

"God *spoke* to you?"

"And I listened. You will hear him, too, if you listen for his voice."

Frowning, she looked away. Caleb had always seemed closer to God than anyone else she knew. While it seemed almost reasonable to believe God did speak to the old man, it had been some time since he had spoken to Annie.

"I'm glad you're asking about these things." Caleb pulled out a chair. "I need to tell you something."

Afraid of what she might hear, she watched him sit down. "You're not sick, are you?"

He chuckled. "I never get sick."

"Then . . . . what?"

"I'll be leaving soon." His words dropped into the warmth of the kitchen with the weight of stones in still water.

Unable to believe what she'd heard, Annie sat perfectly still for a moment, then forced out a reply. "You're *leaving?*"

He nodded. "I was sent here to serve Missy, and now that she's gone home, I expect to be transferred to another post. You're not to worry," his eyes twinkled, "for the Lord will continue to keep his hand upon anyone who lives in this special place. But don't let concern for me cloud your thinking about your future. I know I'll be moving on by the end of the month."

Annie stared wordlessly at him, her heart pounding. Had Olympia's death unhinged him? Aside from his occasional odd comments Caleb had never shown any serious sign of mental instability, but he had never lost two dear people in such a short time. Perhaps grief had ravaged his mind.

If so, she would need to treat him with loving firmness, as if he were a child and she the parent. Taking a deep breath, she forced a note of sternness into her voice. "You can't go, Caleb, so don't even think about it. I don't mean to sound unkind, but you're too old to accept another post."

Reaching out, he squeezed her shoulder. "It's sweet of you to worry about me, child, but completely unnecessary. Don't let this aging body deceive you—I will serve many more years before my work is complete."

"Caleb, you're talking crazy. I don't know how much Aunt Olympia paid you, but you should think about retiring. If I sell the house, I could set you up with a retirement fund—"

"I don't need money. My reward comes from doing the will of the Father."

"But your needs are on earth, right? You've worked your fingers to the bone in this place, so you deserve something for your efforts. I could sell the house. I'll split the proceeds with you and you could get a little apartment in Ogunquit, if you want to stay in the area—"

The shrill ringing of the kitchen phone interrupted, and Caleb rose to answer it. While she waited, the butler croaked out a greeting, then winked and handed her the phone.

The caller had to be A.J.

She accepted the phone, then smiled when Caleb discreetly slipped from the room.

"Hey," she murmured into the receiver. "Thanks for calling. I need to talk to somebody rational, and I think Caleb's slipped a gear."

"Really?" A.J.'s voice rang with surprise. "He seemed to have his act together at the funeral."

"I think maybe it's a delayed stress reaction or something. He just told me he plans to leave Heavenly Daze and take another job."

A.J. laughed. "Maybe he's hinting that he'd like to go with you when you come to New York."

Annie gripped the phone cord. A.J. had never said anything about her moving to New York, so his comment was either a roundabout proposal . . . or something she was misinterpreting entirely.

"Well," she injected a coy note into her

voice, "I'm not so sure I'll be moving to New York. I hear the weather's terrible up there."

Warm baritone laughter rang over the line. "And you think the weather's better in Maine? Honey, you've been on that island too long. You need to come back to civilization."

"I'd be happy to . . . if I had the right motivation. Right now I'm perfectly content to rattle around in this big, old house."

"Would a pair of warm slippers by the fire be motivation enough? Maybe some Kenny G on the CD player, and a nice dinner for two on TV trays?"

Grinning, Annie ran her hand over the worn vinyl tablecloth. "New York doesn't sound terribly romantic. I could have all those things right here in Frenchman's Fairest."

"But you couldn't have tickets to a Broadway show . . . or a gallant young doctor to squire you around Times Square. If you come to New York, you could have all of the above for only $19.99 and the answer *yes.*"

"If the answer is yes," Annie clenched the phone cord until her nails cut into her palm, "what, exactly, is the question?"

A.J. paused, and in the silence Annie

could hear her heart thumping. "The question," he finally said, "would have to be, 'Will you move to New York so we can spend more time together . . . and see what the future might hold?'"

Exhaling, Annie resisted a sudden stab of disappointment. What had she expected after six weeks of dating, an outright proposal? She and A.J. had been out only a few times.

At least he hadn't asked her to move in with him. Too many of her friends thought nothing of living with a man before marriage, but Annie knew she'd never be able to do that. She was no angel, but she did know that a godly relationship ought to begin with respect and commitment, not sex and cohabitation.

She was not so much in love that A.J. Hayes should start counting his chickens, but the man had seemed awfully cocky when he posed the question about moving.

"I'm not sure the answer is yes," she said, her voice cool. "I've been toying with the idea of staying in Heavenly Daze. After all, I now own a house here. Why should I pay rent in Portland when I can own waterfront property on an island?"

"Come on, Annie." She thought she heard a note of exasperation in his voice. "Surely you aren't serious."

"Why not? This isn't the edge of the world, you know. I grew up here, and it is a nice place."

"But it's so isolated! My plane can't land there, and you know what a disaster that ferry is. I don't even like to visit my father on that God-forsaken island, so how can you expect . . ."

His voice trailed away, but Annie had already intuited his unspoken thought—*If I won't visit my father, why would you expect me to visit you?*

Apparently Dr. Alex Hayes wasn't as deeply in love as she had first thought.

He sighed into the phone. "I'm sorry, that didn't come out right. But you're not seriously thinking about keeping that place, are you? It's not easy to take care of a two-hundred-year-old mausoleum."

"It's not a mausoleum, it's a historic residence." She tugged on the phone cord. "I know it'd be hard to maintain, but I can't imagine selling Aunt Olympia's house. She loved this place, and she wanted me to have it."

"But she left it to you, knowing that you live in Portland. Honestly, Annie, you shouldn't beat yourself up about selling it. Your aunt knew you were an independent woman."

"Ayuh, she did. But I know how much she loved Heavenly Daze, how proud she was to belong here. If I sell, there won't be any descendants of Jacques de Cuvier left on the island."

"Descendants of who?"

"Of *whom*. Jacques de Cuvier was the sea captain who founded the town."

"Like *he* really cares if you stay there."

"I don't know—he might. Caleb keeps telling me that people in heaven are watching us down here."

A.J. snorted. "Annie, honey, come on! You're just a little confused because of the funeral, that's all. Once you're back in Portland, you'll see things more clearly. You'll realize how hard it is to manage a property from long-distance, and you'll discover that even selling the place will be a challenge. You'll be lucky to get a hundred grand for it."

Annie blew out her cheeks, then rolled her eyes toward the ceiling. "A.J., I really don't want to talk about this now."

"Okay. So—what else is new?"

She cast about for another topic of conversation and came up empty. "Not much."

"Nothing ever happens on that island. Okay, sweetie, I've got to go. Give my dad a hug for me when you see him, okay? And come back to the real world soon. I miss you."

Annie blinked away a sudden surge of tears. "I miss . . . everybody."

And as she hung up the phone, she wondered if she really missed A.J. . . . or only the way things used to be.

Chapter Seven

After rising with the sun, Annie dressed in a sweater and jeans, then pulled on her slicker and headed out to the beach with Tallulah. No one was stirring at the dock at this early hour, but the lights gleamed from Birdie's Bakery, where Abner Smith would be piping out doughnuts in preparation for the morning coffee crowd.

Tallulah paused at the intersection of Ferry Road and Main Street, then whimpered softly.

"You don't want to go with me to the beach?"

The dog dropped onto her belly, then brought both paws over her nose. The adorable action tore at Annie's heart. What was going to happen to Tallulah? For sure the old dog wouldn't relish living in Annie's apartment with her cat. After the freedom of Heavenly Daze, apartment life would seem like prison to the outgoing terrier.

"Too cold, huh? Okay, girl, run along to see Abner. He just might have a treat for you."

Tallulah didn't need to be told twice. She rose and trotted off at a brisk clip, leaving Annie alone. She gazed wistfully after the dog—why was it that her aunt's dog had no trouble making decisions, while she couldn't even decide when she should return to Portland?

She had not slept during the night, but tossed and turned for what felt like an eternity. Stretched out on her right side, she convinced herself to sell Frenchman's Fairest; when she turned onto her left side, she thought she should keep the house no matter what. Rolling onto her belly, with her face buried in her arms, she worried about Olympia floating all the way to England; flat on her back and staring at the ceiling, she tried to imagine Olympia in heaven, contentedly playing a harp.

How was a woman supposed to find balance in life?

She looked up as a bell jangled in the morning silence—Abner was opening the bakery door to let Tallulah in. He looked up and waved at Annie; stiffly, she pulled her hand from her pocket and returned the greeting.

What was it with the Smith men? Nothing ever ruffled them. And whenever you had a problem, you could count on one of the Smith guys to send you straight to the heavenly throne room for help.

She felt a twinge of guilt as she walked toward the beach. She'd been fretting and worrying for days, but hadn't honestly offered her petition to the Lord.

Alone on the beach, she huddled inside her overcoat and trudged over the damp sand. The southwestern shore offered the only sandy beach on Heavenly Daze, for the northern and eastern coasts were too rocky to allow for easy walking. But the windward side had been worn smooth over the years, and she liked the way the wet sand shifted ever so slightly beneath her rubber boots, then held firm. It was a good place for thinking . . . and even better for praying.

"Dear God," she lifted her eyes to the cloudy skies above the watery horizon, "if ever I needed advice and guidance, I need it now. I don't know what to do, and thinking

only makes me more confused. My head
tells me to do one thing, but my heart tells
me to do something else."

Her head was telling her to sell the house
and take the money. With a decent sales
price for the estate she could make sure
Caleb had enough to buy a little place in
Ogunquit then search for Olympia, bury her
next to Edmund, and buy a really nice monument for both of them. Olympia had
displayed a fondness for monuments, evi-
denced most particularly by the bronze
marker on the lawn of Frenchman's Fairest.
Practically every building on the island had
some historic significance, but Olympia had
been the only resident who felt compelled to
erect a sign on her property.

So selling the house would be a good
thing.

On the other hand, what would Dr. Marc
do if she sold the house? Olympia and Edmund had offered their detached guest
cottage to serve as the island doctor's residence and office, but the new owner of
Frenchman's Fairest might have other ideas
for the building. That would leave Dr. Marc
without a place to live and work, and Heavenly Daze without a clinic.

She frowned, then shook the notion away. The town would have to take care of itself. Birdie would be getting married soon, so perhaps Dr. Marc could move in with Beatrice.

The thought brought a smile to Annie's chapped lips. Bea would up and faint before she'd even entertain the idea of living with a man, even platonically, so Dr. Marc would have to move in with Cleta and Floyd and set up an office in one of their guest rooms. That'd undoubtedly cut into their income during tourist season, but if Barbara and Russell moved out, the doctor could have their rooms—

If Barb and Russ ever moved out.

Annie stared out at the sea, trying to imagine her life without the people of Heavenly Daze. She knew the islanders as well as she knew the inside of her palm. Though life might take the girl off the island, she doubted it could ever take the island out of the girl.

Shivering, she hunched lower in her jacket as the wind whipped over the beach. New York was a wonderful place to visit, Portland was nice and clean, but could she live away from the sea? And the appeal of Heavenly Daze involved far more than sea and shore, for it had always been the nest to which she flew home to rest. Life without that nest would be like living in a house with no bedroom.

So she should keep the house. But how was she supposed to pay for its mainte-nance? Her teacher's salary barely kept her afloat in Portland. The Durpee Seed Com-pany bonus for which she'd been working would never materialize now that her toma-toes had proven inedible.

She could take a second job, but there was no work to be found on the island in win-ter, and only the Lobster Pot required extra employees in the summer. If she worked two jobs in Portland, she'd never have time to visit Heavenly Daze and enjoy the property she was desperately striving to keep.

Weary of the internal debate, she blew out a frosty breath, then turned toward home. The idea of keeping Frenchman's Fairest was highly impractical. The house needed work, Aunt Olympia needed a proper burial, Caleb needed a retirement fund, and Dr. Marc—she felt her heart twist—he needed a property owner who would let him remain in the guest cottage and could afford to maintain it.

Thoughts of the doctor brought a rueful

smile to her face. Why was A.J. so reluctant to visit the island? She knew of no rift between him and his father; each always spoke highly of the other. Annie had watched them carefully at Christmas, and both men had truly enjoyed each other's company. But Dr. Marc was always making excuses for A.J., saying Alex was a busy and successful neurosurgeon . . .

How successful could you be if you were too busy for friends and family? Annie frowned as another thought struck—she was A.J.'s girlfriend, yet he had barely made the funeral of her closest living relative. If she occupied such a low place on his priority list now, what would life be like when they'd been married twenty years?

Her freewheeling friends would laugh off such worries. She ought to marry A.J., they'd say, and quit working altogether. As a surgeon's wife she could entertain and socialize and host benefits for charitable causes. She could travel and mingle with celebrities; she could have a fine apartment in Manhattan and a weekend house in the Hamptons. Closing her eyes, she could visualize the house A.J. would want—a spacious, wide-windowed mansion painted in creams and beiges, with towering ivory statues in the living room and white furs on the bedroom floor.

Her eyes flew open. Try as she might, she couldn't imagine Birdie and Bea inside that house. Vernie, with her boots and leather aviator's cap, would be as out of place as a bucket under a bull. Caleb would be a nervous wreck in such a fine home, and Aunt Olympia's precious rose teacups would look like cast-off bric-a-brac in a modern stainless steel kitchen.

Why, even she wouldn't feel at home in such a place. In the last few days she hadn't felt at home anywhere but in Olympia's parlor. The tattered lace curtains at the window, crackling logs in the fireplace, and the worn sofa before the bookcases refreshed her senses in a way her Portland apartment never could. A.J. would find Olympia's parlor provincial and plain, but the room would suit a man like . . . Dr. Marc.

Turning up the beach she began to retrace her steps, moving along the southern slope of the island and the path to the ferry dock. For beyond the trail lay Frenchman's Fairest and the carriage house, where she knew she'd find the man she sought.

* * *

"Why, Annie!" Marc started to smile at his unexpected visitor, then thought the better of it. The young woman wore a troubled expression, and the cold had stolen all the color from her cheeks. "Are you feeling all right?"

"No—I mean yes. I'm not sick, but I'd like to talk to you."

He opened the door wider. "Come on in. Since this isn't a medical call, we'll go back to the keeping room."

He led the way past his examination room and book-lined office to his private quarters, a comfortable space at the back of the cottage. His sofa bed, now neatly tidied up, lined the wall, while in the center of the room a black woodstove squatted on a brick hearth and radiated with pleasant heat.

"Make yourself at home," he said, stepping forward to tug at her coat. "I'll hang up your coat and get you something warm to drink."

Annie closed her eyes as he lifted the coat from her shoulders, and he had a feeling she was looking for someone to lift her troubles as well. The poor girl had endured a lot in the last few days.

"Have you been out walking?" he asked, moving to a small cabinet to the right of the doorway. The counter, equipped with microwave, coffee maker, sink, and hotplate, served admirably as a kitchen since he rarely had guests.

Annie sank onto the sofa, then held her hands toward the stove. "Ayuh. I needed to get out of the house to think."

"You must be frozen to the bone. I'll make you a cup of hot tea—"

"Don't go to any bother. The heat feels nice."

"It's no bother, Annie. I'll have a cup, too."

Leaving her to enjoy the quiet, he pulled two mugs from the cabinet, then filled them with water and set them in the microwave. He punched on the power for three minutes.

Drumming his nails on the counter, he squinted at the oven and decided that these were the longest three minutes he'd passed in his lifetime. Annie had to be bored silly, and with every passing moment he wondered why she'd shown up at his door. Caleb was her confidant and Dana Klackenbush more her age . . .

What was she doing here? And why did he suddenly feel as flustered as a schoolboy? His cheeks were burning, which meant he was blushing, and Annie was too observant not to notice.

Finally the oven beeped. He removed the mugs, burning his fingers in the process, then left the cups to steam on the counter while he bent to look in a cabinet and pretended to rummage for tea bags.

He had to calm down. He drew in a deep breath, trying to lower his blood pressure and restore his usual color. The young woman who sat across the room might well be his daughter-in-law one day, so there was no reason for him to feel awkward and self-conscious. Besides, she looked like she could use a friend, and he'd been her friend long before Alex noticed her exceptional qualities.

When he was certain his pulse had returned to its normal rhythm, he stood, caught her worried gaze, and smiled. "What's on your mind, hon?"

Maybe the word *hon* broke the dam, or perhaps it was the directness of the question, but tears overtook Annie with a sudden ferocity that surprised him. She threw herself into a mound of sofa pillows, sobbing as if her world had shattered, and the sound of her despair tore at Marc's heart.

He took two steps forward, then hesitated. What should he do? Stand and watch her weep, or offer the comfort of a shoulder to cry on?

He grimaced, annoyed that he was even debating the question. If Cleta were weeping, or Birdie, he wouldn't think twice about hurrying forward to comfort them.

Drawing a deep breath, he crossed the room and sat beside her. "There, now." He gently touched her shoulder, and that was all the encouragement she needed to seek the shelter of his arms.

"Dr. Marc, I'm so confused!"

He slipped one arm around her, pulling her head to his chest. "It's okay, dear, things are going to be just fine."

"It's . . . the house." She sniffed against his sweater. "And Aunt Olympia. I have so many choices, so many obligations. And I don't know who to ask for advice now that Aunt Olympia and Uncle Edmund are gone."

His hand, moving as if it had a mind of its own, smoothed her wind-whipped hair. "You have Caleb. He's always given trustworthy advice."

She shook her head. "I can't ask him about this because he told me he's leaving.

192 Lori Copeland and Angela Hunt

By the end of the month, he said. He's going off to work someplace else, and I'm afraid it's because Aunt Olympia wasn't able to provide for him. I wish I could afford to pay him, but I can't, and I think he doesn't want me to feel obligated—"

"Maybe he wants to work."

She sobbed again. "Who in their right mind wants to work at his age? I don't know what to do."

Marc lifted a brow, then asked a delicate question: "Have you talked to A.J?"

The head against his sweater wobbled up and down. "A.J. says I should sell the house and move to New York. He doesn't really like Heavenly Daze."

Marc chuckled dryly. "That comes as no surprise."

She lifted her bleary eyes. "Well, I don't really like New York. It's a nice place to visit, but I don't think I could ever live there."

Marc let his hand fall on the back of the sofa as the world went silent around them. If this were a casual conversation he would murmur some inane comment and move on, but this didn't feel like a casual conversation. And the longer he looked into Annie's sorrowful eyes, the more his heart yearned for something he had no business considering, much less imagining . . .

Abruptly, he pulled away and stood. "I promised you tea, didn't I?"

"You did . . . but I don't really need it."

"I do."

He strode toward the kitchen, where the two mugs waited on the counter, cooler now, but still useful for keeping his hands busy.

Was that a note of disappointment he heard in her voice just now? Could she be feeling . . . no, she couldn't. Annie was young enough to be his daughter. Her entire lifetime stretched before her. He was a retired doctor living on Heavenly Daze because he'd tired of the rat race. He had moved here after his wife's death, content to spend the rest of his life serving other people . . . alone.

He didn't want to love again. He certainly didn't expect to love again.

And he would not love again. He would rejoice for his son, knowing that Alex had found a woman of whom he was *almost* worthy.

He unwrapped two teabags and dropped one into each mug. "Sugar?"

"Ayuh. Two teaspoons, please."

He smiled. "I like a girl who's not afraid of a few empty calories. You take risks."

"No, I don't." She stood and came toward him, her eyes wide pools of appeal. "I'm scared to death, Dr. Marc. Afraid I'll make the wrong decision. If I sell the house and leave Heavenly Daze, I'm afraid I'll lose a part of myself. I used to think that part wasn't important, but lately I've come to realize it matters . . . a lot."

"Then don't sell the house." He said this with more conviction than was appropriate for an impartial advisor, but she didn't seem to notice.

"But if I don't sell the house, how am I supposed to take care of it? I live and work in Portland, and my annual salary can't handle my living expenses and the cost of maintaining this house, too."

He pulled a teabag from the first cup. "I could help, Annie. Your aunt always let me stay here as a service, but I could pay rent. In fact, I insist upon it—"

"No." A blush burned through her pallor. "I couldn't take money from you, especially not after all you've done for the town. But I could do a lot with the proceeds from the house. For one thing, I could hire a boat to search for Olympia, then bury her properly."

He handed her the mug. "Assuming you could find the casket—which is a long shot—why on earth would you think Olympia cares about being properly buried?"

Annie blinked. "Aunt Olympia always cared about doing the proper thing."

"But what makes you think she's concerned about such things now?"

The question seemed to strike home. "I . . . well, maybe she doesn't. But surely everybody else does. I can only imagine what Vernie and Cleta are saying about me for leaving Olympia to swim with the fishes—"

He laughed softly. "They're not mobsters, dear, and you heard them at the funeral. They think there's a certain poetic justice in the way Olympia went out."

"But Olympia would hate to know they were laughing at her."

"They're not laughing at her—I'd bet my last dollar they're laughing *with* her."

Leaning on the counter, she quietly sipped her tea.

Her silence gave him courage. "Your confusion isn't stemming from the house, Annie, and I think you know that. You're confused about letting go. Are you ready to let go of Heavenly Daze and move to New York with Alex?"

Surprise blossomed on her face. "Do you want me to move to New York with Alex?"

"I want you to be happy, Annie."

"Really?" She lowered her mug and looked away, apparently considering the question, and Marc purposely turned his attention to a painting on the wall, afraid to read her thoughts in her eyes. By all that was right and honorable he ought to push her out of the nest and send her off to New York. One day his son would thank him. Maybe he and Annie would come to visit, bringing his grandchildren with them. The trade-off would be worth it, because life on Heavenly Daze without frequent visits from Annie would be dark and dull.

Did he want a delightful daughter-in-law to cherish forever, or—his heart shrank from shaping the question—did he want Annie for himself?

"You'll have to choose," he said, his voice sounding strangled as he stirred sugar into his tea. And as he took the first sip, he glanced into the dark brew and saw a coward reflected there—a man so afraid of his feelings he was willing to let a young woman make choices for him.

* * *

By 11:00 A.M., the island women were seated in the church sanctuary, cleaning supplies scattered among them. Because the church was too small to hire a cleaning service—and because there were none to be had—the women had always agreed to spend the first Thursday of every month polishing the old pews and dusting the antique woodwork.

Edith had arrived first, to unlock the door and set out the cleaning supplies. She'd been uncharacteristically quiet as the other women arrived—they probably thought she was mourning Olympia. Truth was, she did miss Olympia something fierce, but her silence resulted from the fact that she was trying to plan a strategy for coping with the ladies' lunch that would follow their cleaning session. Each woman always brought a dish, usually a casserole or salad, and after an hour of scrubbing they'd go down to the basement to eat. Trouble was, Edith didn't have a clue how she would survive the hour.

The only day she'd managed successfully was her first day of "Last Meals." The second day, when she'd tried to starve herself, had ended in disaster after her meltdown at the funeral dinner. Yesterday she had tried to diet by eating only half of what she usually ate, but the previous day's starvation had triggered some sort of gorging mechanism and she'd stuffed herself like a hog.

This morning she had risen with new determination—she would arm herself with the low-fat diet plan. She would eat no more than twenty grams of fat per day, thank you very much, so for breakfast she had eaten a low-fat fruit bar that tasted like strawberry-flavored cardboard and three packages of gummy worms. Delicious—and not a smidgen of fat in a single worm.

But how was she supposed to be successful when faced with a table loaded with casseroles and salads, none of which would have *labels?*

Walking among the pews, searching for errant scraps of paper and old bulletins, she pondered the question and half-listened to the other women's conversation.

Cleta sat on the first pew, mending an altar cloth, her head bobbing toward the women around her. "Nobody asked my opinion, but I think Crazy Odell ought to have his neck wrung like a chicken."

"No one can predict a rogue wave, Cleta." Vernie Bidderman, bent over the communion table, paused from dusting long enough to add her two cents.

"Has the Coast Guard seen her?" Bea asked.

Barbara Higgs lifted her head from where she was mending an altar cloth. "Russell said some fishermen spotted a big floating box around Boothbay Harbor, but they weren't able to catch her. The Coast Guard's still keeping an eye out, though."

"I wonder what Annie will do with the house?" Birdie stopped pushing the dust mop down the aisle and stared into space. "Heavenly Daze won't be the same without a de Cuvier in Frenchman's Folly."

"Just goes to show life is fragile," Babette called from the back of the church, where she was spritzing the windows with cleaner. "And we should live each day as if it were our last."

"Anyone talk to Annie lately?" Bea called from the piano. "She puts on her best face when I deliver the mail, but you have to wonder. Poor thing—losing both aunt and uncle in such a short time."

"Annie's doing well—that girl has spunk." Vernie rubbed a spot on the altar table until it squeaked. "I stopped by Frenchmen's Folly last night, and Annie said she and Caleb have a real peace about Olympia's passing. I think she's still a little unnerved about Olympia's *voyage,* though."

A nervous titter erupted, then faded.

By noon the women had made their way down to the basement and the kitchen. Edith felt her eyes water when she beheld the day's feast: Babette's cheesy chive potatoes, Vernie's shrimp scampi, Birdie's hot yeast rolls, Cleta's strawberry-rhubarb pie.

Thursday morning cleaning was a diet ambush, pure and simple.

Edith took a spoonful of everything, resigning herself to the fact that she'd chosen a bad day to count fat grams. She'd start again, and she'd be downright religious about her diet . . . tomorrow.

She ate slowly, watching Dana and Babette pack the food away and envying their metabolism. Both women were as slender as flower stems. Barbara Higgs had a little more meat on her bones, but nothing serious. Edith had once been slim, but the older she got, the harder it was to shed extra pounds. She closed her eyes and bit into a hot roll. My, Birdie could make bread.

"I don't know about you, but I can't seem to get enough to eat these days," Vernie complained. She dished up a second helping of cheesy chive potatoes.

"Oh, you're just in love," Cleta teased.

Color infused Vernie's cheeks, but everyone in town knew her husband, Stanley, had taken to courting her like a man with nothing to lose. Stanley Bidderman, who'd gone missing for twenty years, had returned to the island in December and declared his intention to win Vernie's heart again.

Throughout the months of December and January the townsfolk had waited to see if Vernie would take Stanley back. She had, after considerable soul-searching. Judging by the bloom in Vernie's cheeks these days, Stanley's efforts to woo his wife had been a success.

Vernie wasn't the only woman with roses in her cheeks. After years of being alone, Birdie Wester had fallen hard for the town curmudgeon, Salt Gribbon, and their wedding was only weeks away.

Dana must have followed Edith's thoughts, for she was grinning at the bride-to-be. "Found a wedding dress yet, Birdie?"

Birdie swallowed a bite of scampi before answering. "Ayuh. Ordered one from the Sears catalog."

Bea rolled her eyes.

"From a catalog?" Babette dropped her jaw. "Why, Birdie, I would have been happy to go shopping with you. Half the fun is trying on a lot of different wedding gowns."

"I know you would, Babette, but I don't want to make a fuss."

"But it's your *wedding* day," Barbara protested. "If that isn't a time for fuss, I don't know what is."

"I'm sure the wedding itself will be all the fuss Salt can stand." Birdie chuckled as she buttered another roll. "You ought to see the cake Abner is proposing—six layers, with butter cream frosting and fresh raspberry filling."

Edith wiped drool from her mind.

Bea snorted. "Raspberries give me a rash."

Birdie smiled. "Abner knows that, sister—he's going to make a special cake for you—one without filling."

Edith stared at Dana's pistachio salad, mentally calculating the ingredients—Cool Whip wasn't too bad fat-wise, especially if it was the nonfat variety. The nuts, however, were terribly high in fat—but it was good fat, wasn't it? The pineapple was okay, no fat. Ditto for the marshmallows. But the pistachio pudding . . . the fat content depended on what kind of milk Dana had used.

Edith reached for the bowl, then plopped a teaspoon full onto her paper plate. Okay, so she'd blown the low-fat diet, but maybe she could work it off. She did have a "Sweatin' to the Oldies" videotape gathering dust in the cabinet.

"Does it seem odd to anyone other than me that we're carrying on as if nothing has happened?" Babette lowered her fork as her eyes went misty. "Olympia is barely cold and here we are joking about cakes and weddings."

"Life goes on, Babette," Edith gently reminded her. "Not even Olympia would want us to sit around mourning for days. She certainly wouldn't want Birdie and Salt to delay their wedding. She was looking forward to it."

Babette sighed. "I know. But sometimes it

seems like the world barely notices when a person leaves it."

"People notice," Birdie insisted. "Every life touches some other life, so people notice. Never doubt that."

On the short walk home, Edith wondered if any of the women had noticed her half-hearted attempt to eat less than usual. Probably not, because on her arm she carried a basket loaded with rolls, a container of cheesy chive potatoes, and pistachio pudding. The women always insisted on giving her their leftovers, but their generosity was doing Edith no favors.

She berated herself for her lack of will power. Until lately she had thought of herself as a woman with a strong will and loads of common sense. Today, for instance, she could have eaten a small serving of scampi and a big bowl of plain salad. She could have skipped the rolls, the potatoes, and the two servings of pistachio salad, but she had eaten like a glutton—because of that blasted low-fat diet plan.

It was too difficult, too much trouble.

She had to find another plan, and she would. Right after supper.

Feeling better if not lighter, Edith felt her

confidence begin to return. Why, she could stay on a diet as well or better than the next woman. Tonight she would sit down with her magazines and study the latest dieting advice. And tomorrow, she'd be perfect.

She would have to be careful, however, because Winslow thought diets were all silly fads. Plus, he seemed oblivious to the extra pounds she carried.

Edith stamped her feet with renewed energy on the front porch steps. Tonight she'd prepare a sensible dinner so Winslow wouldn't suspect a thing. Then she'd help him eat the last of the leftovers, and tomorrow she'd begin again with a clean slate.

Tomorrow, she'd be resolute.

* * *

Over dinner, Edith slowly ate her sensible meal (chicken and broccoli and leftovers), then lowered her fork and looked at her husband. "How was your day, dear?"

"Hmm?" He glanced up from a steno pad on the table, then dropped his eyes to his notes.

"What did you do today?"

Winslow usually shared his activities during supper, but tonight he seemed more interested in his notes than in her. Edith knew Olympia's sudden death had affected him, but would it hurt him to make a personal contribution to the conversation?

Sighing, she stood to pour herself another cup of decaf coffee.

Her movement must have signaled something to her absent husband, for he turned a page on his notepad and spoke: "I think I am going to leave Obadiah and center on Nahum for the next twelve weeks. I think my flock is ready for a bit of a change."

Edith groaned. Only the most dedicated Christian could make it through twelve weeks of Nahum without keeling over.

Sinking back into her chair, she changed the subject. "When did you schedule Birdie and Salt for premarital counseling?"

He peered at his notes over the edge of his glasses. "Hmm . . . first of next month."

Edith tore open two packages of aspartame and dumped the contents into her cup. "Birdie ordered her dress from the Sears catalog."

"That's nice."

She stirred the coffee so forcefully her spoon threatened to break the glass.

Winslow was on autopilot. She sipped from her coffee cup, then said, "The color is orange, the bodice is cut to the navel, and the dress is backless."

"That's nice, sweetie." He looked up, his eyes blank orbs, then squinted at her. "Did you say *orange?*"

"Never mind, Win."

Sighing, she took her coffee and walked into the living room, then stepped out onto the front porch. The sun had set an hour before, and lights lit the porches of houses down the street. Across the road, the Grahams would be gathered around the table with Georgie, and just past the church, Cleta, Floyd, Russell, and Barbara would be sitting down to a dinner of crab cakes and potatoes. Cleta had mentioned her dinner plans at lunch, and Edith's mouth had watered at the menu.

What was wrong with her? Instead of learning to live without food, she seemed to be obsessing over it!

Shivering, she took another sip of her coffee. The liquid warmed her throat and brought heat to her cheeks, which were already beginning to feel the effects of the cold.

In the distance a harbor buoy clanged through lowering fog. Edith bit back tears as she stood alone in the darkness, thinking about all the happy times she and Winslow had experienced. God had blessed her with health, meaningful friendships, and a loving and devoted husband. So why was she standing here feeling miserable?

Because she was overweight. Because the last couple of days had proved she had absolutely no self-control. She had always considered herself a leader among the women; in the last three days she had learned she had no backbone at all. She couldn't even stand up to her own foolish desires for food.

Arming herself with resolve, she went back into the house. She reached under the coffee table for the latest issue of *Good Housekeeping,* then spied a provocative headline: *I lost thirty pounds in one month eating bread and potatoes, and you can, too!*

She opened the magazine and ran her finger down the table of contents, searching for the article.

"Edith?"

She glanced up to see Winslow silhouetted in the doorway.

"Honey, are you all right?" He crossed the room and sat beside her on the sofa. When he spotted the betraying shimmer of tears in her eyes, his expression softened. "Is something bothering you?"

Edith longed to confess everything, for Winslow would undoubtedly assure her she was fine, he loved her, she didn't need to worry about her weight. But he saw her every day, and he hadn't noticed how she had changed over the years. Furthermore, he deserved to have a wife who looked pretty by his side.

Sliding into his arms, Edith rested her head on his solid shoulder, then crinkled her nose. He smelled of shrimp and butter.

"I'm feeling a little melancholy tonight, Win. Nothing serious."

"Are you sure?"

"I'm sure. But thanks for asking."

She *was* sure, for tomorrow would bring another day and a fresh start. Armed with this article in *Good Housekeeping,* she'd meet her eating opportunities with courage and resolve. She would win the war against excess pounds one day at a time.

"I adore you, Edith Wickam." Winslow dropped a kiss on her forehead before he stood and walked back to the kitchen where his notes waited.

"I adore you, too, Win," she whispered. "Enough to make you proud of me again."

* * *

"Honey? Where'd you put the new toothpaste?"

"Under the sink, Win." Edith wound the clock and set it on the bed stand. Winslow's and Stanley's recent remodeling job had resulted in a spacious new area beneath the sink to store supplies from the hall closet. She wouldn't wish the remodeling process on her worst enemy, but the results were pretty and added a much-needed update to the parsonage.

She picked up her Bible as Winslow continued to rattle around in the adjoining bathroom. Closing her eyes, she rested the open book across her breast and sighed, trying to summon enough concentration to read a few Scriptures.

An image from a TV commercial blazed on the backs of her eyelids. A giant taco, de-

signed to tantalize, was practically porno-
graphic in the way it drew attention to the
crispy shell, thick shredded cheese, tiny bits
of tangy tomato. Never had a picture been
more carefully designed to arouse the lust of
the flesh—

Opening her eyes, she blinked the image
away. What was wrong with her? She had
never been this fixated on food before. She
had resolved to eat less, but somehow her
brain had translated that into a food preoc-
cupation. . . .

The bed sagged as Winslow sat down
and pulled off his slippers. Removing his
glasses, he placed them on the nightstand,
and then rolled under the covers.

"Ahh." He snuggled beneath the electric
blanket's warmth. "I'll be glad when spring
comes."

Edith nodded. "Me, too. Can't wait to see
my crocus and hyacinths along the front
porch."

Too bad she couldn't eat her spring
flowers—they were undoubtedly low calo-
rie.

She smiled when she heard Winslow sigh
contentedly. Within minutes he would be
asleep.

Lifting the Bible, she tried to concentrate on a verse from Ecclesiastes:

While still seeking wisdom, I clutched at foolishness. In this way, I hoped to experience the only happiness most people find during their brief life in this world.

Why did people insist on reaching for foolish things when they knew wisdom was better? Why did *she?*

Winslow's voice startled her.

"Something *is* bothering you tonight, Edith. What is it?"

Tears sprang to her eyes. She shook her head as she snagged a tissue from the box on the nightstand.

"It's just . . . everything," she said, hating the way her voice trembled. "Olympia and Bea and Annie—it's a time of change, and change isn't easy."

She fell quiet, hoping Winslow would accept her answer at face value. Everyone's emotions had been close to the surface all week, but the reason for her tears went far deeper. She was indulging in her own private pity party because she wasn't as thin as she used to be.

Win's voice drew her back. "Edith?"

Closing the Bible, she shut her eyes. "It's nothing, Win. Nothing important, just . . . foolishness."

"It's the diet thing, isn't it?" His voice held a note of reservation; she knew he disliked diets, always said they never worked. All things in moderation, he believed, but Edith didn't have time for moderation with Birdie's wedding less than two months away. Desperate times called for desperate measures.

She opened her eyes and turned to face him. "I have to lose two dress sizes by the end of next month, Win. Otherwise I have nothing to wear to Birdie's wedding." She reached out to run her hand along his cheek. "I know you don't approve of diets, but I'm asking you to be a little tolerant so I can reach my goal."

"Edith." Sighing, he stroked her arm. "Why do women agonize about their weight?"

She shrugged. "We just do."

Winslow nodded thoughtfully. "Okay, then. I will try to understand your desire to lose a few pounds, but only if you consult Dr. Marc and do *exactly* as he says. I don't want you going on one of those fad diets and making yourself sick."

"Why should I see Dr. Marc? When I had my physical last year he said I was as healthy as a horse." Not the most flattering diagnosis, but welcome nevertheless.

"Dr. Marc will recommend a sound program. I trust him."

And he didn't trust *her?* Edith pulled away, a little hurt, but Winslow didn't understand. Besides, she knew what Dr. Marc would say: Eat according to the food pyramid, exercise, take it slow and easy. Sound advice, sure, but too slow if she was going to wear her peach dress for Birdie's wedding.

When she didn't answer, Win nudged her. "Do I have your promise?"

"Uh hum." Edith felt an urgent need to change the subject. "Can you turn the blanket down, hon? My side is getting too warm."

"Sure." He turned the dial down a notch, then snuggled closer to her side. "I love you like you are, Edith."

"I know, Win." She patted his hand, feeling only a little guilty. She might have to fudge a bit to get around Win's wishes, but she'd be careful. Men just didn't understand. They lost weight quicker than women, they kept it off easier, and they didn't suffer from hormonal rages that made them want to eat everything in sight, particularly if it was made of chocolate. . . .

She'd go see Dr. Marc if it'd make Winslow feel better, then she'd do whatever it took to get the weight off. And when she stood by Winslow's side, mixing with guests at Birdie's wedding reception, she'd be the picture of elegant grace in peach and silver. . . .

Simply lovely.

Chapter Eight

Returning to her tiny office at Portland's Southern Maine Technical College, Annie dropped her book bag to the floor, then leafed through a sheaf of pink messages the division secretary had stacked on her desk. Apparently her students had been delighted to have a week off from her class, but only five students had enrolled in "Herbaceous Plant Design" for the spring term. In a Maine February, the only herbaceous plants around lived in the college greenhouse.

She dropped into her chair and tossed the messages onto her desk. None of them were pressing; they could wait until after she'd gone through the mail.

A rap on her door made her look up. "Ms. Cuvier?"

A freckle-faced young man with hair the color of ripe apples stood in her doorway.

"Can I help you?"

"Yeah." The young man blushed. "I'm Jason Boggs. I wanted to sign up for your class."

She lifted a brow. "You're a bit early, Jason. Registration for the summer term won't begin for weeks."

"But the catalog says instructor approval is required for the summer lab. I wanted to come by early . . . you know, to make sure you approve of me."

Annie had to smile when his ears went the color of strawberries.

"It's not a hugely popular class, Jason. I think you'll be fine."

His tentative grin broadened. "Great! When I read the article, I just knew I had to get into your lab. I want to learn all about how to design plants like your tomatoes."

"The class isn't about designing plants, Jason, it's about designing landscapes." She frowned. "Um, what article did you read?"

"This one." With a flourish, he pulled a magazine from his book bag, then dropped it on her desk. Aghast, she stared at a glossy copy of *Tomato Monthly.* The cover featured her smiling face, and in her hands she held one of her spindly, practically poisonous tomato plants.

Groaning, she dropped her head into her hands. "They were supposed to pull this story. I called them right after the incident."

"What incident?"

"My tomatoes nearly poisoned an entire town. They're worthless."

Jason shrugged. "Doesn't matter, really. The article says you're a genius at hybrid plant design. The writer said he thinks you're going to be a millionaire by the time you're thirty."

Annie laughed aloud. "Don't believe everything you read, Jason." She fingered the glossy cover. "Do you mind if I borrow this? No—wait. I don't want to look at it. Take it with you."

He picked up the magazine and turned, then paused at the door. "So I can sign up for your class?"

"If you want to learn about landscape design, sure. If you want to learn how to poison half the world's population, why not?"

Jason Boggs threw her a grin, then walked away whistling. When he had disappeared around a corner, Annie dropped her head to her desk and covered it with her hands.

What had she ever done to deserve such a streak of bad luck? She'd been blessed with a rich imagination, but apparently she lacked the brainpower to make her ideas work. As a kid, her soda pop concoction had blown a hole through the roof of the barn at Frenchman's Fairest, and her hair dye had turned Barbara Higgs's hair shocking pink for an entire summer. Even those blasted tomatoes, which had actually managed to bloom and produce fruit in a Maine winter, had proven to be all looks and no substance.

Everything she touched ended in disaster, and A.J. would soon learn that she couldn't accomplish anything worthwhile. He'd never understand her failures. He was the proverbial golden child who succeeded in everything he undertook. She had no doubt he had graduated at the head of his class and was probably the best neurosurgeon in New York, well on his way to running a hospital or two. . . .

What had ever made her think he'd be interested in someone like her?

The phone at her elbow rang. Wearily, she lifted the receiver. "Hello?"

"Annie? It's Edmund."

For an instant her frazzled brain wondered if Uncle Edmund had found a way to phone from heaven, then she remembered her cousin. "Edmund! Are you in Boston?"

"Yes." She heard a smile in his voice. "Listen, I don't know if you've already made a decision about Mom's house, but if you're thinking about selling, I think I may have found a buyer. A partner in my law firm is interested in opening a maritime museum, and he thinks Heavenly Daze might be just the place for it. My mother's house would be perfect."

Annie crinkled her nose, trying to imagine Frenchman's Fairest as an institution. "Would he live there?"

"Of course not, the place is practically uninhabitable. The museum would be open only during tourist season. He'd hire someone to manage it, of course, and they'd probably live in the guest cottage."

So Dr. Marc would have to leave. And Caleb.

She drew a deep breath. "I haven't actually decided to sell, Edmund, but it's nice to know someone is interested."

"I think he'll pay up to two hundred thousand for the place. No more, because we both know it needs extensive repairs."

"I know."

"So—can I tell him you'll think about it?"

"I'll think about it. And Edmund?"

"Yes?"

"Are you upset, you know, about not getting the house? I didn't know Olympia was going to leave it to me. I wouldn't want you thinking I asked for it."

He laughed. "I wouldn't have that money pit if you paid me to take it. I'm only recommending it to my friend because I know he won't be operating in the off-season, so he won't have to replace the furnace and insulate all those leaky windows."

Annie sighed. "Thanks for calling. I'll let you know."

She hung up, then propped her chin on her hand. Edmund had given her another reason to sell, a good one. Two hundred thousand dollars would go a long way to settle Caleb in a condo and put a proper monument on Olympia's grave, occupied or not. With that kind of money she could build a little medical clinic for Dr. Marc on Ferry Road, perhaps down by the Lobster Pot. There might even be enough left over to replace her rattling car. . . .

She slammed her hand to the desk. This

ought to be a simple decision, so why wasn't it? She ought to be able to line up the pros and cons of selling and staying and make a definitive decision, yet something in her refused to approach that point.

She needed someone to help her think clearly, but A.J. was no help at all. The last time she'd spoken to him, he'd become almost irritated with her because she couldn't—wouldn't—dismiss Heavenly Daze without a second thought.

Her thoughts drifted toward Dr. Marc. Of all the people she knew on Heavenly Daze, he understood her situation best. But she couldn't call him . . . she had bothered him enough.

Chapter Nine

Two days after promising her husband she'd see the physician, Edith sat in Dr. Marc's office and flipped through a magazine.

Yesterday she'd tried the meat-and-potatoes diet written up in *Good Housekeeping*. It felt strange to eat sausage and potatoes for breakfast, and stranger still to have a huge slice of pot roast with a baked potato for lunch. Win hadn't minded the supper of pork loin and potatoes, but by eight o'clock, when she fixed a plate of beef and potatoes for the required before-bed snack, Edith had figured out why this diet worked—the dieter grew so tired of beef and potatoes by the second day that he or she simply stopped eating . . . or quit.

Edith was ready to quit and move on to something else. The magazine in the doctor's office had no diets to offer, though it did have a dozen glossy pictures of decadent desserts: chocolate pound cake; strawberry soufflés, and a crème brûlée that looked good enough to die for. . . .

When she heard Dr. Marc and Babette Graham coming down the hallway, she set the magazine aside. Her interest shifted into concern when she saw that Babette was as white as snow.

"Hi, Babette."

The younger woman didn't even look up. She nodded in a sort of daze, then pulled her coat from the hook by the door and slipped it on.

"Take your vitamins," Dr. Marc said, his attention focused on Babette. "Remember—this is a very important time."

"Ayuh." Babette spoke in an absent voice.

"And come see me again in a couple of weeks."

"Ayuh." Wearing the bewildered look of a sleepwalker, Babette opened the front door and stepped outside.

When the door had closed, Edith jerked her thumb toward the porch. "Is she—"

"I'm going to count on your discretion,"

Dr. Marc said, grinning. "I think she and Charles should make the announcement."

"Oh, my." Edith winced in sympathy for the young woman. Every mother welcomed children, but Babette already had Georgie, and that boy was a handful.

She nodded to the doctor. "Don't worry. As a pastor's wife, I'm used to zipping my lip."

"Thanks." His friendly expression shifted to a look of concern. "I hope you're not having the same, um, symptoms."

She laughed. "Oh, no. My problem is nothing a little will power can't fix. For the record, I didn't want to bother you with this, but I promised Winslow."

The doctor laughed. "Come on back, then, and let's talk."

As nervous as a cat, she followed him into the small examining room. She didn't want the entire town to know she was dieting, but the doctor was a trustworthy person. He wouldn't spill the . . . She groaned as an image of deep, rich, molasses-covered Boston baked beans rose in her mind.

"Now, then." The doctor leaned against the counter and crossed his arms. "How can I help you?"

Clearing her throat, Edith stared at her

folded hands. "I've been thinking about taking off a few pounds. Winslow wanted me to consult you first."

Lifting one finger to his chin, the doctor studied her. "A diet, huh? Clothes feeling a little too tight?"

She managed a tolerant smile.

"Well, I suppose most of us could afford to drop some excess weight. In the winter, we Mainers tend to be like the animals—we overeat, put on extra padding, then go through a spring shed." He grinned at her. "Don't worry, you won't be the only islander watching what they eat."

He picked up a folder and shuffled through the papers inside. "We did blood work a few months ago, cholesterol's fine . . . triglycerides are only slightly elevated." He glanced up, smiling. "I see no reason why you can't limit your intake of food for a few weeks—as long as you don't get carried away and go for the skin-and-bones look."

Edith had no intention of turning herself into Calista Flockhart. "So I can lose fifteen, maybe twenty pounds?"

Dr. Marc frowned. "Twenty? You'd be shivering come next winter, Edith. For your frame, that's a lot of weight to lose."

She shrugged. "Twenty would give me a little leeway. Summer is right around the corner and I always gain weight in summer—you know how those ice cream socials can get out of hand."

He laughed, patting his midsection. "Do I ever."

"Good." She sighed, feeling better now that she had his blessing. "I won't take up any more of your time. Winslow is such a worry wart."

The doctor led the way out of the exam room. "Remember now—no fad diets. Eat sensibly. Lots of fresh fruits—"

"—and vegetables," Edith finished. "I know the routine, Doc."

"But do you *follow* the routine?" He paused, turning to face her. "I mean it, Edith. You're not as young as you once were—none of us are. Teenagers can get away with fad diets, but we older folks can't. Dropping weight takes time, if done properly. You didn't gain the weight overnight, and you shouldn't take it off overnight. I recommend a program like Pound Pinchers—anything that offers group support. In fact, I believe there's a Pound Pinchers meeting every Thursday morning in Ogunquit."

The island women usually cleaned or quilted on Thursday mornings, and Edith didn't want to miss the fellowship. Besides, she didn't need to have her hand held through a diet. She was a grown woman, and she could manage most anything.

"Eighteen hundred calories a day should be about right for you," the doctor went on "Enjoy a piece of cake or a scoop of ice cream once a week. The body craves variety, so don't deprive yourself of everything you like."

Oh, no. She hated to admit it, but a single taste of a forbidden food meant certain suicide for her diet. She would have to go cold turkey and eat none of her favorites until the weight was gone. The thought of the peach dress in the closet bolstered her confidence.

She could do it. She'd count calories, stop eating after eighteen hundred calories a day, and eat whatever she liked . . . except her red flag foods. Toss in a few fast walks around the island, and she'd be shipshape in no time.

"Thank you, Dr. Marc. I'll be fine."

She left the office feeling lighter in mind, if not in body. By the time Birdie's and Salt's wedding rolled around she would be slim and trim once again.

Delicious aromas drifted from the bakery as she crossed Ferry Road—Abner was making crullers. Her eyes searched the street for Tallulah, then an unexpected thought struck her.

What would become of Tallulah now that Edmund and Olympia were gone?

Chapter Ten

"Isn't this invigorating?" Clad in a sweat suit, tennis shoes, and matching wrist and ankle weights, Edith swung her arms like pistons and plowed ahead, her legs pumping to the rhythm of a rhyme she'd invented:

> *One, two, three, four! You can do a little more!*
> *Five, six, seven, eight! Come on, girl, and lose this weight!*

Twenty paces behind, Winslow followed, his bald head gleaming with sweat despite the chilly temperature. "Hold up, Edith." Puffing, he bent to tie his shoelace.

Not willing to stop moving, Edith doubled back to walk in a circle around him. She was two days into the eighteen-hundred-calorie-a-day-diet-and-exercise plan, and she hadn't lost a pound. Or a half a pound.

Or an inch.

Which convinced her that if she could maintain her pace, surely tomorrow she'd wake up and find that the fat globules on her hips had decided to melt away in the night.

Winslow straightened and shot her a grin. "Okay. Lead on, woman!"

Edith took off, quickening her pace, but she hadn't gone twenty steps when she spied a rock. Suddenly weary, she dropped to it, then rested her hands on her bent knees and hung her head.

Something had gone wrong. Her *energy* globules had decided to melt away; the fat was hanging on.

Waves lapped the shoreline, and the morning sun gleamed silver on the water and streaked the lighthouse with golden rays. On any other day she would have reveled in the sight, but today defeat colored her perceptions.

She stared at the water as Winslow approached. "It's no use. I'm starving myself and getting nowhere. We're going home and I'm making pancakes."

"Now, Edith." Win dropped to the rock beside her, his eyes dark with compassion. "You know losing weight is not an easy process."

"Easy for you to say." She turned envious eyes on him. "How much have you lost in the past couple of days?"

He wouldn't meet her gaze. "That doesn't matter, does it? I wasn't really trying."

Her eyes pierced him. "How much, Win?"

"Two pounds—but Edith, everyone's metabolism is different."

"Ayuh. And mine is out of order." She raked a hand through her windblown hair. She had *religiously* stuck to Dr. Marc's regimen—she'd given up all snacks and desserts and eaten nothing but healthy foods for the last two days. But the new scales she had purchased from the Mercantile refused to budge.

Why didn't she just give up and wear sackcloth to Birdie's wedding?

Giving in was far easier than suffering. She hadn't slept last night; experiencing hunger pangs, she had gotten up and roamed the house, finally finding the will power to munch on carrot sticks instead of

Pringles. All this extra exercise had done something to make her hungrier, and low-fat, low-calorie food just didn't seem to satisfy. . . .

She dropped her face into her hands. "I'm such a wimp about this. I want to be thin, but I can't seem to find the strength to turn that want into reality."

Winslow slipped an arm around her shoulder. "You're making too much of this, Edith. What's the harm if you can't wear that peach dress to Birdie's wedding? You have other dresses."

"None that are elegant!! None that make me feel pretty!"

As Winslow stared at her in bewilderment, Edith shook her head. Men didn't understand. A man could be fifty pounds overweight and people would smile and say that his wife must certainly be a good cook. A woman, on the other hand, would be ridiculed if she began to put on a few pounds. Let a movie star begin to look maternal and suddenly she became fodder for the late-night TV shows.

When did society become so fat-phobic? Fashion magazines promoted anorexia and emaciation, television ads featured actresses who boasted about wearing a size zero.

Zero? A zero was nothing but skin, bones, and hair!

Why was life so unfair? She had never worried about her weight until lately. As a young girl she'd been blessed with an active life and a fully functioning metabolism, now she lived at a slower pace and enjoyed a simpler life. Why should her body punish her for taking it easy? And why was it so hard to eat less when half the world went to bed hungry every night?

Until she'd begun this diet, Edith couldn't remember the last time she'd honestly been hungry. Oh, there were times when she saw a delicious dish and wanted to try a bite, but it had been years since her stomach had actually growled with hunger. Last night, however, it had growled plenty, and the feeling wasn't pleasant.

Sighing, she reached up and patted her husband's face. "I think I'm ready to walk home now."

"Good. We'll get those pounds off!" Winslow gave her an encouraging squeeze and a brief kiss before he sprang up, punching the air like Rocky Balboa gone amuck.

She eyed him with a sour smile and rose slowly. Of course he felt optimistic; he'd lost weight without even trying.

Later, while Winslow showered, Edith called Dr. Marc.

"Dr. Marc? I'm sorry; I hope I didn't interrupt you."

"No, Edith. Is something wrong?"

"I'm hungry—starving. I've drunk three glasses of water and eaten all my allotted breakfast calories. Since the only calorie-free thing in my kitchen at the moment is my sink, I'm thinking of eating it."

His chuckle did nothing to ease her frustration. "Have an extra piece of toast, Edith, and deduct the calories at lunch."

If she did that, she'd be eating the stove by three.

"Remember, slow weight loss is better than fast."

"But I haven't dropped an ounce in two days. I've walked both mornings, and I've stuck to my allotted calories."

"Well, losing weight isn't easy."

"Winslow's lost two pounds."

"Good for him! And soon you'll start to see those numbers drop. Now have another piece of toast, maybe some extra fruit, then find something to do that will keep your mind off food."

Edith made a face at the phone, then hung up. Something to do? Well—she glanced around the kitchen. She did have to go to the Mecantile to pick up a few things. Thank the Lord, Vernie had stocked up for winter . . . and she had a computer.

Ten minutes later, Edith had walked down to the Mercantile and asked Vernie if she could borrow the computer for a moment.

"I just need to look something up on the Internet," she explained. "I would have gone over to use Charles Graham's machine, but since I was coming here anyway . . ."

Vernie flapped a hand in her direction. "Go right ahead, hon, and give me that shopping list. Abner and I will get started on your basket."

Grateful that Vernie wouldn't be reading over her shoulder, Edith sat at the computer desk, then opened the Internet browser. Moving to *www.google.com,* she typed "weight loss" as her search term.

The results filled the screen almost instantly, and her eyes crossed when she realized there were thousands of reference pages. "Would you like to narrow the search?" asked Google.

"You bet . . . along with my hips."

She typed "kinds of diets," then sat back as a list of diets filled the screen.

After tapping the site for the cabbage soup diet, she read: *Eat as much of the soup as you want and you'll feel full, but be prepared . . . some flatulence could occur.*

Cabbage soup? She liked cabbage, and so did Winslow. She liked soup; nothing was better in winter.

She closed her eyes, imagining herself in the peach dress in record time. Cabbage was roughage, so she could fill up on this stuff, never be hungry, and eat practically nothing in the process.

She studied the screen to check the ingredients: cabbage, onions, tomatoes, bouillon, onion soup mix, and tomato juice. Nothing harmful. And hadn't Dr. Marc recommended lots of vegetables? And the diet wasn't only soup—each day offered other foods, too: potatoes, fruit juice, and other vegetables. One day a week, she could even eat beef.

Setting her jaw, she clicked the print icon.

When the page had printed, she hollered for Abner to make sure he had at least three nice cabbages in her basket.

She had no sooner staggered through the parsonage doorway with her groceries when she spied Winslow in the living room. Grinning, he held out a bouquet of red roses. "Happy Valentine's Day, honey."

"Oh!" Dropping her shopping bag by the door, she hurried across the room to give him a hug. "Thank you so much! I'd forgotten what day it was."

He placed the flowers in her arms, then kissed her lightly. "And in addition," he picked up a beribboned satin box from the coffee table, "sweets for the sweet."

Edith's face fell. He had brought a box of her favorite lemon drops . . . and she had decided to begin the cabbage soup diet tomorrow.

Win must have noticed her lack of enthusiasm. "I know you're trying to lose weight, but one every now and then wouldn't hurt, would it?"

Poor, dear Winslow. He had no idea how hard it was for her to give up sweets . . . but his intentions were good. Smiling, she accepted the candy. She'd do something with it later—either roll every last piece in wet salt or offer the box to Tallulah.

"Thank you, Win. And for your Valentine's Day gift, I'm going to fix the best dinner you've had all week—chicken fried steak, candied sweet potatoes, rolls, and gravy."

When his eyes lit up, she knew she couldn't have dreamed up a more appreciated gift.

Chapter Eleven

Marc gave Barbara Higgs a reassuring smile, then moved toward the door. "You're doing fine, Barbara, and everything seems to indicate your surgery was a success. When you think you and Russell have succeeded in conceiving, you come talk to me again. We want your baby to be as healthy as he or she can be."

Barbara's cheeks brightened as she glanced down at her hands. "Russell and I don't know how to thank you, Dr. Marc."

"You just take care of yourself. Go ahead and get dressed, and put your mind at ease. Everything is in the Lord's hands now."

Leaving her alone in the exam room to change clothes, Marc retreated to his office to jot a few notes in her file. Barbara and Russell Higgs had been trying to conceive a child for some time, and last month he'd discovered that Barbara suffered from endometriosis. Surgery had taken care of the problem, so now the matter of children rested in the Lord's hands.

He made his notes, then closed the chart and blew out his cheeks. The townsfolk seemed healthy enough now—Vernie had bounced back from the flu; Stanley, Floyd, and Winslow had recovered from Annie's tomatoes.

A smile crossed his face. Goodness, how he missed her. The big house next door seemed to grow colder and lonelier with each passing month, with Edmund being promoted to heaven in November and Olympia following soon after. Caleb was the only resident now, and Marc wondered how the old man kept from going stir crazy in the creaky old house. But if Annie lived there, the place would hum with activity even on the frostiest winter day. . . .

Why couldn't Alex see that his young woman *needed* Heavenly Daze? Couldn't he see that the spirit of the island fueled her vitality? Like the prodigal, Annie had wandered from home, but the island and its people kept drawing her back.

He heard the jangle of the bell over the front door and mentally noted that Barbara had departed. A moment later he flinched when his thoughts were interrupted by a rusty greeting: "Dr. Marc?"

He turned to see Caleb standing in the office doorway, his cap in his hand. "Caleb! How be you today?"

The old butler waved his hand. "Never better, Dr. Marc, just a little lonesome. Wondered if you might be ready for a coffee break?"

"I'd love one." Leaving Barbara's chart on his desk, Marc stood and led the way to his private quarters. "Did you see Barbara Higgs as you came in?"

"Ayuh. Wearing a big smile, she was."

"We're hoping she'll be expecting soon. She and Russell are ready to start a family."

Caleb flashed an easy, relaxed smile with a good deal of confidence behind it. "The Father has heard their prayers. But Babette Graham is the one carrying new life."

"She told you, did she?" Marc motioned toward a chair as he moved to the counter where his coffee maker steamed with a fresh pot.

The old butler shook his head. "No, I have not spoken to Babette."

"Charles, then?"

Caleb smiled. "No."

Mark grinned. "So you saw her looking shell-shocked and put two and two together."

"No." Caleb folded his hands. "I have been entrusted to give you an important message. Babette is carrying not one new life, but three, and it is important that you be aware of this as soon as possible. When her time is fulfilled, she must be near a hospital."

Mark stared in silence, caught off guard by the sudden vibrancy of the old man's voice. Caleb did not often make such pronouncements, though he often made the occasional odd remark. . . .

The butler was staring at him, waiting for a response.

"Three babies." Marc met his gaze. "Triplets."

Caleb nodded. "I have been chosen to tell you because I am leaving. So you must keep careful watch on our Babette."

Marc cracked a smile and gestured toward the chair again. "Are you becoming psychic in your old age, Caleb? Bringing me messages from the future?"

"No." Caleb moved toward the chair. "I am merely obeying the Lord's command."

Marc turned toward his coffeepot as his thoughts whirled. Caleb's remark was harmless enough, and time would certainly tell if he was right. Babette was not far enough along to tell much through an ultrasound, but he could certainly recommend that she get one as soon as the ferry was running again. . . .

As for Caleb . . . he took a deep breath as he opened a cabinet in search of coffee mugs. He'd keep the butler's bizarre remark to himself and watch the old man a little more carefully over the next few days. If he was losing touch with reality, he'd make other slips.

"So," Caleb sank into the chair, "have you heard from Annie since she returned to Portland?"

Jarred by the mention of Annie's name, Marc gave a half-guilty start. "Why, no."

Caleb gave him a knowing smile. "I thought she might be calling you—I know she respects you tremendously. And something tells me the flame between her and A.J. has cooled a bit."

"Has it?" Marc busied himself with the coffeepot and mugs, grateful for something to do with his hands. "Alex could not do better than Annie when it comes time to choose a wife."

"Perhaps Annie was never meant for A.J."

Marc shrugged. "What is it they say? Every pot has its lid. Annie will find someone soon enough."

"Perhaps she already has. But it'd be a real shame if her someone is too reluctant to declare his feelings."

Marc's hands froze, and for a long moment he dared not look up. When he did lift his eyes, he saw no trace of mischief in Caleb's gentle smile.

"That," he agreed, taking a mug to the older man, "would be a shame."

Caleb accepted the coffee. "Why are you so afraid, Marc? The Lord knows your heart and your intentions toward our Annie."

Stunned, Marc sank into the adjacent chair. Caleb had always been intuitive, and this time he had hit the nail on the head. No sense in trying to deny it.

Marc lifted his own mug. "How can he know my intentions? I'm not sure of them myself."

"You've been distracted by concern for your son."

"Alex is a better partner for Annie. They are closer in age."

Caleb waved a hand in dismissal. "Age matters little once a man or woman reaches maturity. Look at Edmund and Olympia—they were twenty years apart, yet no two human souls were more closely knit."

"Still . . . it doesn't seem right for me to think of Annie that way. She's so young."

"She's nearly thirty."

"She has her entire life ahead of her."

"How do you know how long a life will be? She may live only ten more years, you may live another forty. Why not love and serve the Lord together for as long as you can?"

Marc cast the butler a quizzical look. "Caleb, sometimes you make no sense at all."

"Sometimes I make all the sense in the world."

"Today is not one of those times. Besides," he shrugged, "I'm not the marrying sort."

"You once were."

"Those days are past. My wife is gone and I've grown accustomed to being alone."

"It is not good for man to be alone. And two are better than one, for they have a good reward for their labor."

"I'm ancient, Caleb."

"You're a youngster."

"I'm nearly sixty."

"A mere child."

Marc laughed. "You talk like you're a hundred years old."

"More like ten thousand, but I lost count some time ago."

Marc made a mental note—odd remark number two from Caleb. Three if you counted the butler's assertion that he ought to pursue Annie.

He balanced his coffee cup on his palm. "Caleb, I don't know what's gotten into you, but I've always appreciated a good joke. That's what you're doing, right? Having a good joke at my expense?"

In answer, Caleb lifted his mug and smiled.

* * *

Winslow stared at the bowl of steaming soup in front of him. "What's in it?"

"Cabbage." Edith sat down wearily. The soup was delicious, but this would be her fourth bowl since two o'clock.

Winslow picked up his spoon and proceeded to eat. "How was your day, dear?"

"Fine."

He cast a longing glance toward the bread and butter on the counter.

She nodded. "You can have bread—all you want. I'll stick with the soup." She forced another swallow of the red liquid. "I'm not very hungry."

Winslow slathered butter on a slice of white bread, then dipped it in his soup bowl. He chatted for a few moments about an old friend from seminary, then gave Edith a wink. "Salt stopped by the church this afternoon, and I'd say he's a happy man. Fairly busting to get this wedding planned."

"I would imagine Birdie is excited, too."

"Ayuh. This soup is great, hon. I love cabbage."

Edith parked her chin in her palm and watched him spoon up the dregs. "I'm glad you like it. We'll be eating a lot of it in the next few days."

"Great." He held up his empty bowl. "I'll take another helping, please."

After dinner, when Winslow had wandered into the den to watch the evening news, she cleaned the kitchen and poured leftover soup into Tupperware containers. Her stomach felt bloated with cabbage and onions. She was full, no doubt, but she felt far from satisfied.

She was craving bread.

With butter.

She would have welcomed a hunk of leather to chew on. Something, anything, that wasn't soup.

She spied a package of cookies behind the dish drainer. Winslow must have left them there; the man never put anything back in its proper place.

She walked toward the cookies, reached for them, then drew her hand back. No. She couldn't eat them. She'd come this far, suffered an entire day of soup. If she ate a cookie now, she'd ruin whatever magical things the fat-burning soup molecules were doing in her body. They'd have to stop burning her fat to burn the invading cookie. . . .

But what if she didn't *eat* the cookie? What if she just sort of *enjoyed* it?

After glancing over her shoulder to be sure Winslow hadn't left the den, she turned on the kitchen faucet. As a stream of cold water gurgled down the drain, she took a cookie from the package and placed it in her mouth, chewing slowly.

Ah . . . crunchy. And sweet. And completely, utterly delicious.

She savored the cookie for a full moment, then deliberately, daintily spat the cookie into the sink. The running water swirled it into the disposal.

Edith reached for another.

After chewing three—and not swallowing a single bite—she flipped on the disposal switch and listened as the last evidence of her weakness rumbled down the drain.

Chapter Twelve

Just before the church service was to begin on Sunday morning, Edith looked up from her pew and saw Winslow gesturing to her from behind the piano. Sliding out of her seat, she hurried to him. "What is it, Win?"

His face twisted in a pained expression as he held his stomach. "That cabbage is repeating on me something awful. Do you have any more of those pills?"

Edith shook her head. She'd taken the last two Gas-X tablets five minutes ago. The cabbage soup diet was working—her scale had rewarded her with a two-pound loss this morning—but the dreadful side effects had made her anxious. For the past two days both she and Winslow had popped Beano like jellybeans, but problems still periodically . . . erupted.

"I'm sorry, Win, but I don't have—"

With uncharacteristic abruptness, he interrupted her thought. "Then ask Vernie to open the mercantile and get me some before I have to preach."

Edith had never seen her husband so upset. She bit her lower lip and turned to search the congregation, then spotted Vernie and Stanley coming through the back door. "Hold on," she muttered. "Stay calm and I'll be back in a minute."

"Hurry, please. The service begins in less than ten minutes and I'll be dangerous without that medicine. If Beatrice gets a whiff of the results of your cabbage soup, you'll have to play the piano this morning."

Edith hurried up the aisle, smiling quick greetings to the assembling church members. She grabbed Vernie's arm just as the mercantile owner was about to sit down.

"Quick, Vernie. Winslow needs something from the store."

Vernie glanced at Stanley. "Can it wait?"

Edith tugged the woman out of the pew. "No time for questions. The service starts in a few minutes."

"What in the world?"

"Just hurry, will you?"

Sprinting down the steps, Edith led the way across the church lawn, where melting snow covered the ground in patches. "Edith, this is crazy," Vernie panted. "What's the hurry?"

"No time for questions. Run!"

When they reached the store, Vernie fumbled with the key in the lock. Impatient, Edith commandeered the keys and unlocked the door, then pushed her way into the shop. Behind her, Vernie shouted, "What? What does Winslow need?"

Edith bolted for the apothecary counter and scanned the shelves. Thank the Lord, she saw Gas-X and Beano. She grabbed a package of each, then turned and ran for the door.

"I'll pay you later," she called. "Thanks!"

Rooted to the spot, Vernie blinked. "Winslow has the rumbles? That's your big emergency?"

Bea was pounding out the last chorus of "When the Roll is Called Up Yonder" when Edith rushed back into the sanctuary. Heads turned as a blast of wind from the open door fluttered the hymnals. Relief flooded Winslow's face when Edith calmly walked down the center aisle and approached the altar.

He accepted a small packet from her, then slipped it into his pocket. Apparently oblivious to everything, Micah kept waving his arms, leading the congregation in song.

By the time the tinkling piano had faded to silence, the pastor had popped three orange gel tabs into his mouth. After Micah's brief prayer, Winslow strode confidently to the pulpit.

Back in her pew, Edith exhaled in relief. No more cabbage soup; it wasn't fair to Winslow.

And her heart couldn't take the strain.

* * *

Coming out of church, Edith drew her collar tighter. Her head ached, and all weekend she'd felt like she was coming down with something. The cabbage soup diet offered plenty of food, just not the kind Edith was used to eating. She found herself craving foods with crunch, and throughout Winslow's sermon she had fantasized about her favorite noisy foods, beginning at the start of the alphabet: apples, bacon, Cracker Jack . . . by the time she got to the Ps (pretzels, pistachios, pickles, peanut brittle, and Pringles), Winslow had begun the benediction.

The balmy weather had held over the weekend—temperatures remained in the thirties, leaving the islanders with nothing to complain about but unnaturally sunny skies. Winslow stood in the vestibule to shake hands with the departing congregation, and Edith took her place by his side, still running foods through her mind.

She was listing the crunchy Ss (snicker-doodles, sugar snap beans), when Floyd cornered Winslow and started in again about the ferry.

"I hear it's supposed to be finished at the York Harbor marina sometime tomorrow, Pastor. You want to ride with me up to York to bring her home? I've got a fisherman picking me up at the dock, 10 A.M. sharp."

Winslow squinted at the mayor. "Does that mean I'll have to ride back with you, um, driving the ferry?"

"Of course. But if your wife needs a run into Ogunquit, I'd be happy to take you both along."

Winslow's shoulders slumped as he glanced at Edith. "You need a run into Ogunquit?"

She knew he was hoping she'd say no, but she did have a mile-long list of low-calorie foods she wanted to investigate. "I'd love to go to Ogunquit tomorrow," she said, slipping her arm through Winslow's. "And I'd be honored to ride with Floyd as ferry captain."

Visibly pleased, the mayor grinned at her. "Cleta and I would be tickled if you and Pastor could join us for supper Wednesday night."

Winslow caught Edith's eye again. "Dear? Do you have other plans?"

Edith winced inwardly. Eating out would be murder on her diet, but Winslow enjoyed spending time with his church members. She'd just have to find a way to make it through.

She nodded and forced a smile. "That would be nice, Floyd. Ask Cleta what I can bring."

"Just bring yourself, that's treat enough."

She looked away as Floyd moved on down the church steps, calling for his wife. Cleta would probably make her famous spaghetti and garlic bread—and Edith *adored* spaghetti and garlic bread.

Her head was beginning to pound when Bea emerged from the church and glanced toward the lighthouse. "Has anyone seen Birdie?"

Edith shook her head.

Winslow took Bea's hand. "I was meaning to ask where Birdie went during the sermon. I hope she isn't ill."

The postmistress frowned. "When Salt and the kids didn't show up by the time you started preaching, Birdie ran up to the light-house to check on them." Bea peered toward the north end of the island. "I wonder if something's wrong. Brittany or Bobby could've taken sick during the night. You know how she loves to take care of those kids."

"I'm sure she's fine," Babette said, rocking from side to side as her son Georgie dragged her through the crowd. "But I'd be happy to send Charles up there to see about things."

"Mom!"

Vernie, who stood between Bea and the wall, effectively halted Georgie's progress.

"I can't get out! Vernie's big ole caboose is in the way!"

Babette calmly clapped a hand over her son's mouth and lifted a brow. "Sorry, Vernie," she said, ignoring the boy squirming in her grasp. "We're working on his manners."

Edith gave the frazzled mother a sympathetic look. Babette and Charles had not yet made a public announcement about her pregnancy; perhaps they were still in shock. Edith could only pray the Lord would send them a quiet, sweet little girl to provide balance in their home.

Vernie scowled at Georgie, who promptly scowled back. Babette dragged her son toward Charles, who stood in the center of the church, talking to Zuriel Smith, the potter who lived in their guest cottage.

Edith closed her eyes in relief that Georgie had not veered her way and commented on *her* caboose.

One thing was certain—if she ate another bowl of soup, she'd probably never listen to another of Winslow's sermons without drooling. Twenty minutes of food fantasy accompanied by a lesson on the Minor Prophets had undoubtedly ingrained a Pavlovian psychological response that nothing but New York Cheesecake and butter-brushed lobster could erase.

So—this afternoon they would throw out the leftover cabbage soup and go on a scavenger hunt in the pantry. And as soon as Floyd got the ferry running, she'd go into Ogunquit, attend a Pound Pinchers meeting, and raid the grocery for some of those prepackaged diet foods. The portions were rabbit-sized, but that was okay. Anything was better than endless cabbage soup.

And, though her mind could be playing tricks on her, she was almost certain she was losing weight. No one could see anything in the tent dresses she favored for church, but her underwear wasn't cutting into her thighs like it usually did. . . .

Could anything feel better than that?

From the sidewalk, Babette yelled for their attention. "Look—isn't that Birdie coming?"

Edith joined the others craning their necks. Birdie was approaching in her golf cart, driving like a maniac as she swerved to avoid potholes.

Wheeling the cart into the churchyard, Birdie came to a quick stop, then waved her hand. "Where's Dr. Marc? And Pastor?"

Winslow hurried out of the vestibule. "I'm here, Birdie."

Edith brought her hand to her chest as Dr. Marc, who'd been talking to Caleb and Stanley Bidderman, hurried toward the golf cart.

"There's a problem at the lighthouse. It's Salt." Birdie's eyes were like two burnt holes in a blanket, dark with fear and worry. "I need you to come quick."

Neither man hesitated. Dr. Marc swung into the passenger seat next to Birdie, while Winslow climbed on the back bench and hung on to a post.

"Micah!" Dr. Marc's voice rang with authority. "My medical bag is by the front door of the clinic. Will you bring it?"

Micah Smith nodded, then sprinted around the corner of the church. Edith took two steps forward, curious to see if the man would run all the way to the clinic, but when she looked at the space between the church and the B&B, the gardener had disappeared.

She whistled in appreciation. That fellow was *fast*.

While the townspeople gaped, Birdie wheeled the cart around and drove back to the lighthouse full throttle, the pastor's head bobbing from the back bench. As they pulled away, comments erupted from various sources.

"What in the world?"

"Must be a problem."

"Did she say Salt or one of the kids?"

"Salt."

"Oh my goodness."

"His heart, do you think?"

"You never know. The man *is* seventy."

Forgetting food for the moment, Edith took off for the lighthouse at a fast walk. Win might need her help. She half walked, half jogged to Puffin Cove, pausing twice to catch her breath.

If this didn't count as aerobic exercise, she didn't know what would.

When she reached the lighthouse, she rapped on the open door, then stepped inside. Winslow, Birdie, and Dr. Marc were bent over a cot where Salt sat with his hand cupped to his forehead. Edith looked for the children, then spied Bobby and Brittany sitting in beanbag chairs, their eyes wide and worried.

"Stop all this fussin'," the old sea captain grumbled. "Just had a little dizzy spell. Nothing to get upset about."

Micah came in behind Edith, carrying Dr. Marc's medical bag. After handing the bag to the doctor, he went and sat between the kids.

Dr. Marc gave the old sea captain a kindly smile. "Feeling better now, Salt?"

The old man met the doctor's eyes, and even from a distance Edith could see fear in them. "Got up to pour a cup of coffee. The room spun and down I went."

The doctor unbuttoned Salt's shirt, then pressed a stethoscope to his chest. "Have you been taking your blood pressure medicine?"

Salt nodded. "I don't think it's my blood pressure."

"Oh, Salt." Birdie stood to the side, a wet washcloth in her hand and a helpless look on her face.

Dr. Marc lifted his head and gently addressed his audience. "If you would all be so kind as to wait at the kitchen table, I'll be able to give Captain Gribbon a brief examination."

"Just a little dizzy spell," Salt insisted. "Nothing to get all fussed up about."

Birdie reached out to touch his hand. "I'll be right over there if you need anything."

Edith moved toward the kitchen table, understanding completely. Marc needed room to work, and he didn't need Salt reading the fear on their faces.

Brittany peered up at Edith with earnest blue eyes. "Is the grandfather sick?"

"I'm sure he'll be fine, dear." Edith patted the young girl's head. "Dr. Marc will take good care of him."

Brittany nodded gravely. "Maybe he needs HRT—but people who have a prior history of strokes, cancer, or liver damage must talk to their doctors before commencing treatment."

Edith glanced down. "You watch a lot of television, don't you, dear?"

"Not anymore," Bobby interrupted. "The grandfather's TV only gets one channel."

Edith sighed and drew the little girl closer. HRT indeed. Whatever ailed Salt, she was certain he did not require hormone replacement therapy.

Fifteen minutes passed before Dr. Marc stood and closed his medical bag. Birdie hurried to the captain's side. "Is everything all right?"

Salt nodded. "Right as rain. Like I said, a little dizzy spell."

Dr. Marc snapped his black bag. "I'm not sure what caused the episode. Salt, I'd like you to come to my office tomorrow so we can run a few tests. I don't think it's anything serious, but there's no harm in being sure. Besides, it's been a while since your last physical, hasn't it?"

Salt grudgingly acknowledged that it had been.

"Then we'll kill two birds with one stone. Come down to the clinic tomorrow. I'll run a few tests, check you over, and have you home by lunchtime. Birdie can look after the kids while you're out."

"Ayuh, I can." Birdie clucked over her fiancé, drawing an afghan around his shoulders. "I'll fix you a bowl of soup before I go—you must be starved."

Soup? Edith pressed a hand to her stomach. The thought of soup, particularly if it contained cabbage, made her ill.

"No soup." Salt dismissed the offer. "Give me something I can sink my teeth into—maybe some corned beef?"

Edith looked away as her mouth began to water. If she wasn't careful, she'd be wrestling a sick old man for first-bite rights to his sandwich.

"Win?" She stood. "I think it's time we should head back."

* * *

At 4:30 on Sunday afternoon, Edith wandered into her kitchen, opened the refrigerator, and gazed critically at the contents. Every drop of the cabbage soup had been poured down the disposal. Fortunately, her refrigerator contained several items that fit beautifully into the Pound Pinchers Plan. What she didn't have, she could pick up in Ogunquit tomorrow.

After the excitement at the lighthouse, she had come home and gone through her cookbook collection. Sure enough, she had a Pound Pinchers cookbook she'd picked up at Wal-Mart, and the editors had explained the entire program in the first few pages.

The sensible eating plan centered on the idea of points and portions; she could eat virtually anything she wanted within her permitted points per day. After looking over a few suggested menus, she saw that she could manage pretty well—she could eat all her favorite foods, even a few high-calorie treats, as long as she remembered to cut back somewhere else.

In addition to cookbooks and prepackaged foods, Pound Pinchers also encouraged "losers" to attend group meetings. Edith riffled through the cookbook and thought the plan made sense. Eating sensibly, drinking six to eight glasses of water, getting reasonable exercise—even Dr. Marc would approve.

But the day's excitement had stirred up her appetite, and by three o'clock she had eaten twenty-six points—the most a woman of her height could manage and still remain on the plan.

Trouble was, she was still hungry.

And a bottle of Hershey's chocolate syrup was calling her name.

Moments later Winslow glanced up when she walked into the den. His pleasant expression shifted to disbelief. "Edith! You have a chocolate moustache!"

"I do not!" She hurriedly swiped her sleeve across her mouth, then picked up her knitting needles. Winslow dropped his head, a grin creasing the corners of his mouth.

Before she could begin a row, the doorbell chimed. Winslow got up, nearly tripping over the recliner footrest. "I'll get it."

A moment later he returned to the den, Birdie Wester in tow. As he helped her out of her coat, Birdie cast Edith an apologetic look. "Sorry to barge in on a Sunday afternoon."

"It's no trouble, Birdie." She stood and gave the woman a welcoming smile. "How is Salt?"

"Resting comfortably, thank you. But we've been talking . . . and that's why I'm here."

Winslow gestured toward the worn sofa

against the wall. "Have a seat, Birdie, and tell us what's on your mind."

The bride-to-be sank to the couch and clasped her hands together. For a long moment she said nothing, then she released a long sigh and looked up. "Life is uncertain, Pastor."

"Ayuh," Winslow agreed. "It's a vapor, here one minute and gone the next."

"Ayuh."

Edith went to sit beside her friend. Taking Birdie's hand, she rubbed warmth back into the blue-veined fingers. "You seemed worried. Are you afraid Dr. Marc was wrong about Salt's spell not being serious?"

"No, Salt trusts the doctor." Birdie smiled, tears brightening her eyes. "It's only that Salt and I have just found each other . . . at our ages, you know . . . and life is short, so we have to seize every minute."

Winslow smiled. "You don't have to worry, Birdie. The Lord numbers our days and holds our hearts. If the Lord wills, you and Salt could have years together. And you'll always have eternity."

"Olympia thought she had years, too." Birdie's voice held a note of panic. "And look what happened to her! Besides, I'll have to share Salt in eternity, and I want him all to myself for a while. Selfish, I know."

Edith shook her head. "I know what you mean, hon." She smiled at her pastor-husband. "Sometimes it's hard to share the man you love."

Winslow ran his finger down the arm of his recliner. "It was Olympia's time to go. But Salt's a strong man; I'm sure he'll come through this little dizzy spell like the captain he is."

"Maybe." Clearing her throat, Birdie brushed wetness from her eyes. "That's why I've stopped by. Salt and I have decided to move the wedding up."

Edith's stomach hit the floor. Move the wedding up? They couldn't! She was nowhere near fitting into that dress!

Winslow laughed. "Well, that's fine. There's not a soul on the island who would begrudge you a moment of happiness." While Edith stared at him in horror, he reached for his appointment book and flipped through the pages. "Let's see. When were you thinking, Birdie?"

"Maybe . . . the twenty-eighth?"

Winslow nodded. "The twenty-eighth of March? That's already your date."

"The twenty-eighth of *this* month," Birdie corrected.

He looked up. "You mean—next week? That gives you only eleven days to prepare."

Birdie nodded. "We talked it over, and we don't see any reason to wait. Other than Patrick, everybody is already here. The ferry should be operating by then, in case there are any guests from Ogunquit. Sears should be sending my dress any day, and Abner can bake the wedding cake on a few hours' notice."

Edith gazed at her guest in astonishment. "But . . . what about Salt's health?"

"Doesn't matter to me. The vows say 'in sickness and in health,' don't they?"

Scribbling in his notebook, Winslow paused. "The twenty-eighth is a Thursday."

"Doesn't matter. That's when Patrick finishes his sixty days at that treatment facility he entered, so that's the soonest he can come home." Birdie set her chin. "Salt and I want all the time we can get together."

"Birdie, dear, there's no need for such urgency," Edith soothed. "Eleven days is hardly enough time to arrange flowers and make rice bags and address the invitations—"

"Hang the flowers—hang the bouquet, even. I'll carry my mother's Bible and we'll tuck the money we save into our savings account. I'll ask Vernie if I can borrow some of her ferns to set around the front of the church, and I know Micah can come up with something for flowers." The bakery owner sent Winslow a steely glance. "The twenty-eighth, Pastor. One week from this coming Thursday."

One week from Thursday. The words echoed in Edith's brain like a death sentence.

Winslow nodded. "If that's what you want."

"That's what we want. Thanks for being flexible and all."

Nodding, Birdie got up. She stood for a moment, not speaking, until Winslow peered at her above the rims of his glasses. "Something else, Birdie?"

"No," she said, turning toward the door. "Just dreadin' the thought of telling Bea about the change."

Chapter Thirteen

On Monday morning, Edith's new bathroom scales registered a half-pound loss. Eight pathetic ounces after a weekend of pinching points.

Edith stepped off the gadget and toweled dry. Pound Pinchers would have to wait. Birdie's decision to move the wedding up a full month called for drastic measures.

"Win?" She stuck her head through the bathroom doorway as she rolled deodorant under her arms.

"Yes, dear?"

"Any idea what the weather will be like today?"

She heard the volume of the TV increase as Win checked the weather report.

"High of thirty-five, low twelve degrees."

She shivered at the thought of standing

on the cold dock while they waited for Floyd's friend to pick them up. The ferry ride wouldn't be much warmer, but she really needed to get into Ogunquit.

She snapped the deodorant lid on the container and set it back in the medicine chest. "You almost ready?"

Winslow was still in his pajamas when she stepped out of the bathroom. He gave her a quizzical look. "What's your hurry?"

"I just don't want to miss Floyd, that's all. And I need things."

"Can't you get the things at the Mercantile?"

"Vernie doesn't carry everything I need."

Winslow sighed, then headed toward the shower. "I'll be ready in five minutes." Edith moved to her bureau, then peered into the mirror. "While we're in Ogunquit, want to eat lunch at Hamilton's?"

"Can you eat there and stay on your diet?"

"Sure." Edith picked up a bottle of Revlon Golden Glow foundation and dotted a few drops on her face. She could eat almost anywhere on the diet she planned to follow today. She'd been reading about the high protein regime, and she loved meat, eggs, and cheese. She'd have to avoid carbohydrates—too bad, because she also loved bread—but the freedom to have real whipped cream on fresh strawberries would be a nice consolation.

Who couldn't stick to that diet? According to what she'd read, her excess weight would melt away when her body's internal furnace mechanism fried her fat cells into oblivion. Besides, she wouldn't have to stay on it forever. After Birdie's wedding, she'd switch to Pound Pinchers and eat sensibly.

The trip to Ogunquit went more smoothly than she'd hoped. Floyd's friend, a lobsterman from York, met them at the Heavenly Daze dock promptly at ten and didn't even hesitate when Edith asked if he'd mind dropping her at Perkins Cove before heading up to York Harbor. Cleta, she noticed, had somehow begged out of the excursion, and poor Winslow felt he had to stay with Floyd on the ride to the marina and home again.

She kissed her husband on the cheek at Perkins Cove, then hopped out of the boat and moved to the pay phone to call a taxi.

Two hours later, after a pleasant morning of browsing the grocery store, Winslow tapped her on the shoulder.

She grinned at him. "You survived!"

"Barely." Winslow wiped imaginary sweat from his brow. "Seriously, Floyd is a better pilot than I would have imagined. I think he's been reading up on it or something. The trip went without a hitch."

Edith glanced at her watch. "Do we have time for lunch, or will Floyd want to hurry back to the island?"

"Floyd's having a ball driving that boat. He's already headed back to the island, but he said I should just call him when we want to return. He'll come out and pick us up."

Edith shook her head. "He may get sick of operating the ferry on that basis."

Winslow chuckled. "Stroble will be back in two weeks, dear. I don't think Floyd will grow tired of his new toy in two weeks."

Leaving the groceries to chill on a sidewalk bench, Edith and Winslow entered Hamilton's Family Restaurant. With greedy eyes Edith eyed the menu, then ordered a large hamburger patty, a mound of cottage cheese, and coffee laced with heavy cream.

At the end of the meal, Winslow leaned back in the booth and narrowed his gaze.

She glanced up, wiping the corners of her mouth with a napkin. "What?"

"All that was on your diet?"

"It is—and so is strawberries and whipped cream. Want some?" She motioned for the waitress. The nicest thing about the high-protein diet was that she didn't feel starved, so she wouldn't zing out of control in midafternoon.

Must have something to do with that internal furnace mechanism.

Whatever it was, more power to it.

Chapter Fourteen

Wednesday night at the Lansdowns', Edith sat at the dining table and eyed the bowl of green beans and the steaming platter of spaghetti and meatballs next to it. According to the high-protein diet, she could eat a meatball (maybe two, if there were extra) and a little salad. No pasta, no sauce, and not one bean.

When she glanced at the buffet, where Cleta and Barbara had set out two fragrant loaves of homemade garlic bread, a scolding voice in her brain chanted, "No refined carbohydrates, no sugar, white rice, white bread, or crackers."

She reached up and dotted her salivating mouth with her napkin.

Breathless, Cleta took her seat at the table. "Well, now, shall we thank the Lord?"

As the table occupants joined hands, Floyd cleared his throat. "Pastor? Would you bless the food?"

Winslow leaned forward and shot a conspiratorial grin at their host. "I'd love to, Floyd, but I think Edith should offer thanks tonight."

Edith, who had lowered her head to half-mast, suddenly jerked her chin toward her husband. What was he *doing?* She could understand if he had deferred to Floyd (people always asked preachers to say grace, but Winslow liked to give others an opportunity), but to ask *her?*

This wasn't about being gracious—this was a mischievous poke at her diet.

She looked at him, silently daring him to meet her gaze, but he had closed his eyes. Floyd, Cleta, Russell, and Barbara had bowed their heads, too. Everyone was waiting for her to ask a blessing for a tableful of food she couldn't eat.

She swiveled her eyes and stared at the green beans. She'd never been particularly fond of green beans, but tonight those little green slivers looked like they'd melt on her tongue in pure deliciousness.

"Lord," she began, lowering her lids, "we

thank you for this day. We thank you for friends, for the beautiful weather, for the good health of our friend Salt Gribbon." She swallowed, searching for words. Would Cleta notice if Edith conveniently forgot to thank the Lord for the food? One thing was certain—she couldn't honestly thank the Lord for food she couldn't eat.

"I thank you, Lord, for the loving hands that prepared this meal. Help us be strong to do the work you have called us to do. Be with Floyd as he pilots the ferry, and be with Captain Stroble and Mazie down in Floridy. Be with Birdie and Salt as they plan their wedding; be with Annie as she decides what to do about Frenchman's Fairest. Be with Butchie and Tallulah and Roxie. Bless the Klackenbushes and the Grahams, and help Babette and Charles as they try to teach Georgie some proper manners. Comfort Bea. Help Stanley and Vernie as they renew their commitment to one another. Thank you for Dr. Marc and his tender watchcare over us. Send our love to Olympia and Edmund and all those who have gone before."

Winslow cleared his throat. Ignoring him, she pressed on: "Loving Father, we ask that you would be with our president and national leaders. Give them wisdom and help them remember the important principles that guided our founding fathers. Remind America's citizens that you are God, that you have a plan for this country, indeed, all countries and all men everywhere . . ."

Beside her, Winslow cleared his throat again. She opened one eye and saw him whirling his finger in a "speed it up" gesture.

Poor baby, his food was getting cold.

"We ask all these things in the name of the altogether lovely One, Jesus Christ. Amen."

As heads lifted around the table, Floyd looked at Edith in outright admiration. "I didn't know you could pray like that."

She shrugged off the compliment and lifted her teacup.

Winslow reached for a basket of garlic bread and started it around the table. "How did fishing go today, Russell?"

With a heavy heart, Edith watched the bread pass by, the warm scent of garlic wafting from the cloth-covered basket. As everyone around her talked and laughed and ate with hearty appetites, she picked at her meatball and salad. Toward the end of the meal, when the men had pushed back their chairs to allow for the expansion at their waistlines, she ran her index finger along the rim of her plate to scrape up the last drops of the tasty sauce. Closing her eyes, she licked her finger, savoring the flavors of tangy tomato, basil, and oregano.

Silence crept over the table.

She opened her eyes, appalled to see Cleta, Floyd, Barbara, Russell, and Winslow staring at her. Quickly swiping her finger on her napkin, she stood and lifted her plate. "Let me help you with the cleanup, Cleta."

Barbara pushed back from the table. "Sit down, Edith, you're a guest. I'll help Mom in the kitchen."

"Stay where you are, Barbara." Edith gently pressed the young woman back into her chair. "You're still recovering from surgery. You should take it easy."

"But I'm fine."

"Honey." Russell threw an arm around his wife's shoulders. "Sit."

"Say, Floyd." Patting his stomach, Winslow leaned back in his chair. "Would you have time to take a look at our freezer? It acts like it's got a short—the light keeps flickering."

"I've been awful busy with the ferry, Pastor, but if I can't manage, I'll send Stanley over. The man's been looking for things to do 'cause his bein' underfoot is threatenin' to drive Vernie crazy."

Winslow laughed. "That'll work."

Edith carried a stack of dishes into the kitchen and Cleta followed. "Land's sake, Edith, you ate like a bird tonight. Are you sick?"

Edith shook her head. "I'm not sick."

"Then you're dieting."

"Shh—I don't want everyone to know. Women on diets tend to talk about food all the time. I don't want to put everyone through that kind of misery."

Cleta paused, one hand coming to her ample hip. "What kind of crazy diet are you on?"

Edith scraped the remnants of someone's spaghetti and salad into the garbage disposal. "High protein is not a crazy diet. Why, most of the Hollywood stars choose low-carbohydrate diets when they want to shed a few pounds."

"Diets aren't healthy." Cleta put the lid on the butter and set the dish in the refrigerator. "Why in the world are you dieting? You look fine to me."

"I'm twenty pounds overweight. Practically obese."

"Hogwash. You look fit and healthy. Let's face it, Edith. We're not spring chickens anymore. As we get older, we get a little fleshier."

"As we get older we have to fight harder to avoid weight gain," Edith corrected.

Cleta shook her head. "You can't fight mother nature."

Tears of frustration stung her eyes. "I can try, can't I?"

Sitting down, Edith dabbed at her eyes with a napkin. She could stop this diet any time, but she didn't want to stop. All she had to do was hold on for eight more days, then her agony would end. She would go back to the Pound Pinchers plan and take the remaining weight off slowly.

Cleta dropped into the empty kitchen chair next to her. "What's wrong, honey?"

"I don't know—maybe this diet is driving me a little nuts. I never thought I'd see the day I'd kill for a green bean. I want so badly to fit into this peach dress I have—it's really pretty, and I've never worn it on the island. I want to look nice for Salt's and Birdie's wedding."

"What a thing to say! Edith Wickam, you're a handsome woman. You'd look nice if you came to the wedding in a gunny sack."

Laughing, Edith wiped her eyes. "Thanks, Cleta, but we both know that's not true."

"Honey." The innkeeper poured Edith a cup of hot coffee. "Liz Curtis Higgs, one of my favorite writers, likes to remind women that they often postpone joy until they are in that size eight or ten dress."

"That's not me. I'm happy."

Cleta lifted a brow. "Are you?"

The question struck Edith like an arrow. She used to be happy . . . until she started dieting. Since then she'd spent nearly every other minute worrying or plotting or fretting. Her emotions had run the gamut from irritable to irrational. . . .

She met Cleta's soft gaze. "I *used* to be happy."

Cleta nodded. "Liz says that being thin doesn't guarantee health or happiness. Every day a woman needs to be assured that she is of immeasurable worth and great beauty *now,* not when she's reached some arbitrary goal. She doesn't advocate giving up or living in denial. She just wants women to acknowledge their physiological differences and accept the bodies they've been given."

Edith looked away, digesting the profound thought. Could she go back to thinking of herself as a person of worth and beauty? Winslow had always made her feel beautiful, but lately she had been ignoring him and focusing on that silly peach dress.

"Cleeeeeta!" Floyd's voice whined from the dining room. "Where's that chocolate cake and coffee?"

"That man." When Cleta got up and lifted the crystal lid of the dessert stand, Edith had to look away from the sight of rich chocolate frosting heaped on a devil's food cake.

Cleta rattled a utensil drawer as she searched for a knife. "I'm going to jerk a knot in the man's tail one of these days. I swear, he gets like an old bear when it comes to his dessert." She glanced up, her mouth drooping with apology as Edith's gaze fixated on chocolate frosting.

"I'm sorry, Edith."

Mustering a smile, Edith got up to search for creamer to pour into the pitcher. "Don't worry—I'm fine."

"I have a can of peaches I can open."

"I'll just have coffee."

Edith opened the refrigerator and found the creamer. She had made it through this meal successfully, but her nerves were coiled tighter than a Slinky.

Eight more days . . . she could still lose weight in eight days. But the high-protein diet had to go.

Chapter Fifteen

Thursday morning, Winslow sat at the table and stared at the three peeled bananas on his wife's plate. "What is that?"

"Breakfast."

Last night she'd found a copy of the Wiener Diet in an old magazine. The food plan was simple and it was guaranteed to work. One woman quoted in the article had lost five pounds in two days! If Edith could match that, she'd be into that peach dress with time to spare before the wedding.

"You're eating bananas?"

"Yep. Eat your waffles, Winslow, before they get cold."

Ayuh, she was eating bananas today: three for breakfast, three for lunch, three for dinner. Tomorrow she'd switch gears and eat frankfurters, three at each meal. Win might complain about her cooking, but at least he liked hotdogs. On day three of this diet she would eat boiled eggs, three at each meal. And the pounds would fall off.

She knew she was ignoring Cleta's advice (and Winslow's and Dr. Marc's), but the scale had coughed up another half pound this morning and boosted her confidence.

She bowed her head for a quick blessing of her breakfast: *Lord, I know you love me as I am, but I so want to be slim by the twenty-eighth. I promise I'll diet healthy after that if you'll just let me get into that peach dress a week from today. Oh—and thank you for the bananas.*

Reaching for the syrup, Winslow un-capped the bottle and doused his waffle in the sweet stuff. He shook his head. "I can't imagine Pound Pinchers endorsing nothing but bananas for breakfast."

"You can eat practically anything with Pound Pinchers, remember?" Edith picked up her fork, then sliced off a bit of banana. In only a few more days she'd be back to fol-lowing the Pound Pinchers program. But if she told Win about the Wiener Plan, he would forbid her to continue, and she didn't have the energy to argue.

For now, what he didn't know wouldn't hurt him.

* * *

Later that morning, Edith glanced up from her reading when a knock came at the kitchen door. Laying her book aside, she wiped a stray hair out of her eyes and went to answer.

Her legs trembled as she walked. She felt awful this morning, queasy and weak. The bananas had upset her stomach.

She opened the door and found Stanley at the door, a toolbox in his hand. "Mornin', Edith."

"How be you, Stan?"

"Floyd said you all needed someone to look at your deep freeze."

"Ayuh." She lifted a hand to her throbbing head. "It's in the basement—well, you know where it is."

"Ayuh." Stanley followed her to the basement stairs. She pulled the light on, then pointed downward.

"You say the light's been blinking?"

Edith nodded. "Winslow thinks the freezer might have a short."

"Ayuh." Stanley shrugged out of his heavy pea coat, dropped it on a kitchen chair, then ducked his head and ventured down the stairs. "I'll holler if I need something."

"Thanks."

Edith lingered in the kitchen, not wanting to leave Stanley completely alone. If she went back to reading in the den, she'd never hear him holler.

Spying the mop behind the back door, she decided to clean the floor. Too preoccupied with diets lately, she had let her housework slip.

She poured a healthy dose of Mr. Clean into her pail, then filled the bucket with hot water from the sink. A few minutes later she had swept the floor and stood the chairs on the kitchen table. Her arms felt like limp noodles—as if her internal engine were running on empty.

Moving in a hazy fog, she dunked her mop into the bucket and sloshed it over the vinyl floor. Back and forth, back and forth—wonder how many calories this activity would burn?

Beneath her, Stanley clanked around in the basement, the sounds of banging coming up the stairs. Why did a short circuit require *banging*?

She cleaned under the table, then dipped her mop in the sudsy water. She frowned when the scent of tobacco reached the kitchen. Stanley knew she didn't like smoking in the house. She thought about stomping downstairs and jerking the cigar out of his mouth, but a pastor's wife didn't give in to such urges, however frequently they popped up.

She mopped harder, bearing down to erase a black scuff on the vinyl. Stanley's crusty baritone drifted up the steps: "Listen to the folk singer, feelin' kinda jaunty . . ."

Clang, clang.

Edith pushed the mop bucket with her toe, moving it toward the back door. They always tracked in mud here; the spot was impossible to keep clean.

"Edith?"

"Need something, Stan?"

"I'm gonna be working with electricity down here."

"I know, Stan." What'd he think she was, thick as a plank?

She bent low to scrub a particularly dirty spot. Amazing, how a floor could go from clean to filthy in the space of a few hours. Things got especially bad in mud season, a phrase she'd never heard until they moved to Heavenly Daze. The state of Maine had five seasons, the old-timers insisted, mud season being accompanied by fall, winter, spring, and July.

Backing up to her bucket, she nudged it with the heel of her shoe. When it stuck to the wet floor, she nudged it harder, sending a splash of gray water over the side but effecting no movement whatsoever. In no mood for bucket defiance, she turned and kicked the darn thing. The pail tilted for an instant, then fell, splashing a stream of sudsy water over the floor . . . and down the basement stairs.

She froze as Stanley's warning came back to her: *"I'm working with electricity down here."*

Oops.

"Fire in the hole!" Stanley shouted. "Aeei-iiiiieeeeeeee!"

Sounds of frantic movement rose from the basement—Stanley's shouts, the splash of water, and the clunking sound of something heavy smacking the top of her clothes dryer.

Wading through the puddle, she approached the stairs and looked down. To the right of the staircase, Stanley crouched on the dryer, his face white and his cigar protruding from a pair of tightly clenched lips.

"Sorry, Stanley," she said weakly. "I was mopping and the bucket tipped over."

Stanley's hand trembled as he reached up to remove the cigar from his mouth. "Confound it, woman! You could've boiled me like a lobster."

"I said I was sorry!" Edith bit her lip, resisting the urge to burst into tears. Dieting was making her crazy! If she hadn't been so testy and impatient she would never have spilled that bucket.

She dared to look into the basement again. "You did cut the power, didn't you?"

"Not yet!"

"Oh. Just a minute, then." Grabbing a towel, she moved down the stairs until she found the circuit panel on the wall. She quickly flipped the breakers for the basement, then ducked to give Stanley an apologetic smile. "Okay—and no harm done, right?"

Stanley gently eased himself off the dryer, then bent to gather his tools. Ramming the cigar stub back into his mouth, he gave her a look of wide-eyed wonder. "Not even Vernie's ever tried to electrocute me. I'll be back when the floor's dry."

"Okay. Thanks, Stan. I'm so sorry."

He brushed past her as he climbed the stairs, and as he pulled his coat from the chair on the table she heard him mumble something about dumb luck and fried handymen.

As the strength ran out of her legs, Edith sank to the steps and pondered what else could possibly go wrong.

Chapter Sixteen

On day two of the Wiener Diet, Edith ate three frankfurters for breakfast and three for brunch, deliberately planning to plead that she wasn't hungry when the other women brought out their casseroles and desserts. Vernie had called last night, announcing an emergency rice-bag-making session in the church basement, and could Edith come?

Of course she could come, and she would—but she would not eat the goodies that always seemed to accompany these public service events.

Wearing a pair of stretch pants and a heavy sweater, she paused by the full-length mirror on her closet door before slipping into her coat and heading out. She hadn't lost much weight—only a few pounds—but she thought she could see a difference, especially in her face. Her jaw line seemed sharper now, her double chin a little less evident.

Surely someone would notice.

When she came down the stairs that led into the church fellowship hall, Cleta glanced up and smiled. "There she is. We were beginning to worry about you, Edith."

"Worry?" Edith laid her purse on the table, smoothing her sweater over her slimmer frame. "Why would you worry?"

"Well, you and your diet. We don't want you getting sick so close to the wedding."

Edith stifled a groan. She had wanted the women to notice that she looked good, not that she'd been on a diet. Now everyone would know, and everyone would want to talk about food.

Sinking into a chair before a mound of lilac tulle, she sent a smile around the circle, then covered her mouth and burped lightly, tasting wieners. "Birdie, how is Salt doing today?"

"He's raring to go." Color flooded the bride-to-be's cheeks. "I mean, he's feeling fine. Better than ever."

"Good." Edith picked up a square of tulle, then looked at the mountain of rice on the table. The women were dropping tablespoonfuls of rice into the square, gathering the edges, and tying the packets with white ribbon. Simple.

Dana Klackenbush leaned forward to grin at Edith. "What diet are you doing? Low fat? High carbs? Sugar Busters, Pound Pinchers, Dr. Atkins, Pritkin, the Zone, or the Blood Type?"

Edith sighed, resigning herself to the conversation. "I've done a little of this, a little of that. I'm pretty close to reaching my goal."

Babette gave Edith a rueful smile. "I'd love to take off a few pounds, but I don't think it's going to be possible for a while."

Edith lifted a brow, waiting. This was the perfect time to announce Babette's good news . . . but the younger woman only lowered her gaze and dropped another spoonful of rice into lilac netting.

"Well," Cleta said, unable to resist adding her two cents. "I know thin is in, but I think too many women are obsessed with weight. It's as if they're telling God he created a faulty product and it's up to us to correct it."

"But too much weight can be dangerous to one's health," Bea inserted.

"I don't think I've ever heard of anyone dying of thirty extra pounds," Birdie said.

Bea tossed a finished rice bag at her sister. "But there's the blood pressure factor associated with weight."

Cleta thumped the table with her scissors. "I know people skinny as fence posts with high blood pressure."

"What about cholesterol?" Dana said. "Cholesterol is a big problem these days with all the red meat and junk food we eat. Even small children are showing signs of high cholesterol."

Vernie dropped a handful of ribbon pieces into the center of the table. "Do you know what the average cholesterol level was just a few years back?"

"Two hundred?" Edith guessed.

"Two fifty," Vernie answered. "Then some expert decided two hundred was ideal. Today, doctors want it below one-sixty. Most folks can't get their cholesterol below one-sixty without cholesterol-lowering medicine, and I hear that eats up your liver. Beef and eggs have become forbidden foods in our society. And butter?" She heaved a sigh. "A sure death sentence."

"But you can't dispute facts," Babette argued. "They say type two diabetes is reaching epidemic proportions among young kids because of the French fries, bread, and junk food they eat. I don't let Georgie have sugar. He eats sugar-free desserts except for the occasional cookie he wheedles out of Birdie or Abner."

"You give that boy desserts made with *aspartame?*" Birdie shook her head. "I'm leery of artificial sweeteners. They can cause all kinds of side effects."

"But refined sugar is bad for you."

"Artificial sweeteners are killing us." Vernie let another load of ribbons fall onto the table, causing Edith to wonder just how many rice bags they were supposed to make. She sighed. "I understand white bread, potatoes, and rice are harmful to your system. They raise the glycemic level or something. The experts say you should eat only whole wheat, nonprocessed food, sweet potatoes, and brown rice."

"I can't eat like that," Birdie said flatly. "I'd be in the kitchen all day, and my bread loaves would weigh twenty pounds."

Comments erupted from all around the table:

"God made sugar, didn't he? How could he be wrong?"

"It wasn't refined when he made it."

"What about caffeine? It'll shorten your life, too."

"That's an old wives' tale!"

"I'm an old wife!"

"Well, I'm not giving up my coffee. Eventually they say everything is bad for you. I don't know who to trust anymore, so I'm going to eat what I like."

"They say diet soda will rot your bones and hasten osteoporosis."

Cleta grinned. "Then you're a goner, Vernie, with all those diet vanilla cokes you drink."

Vernie snorted. "The world needs more vanilla cokes—most folks could use a little sweetening."

Cleta laughed. "What about all the hormones in our milk and poultry? No wonder I've got all these ugly coarse black hairs sprouting on my chin. They'll be coming out of my back before long."

"I believe that's caused by *lack* of hormones, Cleta."

"Whatever. I still have to pluck every day."

Edith glanced up. "If we can't eat refined sugar, meat, or soda . . . if we can't drink the water because of the fluoride and chlorine, eat fruits and vegetables because of insecticide, or eat fish because of the mercury, what are we supposed to eat?"

The women babbled in confusion until Birdie nodded decisively. "We eat all things in moderation." She looked around the table as if daring someone to contradict her. "The good Lord made each of us different, and that includes bodies and metabolisms. We enjoy the things he has given us, the things available to us, and we don't worry about things we can't help."

She tossed a beribboned rice bag into the basket at the end of the table, then stood to drive her point home. "Animals, vegetables, fish, fruits, and grains were given to us for nourishment. It's only when we abuse our abundance that problems arise. And I speak for myself, ladies." She patted her stomach. "With all the good food I've been eating, if next Thursday doesn't hurry and get here I'm not going to be able to squeeze into my wedding dress."

Edith sighed in relief when the topic shifted to the upcoming wedding.

Dana clapped her hands. "Did your dress arrive?"

"Yesterday," Birdie said, beaming. "Floyd

brought three bags of mail over, and my dress was sitting in a big box right on top!"

"Do you like it?"

"I love it!"

Babette waved to break into the conversation. "By the way, how many of these rice bags are we making?"

"Well," Birdie stopped to count on her fingers. "Fifty ought to do it."

"Fifty?" Vernie dropped her jaw, then pointed to the mountain of tulle on the table. "Birdie, you've got enough stuff here to make three hundred."

Birdie's eyes twinkled above an impish smile. "Well . . . you never know. We might be having another celebration before long."

She winked at Vernie, who promptly threw up her hands.

"Oh, no. I married Stanley once already; that was enough."

"Come on, Vernie. If any couple ever deserved a wedding renewal ceremony, you and Stanley do."

"Nope." But Vernie smiled as she picked up another piece of netting and spread it on the table.

Babette fluttered her fingers. "Maybe we could use them for Annie and A.J."

"I wouldn't hold my breath for *that* one." Vernie brought her scissors down on another hank of ribbon with a decisive *snip*. "I asked Caleb how A.J. and Annie were doing, and he said they weren't."

Birdie squinted. "Weren't what?"

"Weren't *doing,* weren't getting along! Apparently things have cooled between those two."

"I wouldn't blame Annie for giving that particular young man the heave-ho." Cleta sat straighter in her chair. "After the funeral, I offered him a room at the B&B—for free, mind you—and he said that although the place was nice and rustic, he had to be getting back to New York." Her nostrils flared as she snatched a square of netting from the table. "Rustic! Our place is anything *but!* We have all the modern amenities but cable, which, I understand, is nothing but a pipeline for pornography these days—"

"Still," Dana interrupted, her voice dreamy, "I was hoping Annie and A.J. would get together. They were such an attractive couple."

Vernie snorted. "What's looks got to do with anything?"

"Indeed." Edith nodded her agreement. "Besides, if Annie married A.J., she'd have to move to New York. Now, tell the truth—can you see that girl living in New York?"

Dana bit her lip as Edith tightened the knot on another rice bag.

Young people. At times you had to wonder if they could discern glitter from gold.

Chapter Seventeen

At the weekly Sunday evening angel meeting in the church basement, Abner pulled out a white pastry box and opened it with a grand gesture.

"Astounding!" Sniffing the rich aromas drifting from the box, Zuriel rose out of his chair. "What is it?"

"It is a calzone," Abner explained, slipping his hands into plastic gloves. "A handheld pastry pie filled with pepperoni and cheeses. Birdie is thinking about selling these during tourist season."

"They smell heavenly." Gavriel winked at Caleb, who smiled in response. In honor of this special occasion, the angel captain had taken the seat next to Caleb, and Abner had baked a special treat—what more could a ministering angel ask of his farewell party?

"Everyone, please enjoy them." Abner began passing out the calzones. "Take one and wrap it in a napkin, no forks needed. Enjoy them while they're hot."

Mingled murmurs of appreciation filled the fellowship hall as the angels filled the bellies of their mortal bodies. As Caleb ate, he studied his fellow ministers and realized how much he would miss these fine servants of the Most High God. Gavriel had been a just and honorable captain, Zuriel had never failed to offer a wise word, and Abner had been a delicious delight. Yakov, with his firsthand knowledge of European history and God's chosen people, had taught him many things, and Elezar's patient nature had blessed not only Vernie Bidderman but Caleb as well. And while all angels had strong voices with which to praise the Creator, Micah had been given a special musical gift. His melodies could lift the souls of men and angels to the heavenlies with one refrain.

While they ate, each angel gave a brief report about the mortals in the household he guarded.

"Charles, Babette, and Georgie are doing well," Zuriel announced. "Babette has learned that she carries new life, but I doubt she has any idea how many new souls reside in her womb!"

Caleb grinned. "I have relayed the news to the doctor," he said. "I don't think he believed me, but he will keep an eye on Babette. He is curious, at least."

Micah paused to wipe his mouth with a napkin. "All is well at the bed and breakfast," he reported. "Barbara and Russell have continued to look for an apartment in Ogunquit, and Cleta is learning how to let go. By the time the Lord sends them a child, all three will have matured in wisdom and grace."

"That is good," Gavriel said. "Salt Gribbon has matured as well, and his health is much improved." He shook his head. "One would think that a man of seventy years would be wise in all things, but humans often have blind spots. Salt overexerted himself the other day, but he is learning to rest in the Lord and accept each day as a precious treasure."

"Bea and Birdie are growing, too," Abner said. "Bea is a little sad at the thought of Birdie's moving to the lighthouse, but I'm sure the sisters will remain close. Bea experienced the intimacy of human marriage early in her life; Birdie will discover it in her later years. Both sisters now understand that marital love is a precious picture of the passion the Father feels for them."

"Love is stirring in Dr. Marc's heart, too." Caleb smiled when several angels looked at him with surprise on their faces. "He loves our Annie, though he is not confident about expressing his feelings. I have not spoken to Annie to know if this feeling is reciprocated."

Gavriel shook his head. "I have not heard from the Father regarding this matter, either. But the Lord will guide you, Caleb, as you guide those to whom you minister."

Yakov wiped his hands on a napkin. "Mike and Dana have begun to think about expanding their family, but I'm most thrilled about the changes in Buddy Franklin. He is hungry for the Word and seeking the Father's will in many areas. He has been a delight to serve."

"Edith Wickam is hungry, too, but lately her thoughts have been too much on physical food." A shadow moved in Gavriel's bright eyes. "Many around her have offered wisdom, but she is also surrounded by the foolish voices of men who would bind her with foolish rules and false idols. Edith has yet to learn how to trust the Father in the area of her physical appetite."

Abner patted his round tummy. "These mortal bodies are easy to overload. Especially in winter, when we do not exercise as much."

"Still," Yakov countered, "the human body is easy to operate. It growls when it needs food. It stops growling when it does not. What could be simpler?"

"Humans have a gift," Gavriel said, standing, "for making the simple complicated. But the Father is faithful, and he will give them light when they are ready to receive it."

Their meal completed, the other angels stood as well, their chairs scraping the painted concrete floor as they lifted their hands and hearts toward heaven.

Micah began the song. One by one, the other angels joined in:

> I will sing of the tender mercies of the Lord forever!
> Young and old will hear of your faithfulness.
> Your unfailing love will last forever.
> Your faithfulness is as enduring as the heavens.

All heaven will praise your miracles, Lord;

Myriads of angels will praise you for your
faithfulness.

For who in all of heaven can compare with
the Lord?

What mightiest angel is anything like the
Lord?

The highest angelic powers stand in awe
of God.

He is far more awesome than those who
surround his throne.

O Lord God Almighty!

Where is there anyone as mighty as you,
Lord?

Faithfulness is your very character.

You are the one who rules the oceans.

When their waves rise in fearful storms,
you subdue them.

You are the one who crushed the great
sea monster.

You scattered your enemies with your
mighty arm.

The heavens are yours, and the earth is
yours;

Everything in the world is yours—you created it all.

Your throne is founded on two strong pillars—righteousness and justice.

Unfailing love and truth walk before you as
  attendants.
Happy are those who hear the joyful call to
  worship,
For they will walk in the light of your presence.

Caleb felt a lump rise in his throat as he
whispered the final words. His angelic brothers were wondrous beings, but they were
still only pale shadows of the One who
loved, sustained, and held the universe together by the sheer force of his will.

Faithfulness was his character. Faithfulness was his name.

Chapter Eighteen

Wiping a tear from her cheek, Annie switched off the *E.R.* rerun before the local news could come on and destroy the mood. Doctors Carter and Corday had been unable to save an elderly woman with heart trouble, and the sad scene where Dr. Carter had to face the woman's weeping daughter had cut a little too close to Annie's reality.

She pulled a tissue from the box on the nightstand, then blew her nose so forcefully her ears popped. She'd wept like a baby through the last ten minutes of the TV drama, and now her head felt swollen.

Three weeks had passed since Olympia had sailed away, and not a single lobster-man, pleasure boat, or Coast Guard cutter had been able to capture the casket. The last report, called in by a Canadian cruise ship, had the casket moving toward Greenland.

Annie felt more helpless than Dr. Carter.

"Stupid show," she muttered, wadding the tissue into a ball. She tossed it in the general direction of the trashcan, then hesitated when she saw the lilac envelope on the bedside table.

The invitation to Salt's and Birdie's wedding had arrived in the afternoon mail, and Annie had been surprised to read that the great event had been pushed forward. They were planning to tie the knot at four o'clock on Thursday afternoon, a mere three days away.

Annie regarded the invitation with mixed feelings. She was genuinely happy for the couple, but it was hard to rejoice for friends when your own heart was heavy with loss and discouragement. It would be hard to face the islanders as a failure in Olympia's cause . . . and even harder to tell them that she and A.J. were kaput.

Lately Annie had begun to wonder if she would ever find love at all.

Maybe she could come up with some project to work on later in the week. Then she could call Caleb and beg out of the wedding. Salt and Birdie would have eyes for only each other; they certainly wouldn't miss her. The only locals who'd even notice her absence would be Tallulah, Caleb, and— she drew in a sharp breath. Would Dr. Marc care if she didn't come?

A silly question, really. The man had a lot on his plate; he certainly didn't have time to entertain fond feelings for his son's ex-girl-friend.

Sighing, she leaned over and turned out the lamp. Darkness engulfed her bedroom, held at bay only by the thin sliver of light edging the bottom of her window shade.

After beating her lumpy pillow into sub-mission, Annie curled up beneath her com-forter and tucked her hands beneath her chin. She had felt listless and irritable all day, feelings that had bloomed into outright de-pression when she had picked up the mail and discovered an official letter from the Durpee Seed Company behind the wedding invitation. Jack Wilson, president of hybrid development, had written to announce offi-cially that she would not receive any com-pensation for her tomato hybrid. The Durpee Seed Company, however, appreciated her fine efforts and wished her the best in her future endeavors. . . .

"Yada, yada, yada," she murmured into her pillow. "Sure, you wish me the best. Everyone wishes me well, including A.J."

The man hadn't called all this week, not once. If she called him, he'd undoubtedly be pleasant and polite, but she knew her refusal to drop everything and move to New York had frosted his feelings. Any other girl would have been highly flattered by his invitation, but Olympia had always said Annie wasn't like other girls.

A drowsy smile curved her mouth as she drifted toward sleep. Olympia used to stand at the threshold of Annie's bedroom and shake her head. *Honestly, girl, what's wrong with you? You're too much like your mother, going around with your head in the clouds, without a lick of horse sense. . . .*

Weeks of frustration and indecision were bearing Annie down with an irresistible warm weight. Her mind went fuzzy, surrendering to the relentless pull of sleep, and her thoughts drifted amid memories of the day until a sharp voice called her brain back to attention: "Wake up, Annie. We need to talk."

Her eyes flew open. She was still curled in bed, the streetlights still fringed the edges of the window shade, but something in the room had changed. Another light had brought a pale luminescence to the room, for something glowed at the foot of her bed.

A thrill of fear shot through Annie as she lifted her head and saw Olympia sitting on the edge of the mattress, her lips set in a firm line, her hands folded primly upon her lap.

Annie squinched her eyelids tight. "Go away! I don't believe in ghosts!"

"Neither do I, so sit up and speak to me properly. I'm not a ghost, I'm your aunt."

"But you're . . . gone."

"I'm spirit now, and I'm in heaven. But I see what's going on with you, and you're about to drive me crazy with all your teeter-tottering back and forth. For heaven's sake, Annie, I didn't leave you the house so you'd be miserable." The visitor's voice softened. "I meant it to be a gift, not a burden."

Annie opened one eye. Olympia no longer sat at the foot of the bed; she had moved to the empty chair by the nightstand.

Right in Annie's line of vision.

"I don't believe in ghosts," she repeated. "Go away."

The phantom exhaled loudly. "For the last time, Annie, I'm not a ghost. This is a vision the Lord's allowing you to experience. Didn't you pray for guidance?"

Annie rose to one elbow. "Well . . . yeah, I guess I did. But I didn't ask for this. And I don't feel like I'm sleeping."

"Dreamers rarely know they're dreaming until they wake. But I didn't come here to talk about your sleep patterns. I came to talk some sense into your head."

Despite the bizarre quality of this dream, Annie couldn't resist rolling her eyes. Whether this was a byproduct of sleep or hysteria, her subconscious had done a dandy job of replicating Aunt Olympia. The stiff image in her chair was somber and serious, but definitely not malevolent.

"Okay." Annie propped her head on her hand. "Talk away. I guess I'm a captive audience."

Olympia's right brow arched. "If I'd known talking to you in your sleep would make you listen, I'd have done it years ago—"

Annie cut her off with a yawn. "Aunt Olympia, I'm too tired for this, I need my sleep. Can you please get to the point?"

Her glowing visitor drew back as if affronted. "Have it your way. I'm here to tell you that you're making yourself miserable. The Lord doesn't want you to be miserable; he wants you to rejoice in his perfect will. So find it, follow it, and you'll be fine."

Annie guffawed. "That's easier said than done. How in the world am I supposed to find God's will? He doesn't exactly carve life directions on stone tablets these days, in case you hadn't noticed."

Olympia made a huffing noise. "Of all people, you should find it easy. You've got Caleb—"

"Caleb's talking nonsense these days. He wants to leave Frenchman's Fairest and find another employer."

"—and you've got a town full of people who love the Lord and love you. They wouldn't steer you wrong."

"I've been talking to people." Annie sat up straighter. "I've talked to Dr. Marc and A.J. Neither of them will tell me what to do."

"You're not a child, Annie." A faint light of reproof glowed in the visitor's eyes. "You're old enough to make your own decisions. All you lack is the courage."

Drawing a deep breath, Annie rose to a full sitting position, then bent her knees beneath the covers. Wrapping her arms around her legs, she lowered her head and sighed. "It's not that easy," she mumbled into her comforter. "This decision is such a big one; it will affect everything for the rest of my life."

"A crossroad," Olympia said. "We all come to them. And the Lord promises to guide us if we listen."

"I've been listening!" Annie's brittle laugh sounded more like a cry of pain. "I'm so confused, Aunt Olympia. I thought I loved A.J., but lately I don't think I do. I was all excited when I first met him—he was handsome, successful, and wealthy enough to do exciting things—but now, I don't know. He's awfully focused on his career, he's terribly busy, and I find myself wondering if he cares enough . . . for me, that is."

"Honey, listen to me."

Annie turned her head to better see the figment of her overactive imagination.

"Sweetheart, love isn't a feeling—feelings are the byproducts of love. Love is a choice. It's a decision you make when you find someone you want to make precious to you."

Annie blinked slowly, wondering if she was losing the dream signal or something. The figment was beginning to speak in riddles.

Soon Olympia would start to fade away, or maybe she'd morph into Birdie or Bea or the wicked witch from *The Wizard of Oz.*

"A decision?" she echoed.

"Of course." The preternatural Olympia leaned forward, her hands folded. "When you came to live with us, I didn't love you all at once. But Edmund and I decided that you'd become precious to us, and you did. Love followed naturally." A glow rose in the woman's face, like a lantern burning behind an oilskin shade. "I still love you, Annie, and so does Edmund. Most of all, our Lord loves you. He cares for you more than you realize, and he is waiting for you to take a step. He'll guide you . . . once you start walking."

Annie lifted her head. Why not promise this fabrication of her overtired brain that she'd make a decision? What would it hurt if she made a dream decision right now?

"All right," she said, nodding. "I'll start walking. Tomorrow I'll go into the office at school and tell them I won't be back next term. Then I'll call Caleb and tell him I'm coming home to stay. And then I'll go to the island and be unemployed and lonely and broke."

"Oh, honey." Olympia giggled so irrepressibly that Annie couldn't help chuckling herself. "You won't be lonely. Someone on the island loves you dearly, for months ago he decided you were precious to him. He has treated you with the respect and care he would show a priceless treasure, but you've been too blind to see."

Annie stared at her guest. "I love him dearly, but Caleb is not my idea of a soul mate, Aunt Olympia."

"Not Caleb." Olympia stood, the glow of her smile brightening the corner of the room. "But someone close."

Then Olympia bent and embraced Annie with a touch as light as air. Annie closed her eyes and inhaled the aroma surrounding her aunt. The scent was unlike anything she had ever breathed—pure and sweet, light and vaguely floral.

"Olympia," she whispered, keeping her eyes closed. "You smell like heaven."

Something like a feathery kiss brushed her cheek, then Annie opened her eyes and saw . . . nothing.

But in the morning, when she threw back the covers and breathed in the courage to face another day, she caught the sweet scent of eternity on her pajamas.

Chapter Nineteen

Standing before the mirror in her bathroom, Edith inhaled and tugged on the zipper in the side of the peach dress. Holding her breath, she pulled, biting her lip as the metal zipper slid smoothly over the plastic teeth . . . and the zipper went up!

Suppressing a whoop of joy, Edith exhaled slowly, bracing herself for the sound of ripping fabric. The dress had been hanging in her closet for a while, and it wouldn't surprise her if some of the seams had weakened . . . but the fabric held.

Stepping back, she lifted her eyes to the mirror.

Instantly, she remembered why she had bought this dress—the peach color complimented her golden skin tones, and the silver edging on the lace brought out the blue in her eyes. The bodice was a little snug, but that was okay, and the fitted waistline seemed smooth.

But the hips. She frowned at the sight of ripples in what should have been a smooth drop to the floor. She carried a tire around her abdomen that would rival the Michelin man's, and there was no hiding it in the fitted skirt.

But she still had two days until the wedding. She'd just have to try something else . . .

Liquid meals. If it had worked for Oprah, it would work for her. Trouble was, Vernie didn't carry liquid meal replacements at the Mercantile, so Edith would have to slip over to Ogunquit.

Thank the Lord Floyd was operating the ferry.

Moving carefully, Edith unzipped the dress and returned it to the hanger. Placing it in the back of the closet, she stepped into her familiar stretch pants and a sweatshirt. The ladies were meeting this morning at the Bed and Breakfast, where Micah had miraculously coaxed all his orchids into bloom.

"They're really beautiful," Cleta had said when she called last night. "Best of all, half of them are purple or lilac! They'll be perfect for Birdie's bouquet and the pew ribbons; we just need a little help arranging everything."

When Edith crossed the threshold of the bed and breakfast, work had already begun in the kitchen. Micah had set all the orchid pots on the table, and Cleta was passing out little tubes with rubber stoppers to water the flowers once they were placed in arrangements.

Edith gasped at the bounty of orchids—luscious purple cattleya blossoms, lovely phalaenopsis blooms, and a delicate cascade of lilac flowers she had never seen before.

"What is this one?" She slipped her hand beneath a spray of blossoms that reminded her of a bridal veil.

Micah smiled. "It's called *aerangis citrate*. It will be beautiful trailing out of Birdie's bouquet, don't you think?"

Edith smiled her agreement as she moved through the room. Dana and Babette were making ribbon roses for the pew markers, while Vernie kept tramping in and out with ferns from her family room. In tourist season, her famous ferns hung from the porch of the Mercantile; in winter, they crowded the windows of her back room, drinking in the shaded sunlight.

The most precious sight was Birdie, who sat in a chair with a rectangle of florist's foam. She and little Brittany were creating the bouquet she would carry down the aisle.

While Birdie twittered with excitement, her sister sat silently at the table, one hand idly stroking an empty ribbon spool. Edith had never seen Birdie looking happier, or Bea more depressed.

Edith lifted her hands. "How can I help?"

Cleta welcomed her with a smile. "Play hostess, will you, Edith? My hands are full, and some of these ladies could use a cup of coffee to perk them up." Cleta accented her words with a sly wink and a nod toward Bea, and Edith understood instantly.

After pouring a cup of coffee for the postmistress, Edith sat next to Bea and pushed the steaming mug toward her. "Enjoy the coffee, Bea. How be you this morning?"

Bea shrugged. "Fine."

Edith knew she *wasn't* fine; she was barely pretending. Her face hung in weary folds, and the creases under her eyes were deep enough to hold water.

"You know, Bea," Edith began, "you're not losing a sister—you're gaining a brother-in-law and two wonderful children."

"I know." Bea pulled a handkerchief from her pocket and pressed it to the corners of her watery eyes.

"Why, you never know what life has in store for you—one of these days some fine-looking gentleman might come along and you'll consider matrimony again."

Bea snorted softly. "When pigs fly."

Edith lightly touched Bea's hand. "You can come visit me anytime you like—and Birdie will be only moments away."

"She'll be too busy to go neighborin' with me. She'll have her new family to think about."

"But you'll see her every day in the bakery."

"It won't be the same."

Edith knew Bea was probably imagining a long stretch of lonely nights in the living quarters behind the bakery. The two sisters used to spend hours knitting peacefully before the fire, laughing and discussing the day's events.

Loneliness could be a painful thing.

Wiping her eyes again, Bea got up. "I

ought to be helping Vernie with those ferns. After Micah ties a ribbon in them, we still have to carry them to the church."

"We'll both help," Edith said. "And you know what? Winslow and I would love to have you come for dinner Friday night. It's been way too long since you shared a meal with us."

Bea nodded absently, and Edith knew she'd have to remind the postmistress of the invitation. But that was okay.

By Friday the wedding would be over and life would be back to normal.

And she'd be able to cook an ordinary meal and eat sensibly.

* * *

After every available orchid had been set into a bouquet, an arrangement, or a pew marker, Edith went home and slipped into her bedroom. Before leaving the B&B she had asked Floyd if he'd be willing to take the ferry out at two, and to her delight he'd agreed to make a run to the mainland.

Moving quietly so she wouldn't disturb Winslow in his study, she pulled on an old coat she hadn't worn in years, then tied a scarf over her head and donned a pair of dark sunglasses.

Dieting had turned her into a crazed criminal. But Winslow would put his foot down if he knew about her plan, and Edith couldn't let anything stop her when she was this close to success.

"How be you this afternoon, Edith?" Floyd called as she came aboard the ferry. Floyd was obviously having a ball driving the boat.

"Afternoon, Floyd." Edith stepped into the warmth of the cabin, then settled on a bench. Floyd began checking things off a printed list at the helm, and Edith crossed her arms as he checked everything from mooring lines to the oil in the engine. When he was convinced the boat was ready—the instant that coincided with the moment Edith nearly screamed in impatience—the motor roared to life and the boat pulled away from the dock.

Wind rattled the windows of the cabin as the stately boat plowed through the waters. Finally Perkins Cove loomed into view, and Edith stood up, ready to make a quick dash to the pay phone to call a cab.

The docking was rough—apparently

Floyd hadn't quite mastered the trick of cutting the engine *before* coasting up to the dock—but Edith exited the boat on shaky legs and wobbled toward the phone.

"You gonna wanna go back soon?" Floyd called, the brisk air carrying his voice.

She turned and pointed toward the phone. "I'm going to run to the grocery. Will you wait thirty minutes?"

The mayor snapped a salute to the brim of his new captain's hat. "Will do. But—" his cocky grin softened, "I kind of like to take a nap around three, if you wouldn't mind hurrying a bit."

"I'll be right back."

Edith trudged toward the phone, wondering how much a case of diet shakes weighed. Maybe she should ask Floyd to come along and help—but Floyd might tell Cleta about her shakes, and once Cleta knew a secret, the whole island knew. She'd just have to carry the case herself. After all, lifting and toting was bound to burn off a few calories.

The image of the peach dress sliding loose and easy over her hips drove her on.

Once she reached the store, she tossed an assortment of delicious-sounding diet shakes into her cart: Dutch Chocolate, Mocha, Passion Fruit, French Vanilla. This diet would be heaven compared to the cabbage soup and wieners.

She paid for her purchases, loaded all the cans into a box, then hauled the carton into the waiting taxi. The driver rolled his eyes at her approach, but didn't lift a finger to help either at the store or at the ferry landing.

She tossed him the exact fare without a tip, then wrapped her arms around the box and waddled to the boat. Floyd eyed the case when she came aboard and offered to set it in the cargo hold.

"No, thank you." She sat on the bench and kept the box on her lap.

Shrugging, Floyd turned to the helm. Twenty minutes later (another checklist), the ferry began to churn back across the water.

At the Heavenly Daze dock, Floyd offered to carry her package to the parsonage, but Edith politely refused his help. Setting the heavy box on her left hip, she made it as far as the B&B. Shifting it to the other hip, she managed to pass the church and the parsonage.

She had a special hiding place in mind for these beauties—the public restrooms. Floyd kept a key on the doorframe above the women's restroom, and nobody ever ventured up here in the off-season. The rooms were vented, too, which kept a stream of fresh, cold air moving through the place— ideal for chilling diet milkshakes.

She had no sooner set the box down to reach for the key when Tallulah and Butch appeared, sniffing at her box.

"Go away, doggies," she said, protecting her treasures with her foot.

Tallulah growled at the container, and the bulldog began to bark.

"Hey!" Edith stomped her foot, sending the dogs back a half-step. "Go home, you two!"

She pulled the heavy door open, then bent to pick up the box. Some muscle in her back—she wasn't sure which—complained about having to pick up a heavy load, but Edith ignored the twinge and lifted the shakes to her hip.

The concrete bathroom was as cold as an arctic tomb. Butch preceded her into the building, poking his nose into corners and sniffing. Edith ignored him and set the box on the floor, then selected six cans and stuffed them in her large purse. That should last her a couple of days—and Thursday she would eat lightly before the wedding.

After the wedding she would devour everything on the buffet table and eat two pieces of wedding cake as a reward for getting into her peach dress. The next week she'd be sensible and take in a Pound Pinchers meeting.

Stepping out of the bathrooms, she locked the door, then turned toward the parsonage. As far as she knew, no one from Heavenly Daze had seen her but Floyd and the dogs. Her secret was safe.

She hadn't gone ten steps when she spied Tallulah . . . alone. Her hand flew to her throat. She had locked Butch in the bathroom!

Hurrying back to the restroom, she fished the key from the doorframe, then freed the grateful bulldog. Edith slumped in relief as she locked the door again. If Butch had remained locked in, after an hour or two he would have started howling. The entire town might have come running, and Floyd has been known to bring out the fire truck for less crucial situations. What a fiasco that would have been!

The house was empty when she got home. Kicking off her flats, she dropped into the wing chair and ripped the tab off a can of Chocolate Mocha. She took a sip, then ran her tongue over her lips. Not bad.

Not bad at all.

Slowly lowering the can, she rested her head on the back of the chair and closed her eyes. Two more days. She wouldn't eat anything on the morning of the twenty-eighth—and maybe she could bundle up and go out for a run. She might lose a pound of water weight. An inch from the tire riding her hips.

Sighing, she leaned back and savored another sip. Winslow had his last counseling session with Birdie and Salt tonight. When he got home she'd feed him a can of Beefaroni. If he asked why she wasn't eating she'd tell him she'd already had dinner—which would be the truth. A delicious, highly nutritious—

She turned the can around to read the ingredients: fat-free milk, water, sugar, gum Arabic, calcium casenate, cellulose gel, canola oil . . .

Canola Oil?

. . . potassium phosphate, soy bean lecithin, cellulose gum, mono and diglycerides, maltodexitrin, artificial flavor, carrageenan, and dextrose.

She frowned. What in the world *was* all that stuff? She took another swallow. Whatever it was, it wasn't bad.

Confident that she was finally getting somewhere, she downed the first can.

* * *

Marc was reading a medical journal when the ringing of the phone snapped his concentration. Hurrying to answer it, he stubbed his toe and nearly broke his neck. "Hello?"

"Dr. Marc, it's Annie."

Suddenly his toe hurt much less. "Annie? Where are you?"

"In my car, driving to Ogunquit. I'm coming home."

A moment of silence stretched between them, then, like a fool he blurted out the first thought to cross his mind: "You're coming for the wedding, I suppose."

"Not entirely." She laughed, the sound musical in his ears. "I'm coming because I need to give the house a good going over, you know, to see what needs to be done. And I want to be there for Caleb, to try to talk him out of leaving. I'm calling because I wondered if you'd ask him to have a room ready for me tonight."

"Sure." Biting back disappointment, Marc settled into his chair. So . . . she'd decided to sell the house. Which meant his world would soon be turned upside down in more than one way.

Oblivious to his pain, she kept rattling on. "If Caleb insists on leaving, I was thinking a little town get-together might be nice—you know, a reception in his honor. As long as it doesn't interfere with Salt's and Birdie's wedding."

Marc looked at the ceiling. "I don't think Caleb would want you to make a lot of fuss. Why don't you discuss it with him when you arrive? I've a feeling he might enjoy a quiet dinner, just the two of you."

"Would you come, too? After all," she laughed softly, "you're part of our house-hold."

She saw him as part of her household . . . perhaps a genial father figure. Certainly no more.

"I'll come," he promised, knowing it might be the last dinner they ever shared together. "Now you drive safely and come on home. We'll be waiting for you."

* * *

Her heart singing, Annie clicked off her cell phone and dropped it into the passenger's seat. For the first time in her life, she knew what she wanted and felt right about pursuing it.

After her strange experience last night she had dreamed again, but the second dream had a more surreal quality. She saw herself sitting on the sofa with A.J. and Dr. Marc in the parlor of Frenchman's Fairest. Because she was weeping for Olympia and Edmund, someone had drawn her into strong arms and comforted her. She had opened her eyes, expecting to see A.J., but he was standing against the wall, his hands shoved into his pockets, his wide eyes focused on the window and the world beyond Heavenly Daze.

And in that moment she knew.

Alexander James Hayes was a fine man, a wonderful surgeon, and a dutiful son, but he would not make her a good husband. On the other hand, the man who had instilled those fine qualities in A.J. was the one who understood her. Marc Hayes had comforted her and wiped her tears, he had given her wise advice and treated her—how had Olympia put it?—as a priceless treasure.

Love had been blooming along with the tomato plants all last autumn, but she'd been too preoccupied to see the tender bud.

* * *

"Hello? Anybody home?"

Annie's voice rang through the foyer and echoed up the stairs. She dropped her purse and gloves on the table by the door, then ventured farther into the house. Nothing had changed physically in Frenchman's Fairest, but the place seemed empty without Olympia's formidable presence.

"Caleb?" She walked toward the kitchen and pushed on the swinging door, but the butler was nowhere in sight. For an instant she worried, then remembered the upcoming wedding. Caleb was probably at the church, offering his services to Birdie and Edith.

She had just begun to unbutton her coat when she heard a rap at the back door. Dr. Marc was peering through the glass.

She felt herself flush as she hurried to let him in. "Dr. Marc!"

"Welcome home, Annie." He stomped his boots on the mat, then stepped in and rubbed his hands together. "Have any trouble getting here?"

"No. Floyd brought me over on the ferry. I'm afraid Captain Stroble is going to have to fight our mayor for control of the boat when he gets back."

Marc laughed, and for the first time she noticed the way his eyes crinkled at the corners. He had the kindest eyes she had ever seen in a man's face.

She motioned toward the refrigerator. "Can I get you anything?"

"No, I'm fine. But if you're hungry, feel free—"

"I'm not hungry."

For a moment neither of them spoke, then the doctor gestured toward the table. "Shall we sit? I believe we have some things to discuss."

"Ayuh, we do." Gratefully, she sank into the nearest chair. She had so much to tell him, but how did you tell a good friend that your feelings had ripened into something that could lead to love? What if he didn't welcome the news?

"I'm glad you've come home, Annie."

Her heart leapt. "Are you?"

"Of course. Caleb gets lonely rattling around in this big house. I can see why he's ready to move on."

She smiled, though her heart felt the sting of disappointment. "Is he still talking about leaving?"

"Ayuh."

"I wish he wouldn't." She bit her lip. "I'd like him to stay."

A flicker of a smile rose at the edges of Marc's mouth, then died out. "I suppose I'll be leaving, too. I was going to talk to Floyd about building a clinic at the north end of the island, but perhaps he and Cleta can put me up until we're able to afford that."

She caught her breath. "Why would *you* leave?"

"Well . . . because you're selling the house."

"Selling?" She stared at him in dismay. "Why would I sell?"

His brows drew together. "You *said* you were going to sell it. You're here to get the house ready for the realtor, aren't you?"

"I never said that."

"You did."

"I said I was coming home to look the

house over—because I plan to live here. I don't know how I'm going to afford it, but sometimes you just have to step out in faith and do what you know is right. But Marc . . . I don't want to live here alone."

"You don't?"

"No."

He peered at her intently. "What did you have in mind?"

As a tingling numbed the pit of her stomach, she carefully met his gaze. "First of all, you'll stay put. Then, maybe a courtship. Six months, maybe eight. However long you think is proper . . . just to see where things might lead."

He drew in a quick breath, but a flame smoldered in his eyes. "A courtship, you say."

She nodded.

He looked away, but an easy smile began to play at the corners of his lips. "I suppose you're thinking I should court Beatrice, now that Birdie will be married to Salt."

She narrowed her gaze. "Not exactly. Miss Bea is a nice lady, but she's not exactly your type."

He tilted his head and looked at her. "And who, pray tell, *is* my type?"

"Someone," she pushed her hair back, "who will decide to treat you as a precious treasure." She placed one hand on his shoulder, then bent her head and looked up into his eyes. "Someone who is willing to be precious to you."

"And who," his voice sounded strangled, "might that be?"

"I'm a good candidate."

He straightened in his chair, his brows rising like flags, but in that instant the back door opened and a breath of winter wind blustered into the kitchen.

Caleb appeared in the kitchen doorway. "Well," he said, his smile broadening as his brows lifted. "Look what the wind blew in!"

* * *

Caleb felt his spirit warm as he beheld Annie and Marc together. God was good.

"Annie," he cut off her flustered explanation with an uplifted hand, "I've been given another assignment. I'll be leaving Thursday, probably right before the wedding."

Her face fell. "Is there nothing I can do to convince you to stay? Caleb, you've been by my side for so many years—let me do something for you. I've decided to keep the house, so you don't have to go."

He dropped his hand to the top of her head. "Do not hold me, child, or keep me from obeying the Lord's will. Thank you for the generous offer, but my orders come from on high. I must be off."

Her chin wobbled then, as it always had just before she burst into tears, and Caleb closed his eyes to the sight of them. Placing both hands firmly upon her head, he lifted his face to the heavens.

"Bless this young woman, Lord, and hold her in the palm of your hand. Direct her in the path you have prepared for her, and fill her days with light and love. Give her joy enough to lighten her heart, and pain enough to make her sensitive to the needs of others. I love her, Lord, and it has been my privilege to serve her."

At the sound of Annie's quiet weeping, for the first time in his ministry Caleb wished he had permission to fade into the wallpaper and avoid the pain of human sorrow.

Chapter Twenty

On Wednesday, Edith phoned Floyd as soon as the grandfather clock struck eight. Would he mind taking the ferry to Ogunquit this morning? She had an emergency she had to take care of in town.

She could almost see Floyd's skeptical expression, but he promised to meet her on the dock in twenty minutes. Grateful, Edith hung up the phone, then slipped on her dark coat, scarf and sunglasses. Winslow was singing in the shower, so he wouldn't hear her slip away. Soon he'd dress and go to his study to work on his sermon; with a little luck it'd be lunchtime before he noticed she'd gone out.

She left the house and hurried to the public restrooms. Only two shakes remained in the cardboard box—two out of twenty-four.

My heaven. Had she really drunk *twenty* shakes since yesterday?

She popped the top of a strawberry can and drained the contents like a lobsterman guzzling beer. As she exhaled a contented sigh, she looked at the can and lifted a brow.

Funny, how they'd gone from being "not bad" to "delicious" in the space of a few hours.

Fortified by another dose of fake food, she tied the scarf under her chin and set out for the ferry.

An hour later she stood in the Ogunquit grocery, watching the clerk ring up another two dozen drinks. The young woman behind the cash register eyed the cans as she ran them through the scanner. "Are these any good?"

Edith couldn't lie. "They're delicious, but I get a little hungry on them."

The woman laughed. "I don't see how you could. Didn't you buy a case yesterday?"

Her cheeks burning, Edith searched for her checkbook. "I'm concerned the weather will turn bad and I might not get back over for awhile." She paid for her purchase and picked up the box.

This time she didn't possess the energy for

pride. When Floyd offered to take the box from her at the dock, she handed it over without a word. He scowled as he shifted it to his hip. "What have you got in here? Lead?"

Edith didn't answer; she trudged into the cabin, then sank to the seat and stared straight ahead. She ought to be feeling great—according to her calculations, yesterday she'd ingested five thousand calories. She ought to have energy to spare, so why did she feel so listless and unsatisfied?

Maybe the wedding was to blame, or the emotional rollercoaster she'd been riding this month with Olympia's funeral and Birdie's wedding coming so close together. Maybe the problem was Win's lack of sympathy . . . and the fact that he had lost weight on her diet without even trying.

Life wasn't fair, and it certainly didn't make sense.

* * *

After safely docking at Heavenly Daze (he was getting the hang of it and had timed this landing perfectly), Floyd Lansdown watched Edith trudge up the hill with her heavy box. Rubbing his whiskered chin, he glanced down at Butch, who had boarded the boat when they landed.

"I don't know, old boy, but I think that woman's in trouble."

Butch whined, his tail wagging, until Floyd fished a doggie treat out of a canister Stroble kept at the helm. He tossed the cookie to Butch, then leaned on the wheel and stared at Edith's retreating figure. "I ain't one for buttin' in anybody's business, you understand, but I am a mite concerned for the preacher's wife."

Butch crunched the biscuit, showering crumbs on the fiberglass floor.

Floyd squinted as the pastor's wife moved past the parsonage and kept walking. Where in tarnation was she taking that load? To the *bathrooms?* He pulled back, his dignity affronted, and Edith disappeared through a brick doorway. Why, those were public restrooms, not community lockers. Nobody used 'em in winter, so she wasn't doing any harm, but if everybody decided to hide their goodies in the bathroom, they'd have a real mess come tourist season.

Floyd pulled his pipe from his pocket, then thrust it between his teeth. He usually minded his own business; didn't like to stir the waters, but he could spot trouble a mile away—in this instance, fifty yards off.

Something had to be done. Edith hadn't looked herself this morning, and it was a sure bet Pastor Winslow didn't know about her gallivantin' around in a Jackie O disguise.

As mayor of Heavenly Daze, he had an obligation to look after his constituents.

Ayuh.

He did.

* * *

Strains of the "Wedding March" drifted from the church as Floyd climbed the hill just before dusk. He'd meant to visit the pastor as soon as possible, but then Babette and Dana had wanted to run over to Ogunquit to shop. After he had taken them over, Stanley had called and asked if he could ride with Floyd just to get out of the house—Vernie was getting anxious about her wedding solo, and Stanley was afraid of getting his head bit off.

So Stanley had come over and they'd taken the ferry to pick up Babette and Dana, but he was no further than half-way across when Cleta had called him back to pick her up because she had to get her dress from the dry cleaners . . . and so it went. Before he knew it, the day had faded away, and he'd lost count of how many times he'd piloted the ferry to Ogunquit and back.

No wonder Stroble insisted upon only three ferry runs per day in the off-season.

Shadows were settling beneath the trees as he trudged toward the church, but lights glowed in the old building's stained-glass windows.

He opened the door and walked through the vestibule, where painted portraits of Captain Jacques de Cuvier and Winslow Wickam peered down at him. In the sanctuary beyond, Salt and Birdie, Bobbie and Brittany, Cleta and Stanley stood at the front. Vernie sat on the front pew, across from Bea at the ivories.

Floyd lingered in the doorway, figuring Cleta would have his head if he interrupted the rehearsal. Bea caught sight of him, though, and slipped away from the piano.

"Floyd?" she asked, approaching. "What are you doing here this late in the day?"

Floyd shrugged and clasped his hands. "I'm here to talk to the pastor."

Bea's eyes narrowed. "If it's about the ferry, it can wait. He's busy."

Floyd bristled. "It's not about the ferry. And I'm perfectly willing to wait."

Her hand rose to her hip. "Then what *is* it about? We're in the middle of a rehearsal."

He crossed his arms. "None of your business, Beatrice. You just go about your piano playing and leave me in peace. This thing can't take much longer, so I'll sit here and wait."

"Hmmpf." Bea whirled away and went back to her piano bench, but not before pecking the pastor on the shoulder and jerking her thumb toward Floyd. Winslow nodded, murmured a few more things to Salt and Birdie, then held up his hands and announced that he'd see them all tomorrow at four o'clock.

Leaving the wedding party to gab about last-minute details, the pastor excused himself and proceeded down the aisle. He greeted Floyd with a smile. "Something up, Floyd?"

The mayor twisted the brim of his captain's hat. "Maybe—but we ought to talk in private."

Floyd glanced around. The church had no office, only the sanctuary and the fellowship hall.

"Shall we go to the parsonage?" Winslow asked.

Floyd hesitated. "Maybe the fellowship hall would be better."

Winslow gave him a curious look, but said nothing as he led Floyd toward the stairs.

A few minutes later they sat at a long folding table. Winslow's eyes shone with frank curiosity. "Tell me what's on your mind, friend."

Floyd scratched the edge of his thumbnail. "I know something I think you ought to know—but I don't want you thinking that I'm sticking my nose in where it don't belong."

The pastor leaned back in his chair. "I won't think that. And I'm here to offer assistance if one of our people needs it. So—" he leaned closer—"who needs help?"

"Edith."

Winslow's smile faded. *"My* Edith?"

"Ayuh. I think she's in trouble."

Winslow paled, coming halfway out of his seat. "What do you mean, trouble? Is she sick?" He glanced toward the door as if he might have to make a hasty exit.

"I think she will be if she keeps this up."

As Winslow stared in disbelief, Floyd told the story of Edith's grocery trips and her surreptitious deposits in the public restrooms. "I know that box was full of meal replacement drinks because I recognized one of the cans. Barbara drinks those things ever now and then. They don't seem to do her a lick of good."

Winslow sank back into his chair. "Edith wouldn't do anything so foolhardy—she promised me she would lose weight sensibly."

"Aw, Pastor, you know women and their weight. None of 'em are sensible when it comes to dieting. But I thought you ought to know your wife was looking a mite streak-ed this morning." Slapping his hands on his thighs, Floyd stood up. "Well, I've got to be getting home. Cleta's making goulash tonight."

Obviously preoccupied with the bombshell he had just dropped, Winslow nodded. "Thank you. I appreciate it."

Floyd paused before heading out the side door. "Don't mean to cause trouble between you and your missus—just thought you ought to know. There's been enough excitement around here lately."

"Indeed," Winslow murmured. "Far too much."

* * *

Winslow had intended to go straight home and talk to Edith, but Bea caught him in the sanctuary. After he had spent twenty minutes artfully dodging questions about what Floyd had wanted (Heavens! He couldn't have this story known around town!), the postmistress changed gears and began to talk about how much she'd miss Birdie after the wedding.

In those words Winslow recognized the ring of truth, so for thirty minutes he sat quietly on the front pew while Bea poured out her heart. "I know I shouldn't feel this way, Pastor," she finished, "but I can't help it."

That's when Abner Smith appeared. Standing quietly at the back of the sanctuary, he walked forward when Bea began to wind down, then slipped onto the pew and took her hand.

"Miss Bea, it's getting late. Birdie sent me to walk you home."

Bea turned wide eyes upon him. "Birdie was worried about me?"

"Of course." Abner smiled when he met Winslow's gaze. "Birdie will always worry about you. You're her sister, and no one can take your place—no more than anyone can take your place in the family of God."

Bea's face softened in the church's golden lights. "That's a lovely thought, Abner."

The baker smiled, then lifted Bea to her feet. "Come on home where it's warm. The temperature's falling outside, and Birdie doesn't want you coming down with a cold."

A little of the glow went out of Bea's face. "She doesn't want me taking sick before the wedding, you mean."

Abner shook his head. "She didn't mention the wedding. She was only thinking about you."

Winslow sat quietly as the baker and the postmistress exited the church. The interaction had been simple and casual, but he had the feeling he'd just witnessed a sort of miracle. All the townsfolk had been trying to convince Bea that she wouldn't miss Birdie . . . when what Bea yearned to hear was that Birdie still loved her.

So simple.

He frowned at the memory of his conversation with Floyd. Things wouldn't be so simple at his house. Edith had been sneaking around on him, and it wasn't like her to be deceitful. Other than the occasional

Christmas or birthday present, he couldn't think of a single time she'd purposely hidden something from him.

When Winslow finally let himself into the parsonage, he noticed Edith had left the lamp in the kitchen burning. A foil-wrapped plate sat on the counter, with a note: *Here's your dinner, Win. I ate earlier.*

Sure she did.

He closed his eyes and took a deep breath. He and Edith had agreed never to confront each other in the heat of anger, and right now Winslow felt more irritated with his wife than he had ever been. Fad diets were dangerous, and she had promised not to do anything foolish. She had promised him and Dr. Marc, yet she had thought nothing of breaking those promises.

I'm not hungry, Win.

I guess the diet is working! My appetite is finally manageable.

Manageable, my foot! She'd been following every fad under the sun—cabbage soup and high protein, wieners and bananas. He could kick himself for his blindness. He should have noticed her bizarre eating patterns, but Salt's wedding and Olympia's death had distracted him.

Goaded by the realization, he moved into the hall. "Edith!"

No answer. He moved through the dark hall, then passed the guest bedroom. He should cool down before confronting her. Quarreling would upset her, but maybe she needed to be upset. Maybe she needed to see just how foolish she'd become.

The door to their bedroom was closed. He stood in the hall, his palms pressed to the wood, and slowly lowered his forehead to the painted surface. What if he lost Edith? He'd heard of people dying of heart attacks from taking too many diet pills and not drinking enough water. The human body was strong and usually adaptable, but it didn't take much to throw it off kilter.

If he lost Edith . . . he couldn't finish the thought. Their little town had lost too many people lately, and he'd suffered along with those folks. But losing Edith would be like losing half his body. She was his rock; his soul mate. She was the first thing he reached for each morning, and the last person he asked God to bless every night.

He opened the door a crack and peered inside the bedroom's dark interior. When his eyes adjusted, he glimpsed her tousled hair upon the pillow, her form beneath the mounded comforter.

She was either sleeping like the dead—unusual for Edith—or she'd heard him come home and was pretending to sleep.

Deceiving him again.

Wheeling on the ball of his foot, he marched back to the guest room and slammed the door behind him. She must have heard *that,* but still he heard no movement from the master bedroom.

He sat on the edge of the bed and kicked off his shoes, then grabbed a handful of the lacy decorator pillows on the bed and flung them to the floor.

Not once in the winding length of their marriage had he and Edith gone to bed mad at one another.

Tonight would be the exception.

Chapter Twenty-one

Edith had just tied the scarf under her chin Thursday morning when Winslow stepped into the kitchen wearing nothing but long underwear and an angry expression. He stared at her for a moment, then took a deep breath. "What's with the disguise, Edith?"

She stammered before his hot gaze. "N-n-nothing, Win. I was just going out for a bit of air."

"Don't lie to me. I know about the diet shakes in the restroom. I know you've been following fad diets when you promised you would eat sensibly."

Edith felt the room sway around her. Reaching out for the back of a chair, she met her husband's gaze. His face was hotter than a burnt boot.

"Now, Win—"

"Edith Wickam!" He slammed his hand down on the kitchen table "I have *never* been so angry with you." His mottled face flushed a deeper shade.

As her stomach gnawed at her backbone, Edith went on the defensive. "Who told you about my shakes? Floyd—it had to be big-mouthed Floyd!"

"He's concerned about you, Edith! As am I!"

"He's a gossip! Tell something to that basket, and it's all over town!"

"You're calling our mayor and good friend a gossip? You've lost your *mind,* woman."

"Have not." She drew herself up to her full height and smiled. "And I've lost weight. This morning I got into that peach dress—and it looks great. So now I'm done. It's over."

Winslow obviously didn't appreciate her proclamation of victory. "It's far from over, Edith. You lied to me."

She felt her smile fade as she looked at him. He was right about that—she had ig-nored his wishes and warnings and done as she pleased.

"I'm sorry," she whispered, recognizing the pain of betrayal in his eyes. "I thought it'd make you happy."

His eyes widened. "You thought risking your health would make me *happy?*"

"No, of course not. I love you, Winslow. I thought being slim would make you proud of me."

His eyes locked with hers as a muscle worked in his jaw. Edith wanted to fly into his arms and kiss away the hurt she had caused, but his expression had not softened.

She tried another tactic. "Please, Win, let's not argue on Birdie's wedding day. Tomorrow I promise I'll investigate Pound Pinchers and get myself back on a reasonable eating program."

"You don't have the will power. You didn't last on that program two days, did you?"

"I have will power. You wait, and I'll show you." She reached out to touch him and he drew back. The gesture broke her heart. "Win . . . don't be mad. I did it for you."

"Oh, yeah? So you won't mind if I take those cans you stashed in the restroom?"

For a moment her spirit rebelled—those were *her* cans, bought and paid for, and she'd gone through a lot of trouble to transport them—but then she saw the look in Winslow's eye and knew he wouldn't budge.

"Go ahead." She waved as if the diet shakes meant nothing to her. "Take them. Drink them. Serve them at the wedding reception. I don't care."

Winslow's head dipped in an abrupt nod. "Fine."

"Fine."

She stood, hands on her hips, as he moved toward the front door, then abruptly doubled back toward their bedroom, probably remembering that he wasn't dressed.

She turned toward the sink and clutched the edge of the counter, anger and grief welling within her. Why couldn't a man think like a woman? Why couldn't he understand how and *why* she'd suffered?

She found no answers in the heavy silence, no comfort but the sight of the cookies tucked behind the dish drainer. Sobbing, Edith turned on the faucet, then took out three cookies, chewing and spitting them under the water as tears rained down her cheeks.

She'd show Winslow. If he wanted to see will power, she'd give him will power. He had taken her diet shakes, so today she'd eat *nothing* until the wedding reception. There she'd look like a dream in her peach dress, and everyone in town would be pea green with envy.

* * *

At noon, Edith opened the parsonage door and peered left and right for a sign of her husband. Winslow hadn't come home since their blowup this morning, and he usually appeared promptly at 11:30 for his lunch.

Not that she'd be eating lunch today— she was going to take a shower and head over to the church to help the ladies decorate, then come home, do her hair, and slip into her peach dress.

With no sign of her husband, she closed the door, then padded to her bedroom. The peach dress, freshly pressed, hung on the back of the bedroom door, ready for the wedding celebration.

She took a moment to finger the silver-spangled lace that would adorn her throat in a few hours. She had never worked so hard for a dress, so wearing it would be extra-special. Once he saw her in it, Winslow would understand.

She moved into the bathroom, then turned on the faucets full force. Golden sunlight streamed through the tiny window and spangled the new floor, and tears swelled to her eyes when she thought of all the work Win and Stanley had put into this room last month. They had suffered, too, through the remodeling, but the result was worth it. Wasn't her diet the same kind of thing?

As steam began to mist the mirror, Edith slipped out of her robe and stepped into the warm stream. The pressure of the water on her neck and shoulders felt wonderful, easing away worries and tenseness. She tilted her head back and felt rivulets stream through her hair, rinsing away the thick shampoo she'd applied.

This shower had been a good idea—she felt hopeful again. And presiding over today's nuptials would remind Winslow of the preciousness and sanctity of marriage. After the wedding, they'd come home and make up. They'd never been able to stay mad after a tiff.

She stepped out of the shower, toweled off, and slipped into her robe. As she picked up her toothbrush, her hand began to tremble so that the brush slipped from between her fingers.

"Clumsy," she murmured, bending to pick

up the toothbrush. The room spun as she bent forward, and she saw the pretty new floor rising up to meet her when suddenly the world went black.

* * *

"You didn't eat a bite of your lunch," Cleta berated the pastor as he stood at the kitchen window, peering toward the church. He saw no sign of Edith, but surely she'd be along soon. No matter how upset she was with him, she wouldn't back out on her promise to help with the wedding decorations.

From across the room, Cleta continued to nag at him. "You're liable to keel over in a faint during the ceremony, Winslow, and won't that be a fine how-de-do? You need to eat something."

"I'm not hungry." Winslow had never spent a more wretched morning. He missed Edith, missed the security of knowing they were in tune with each other.

Cleta cleared the lunch dishes off the table. "Winslow, I don't know why you decided to eat lunch with us today, but I've a hunch all's not well between you and your missus. So take it from me—you need to go home and make things right. You look like a sick goat, and Birdie won't want a goat presiding over her wedding ceremony."

At the mention of the ceremony, Winslow glanced down at his shirt. He'd picked up his suit coat and trousers as he went out the door, but he'd forgotten to grab a tie. And until Edith left the house, the parsonage was anything but neutral territory.

He turned to the table, where Floyd was sipping a cup of hot coffee, fortifying himself, he said, for his last ferry run before the wedding.

"Floyd, can you run over to the parsonage and get me a tie? There's a nice black one hanging from the hook on the back of the bedroom door." His mouth twisted in a rueful smile. "You'll need to pick up my electric razor, too."

Floyd shot Winslow a look filled with meaning, then nodded. "Ayuh. I can."

At least Floyd understood what was going on.

In the cooler light of hindsight, Winslow realized he'd been hard on Edith this morning. He shouldn't have been so angry; after all, he knew what it was like to look in the mirror and be unsatisfied with the reflection.

A few months ago he'd undergone a similar crisis, but he'd been preoccupied with hair, not weight.

Maybe his own insecurities had fueled his anger this morning. In any case, he'd come down hard on his wife when she most needed understanding and sympathy. He'd go home and apologize as soon as he saw her begin to bend a little.

Cleta dropped a pot into the dishwasher, then slammed the door. "Floyd, sit down and enjoy your coffee. I'll go get the tie and razor. Unless I miss my guess, Edith could use a sympathetic ear about now."

Winslow threw Cleta a grateful smile as she moved toward the back door. "Tell her . . . tell her I'm sorry I was so harsh this morning, okay? And I'll see her at the wedding."

Cleta paused, her hand on the knob. "You could go tell her yourself."

Winslow shook his head. "Not yet. She's got to meet me halfway."

Cleta opened the door, sending a blast of frigid air into the cozy kitchen. "Hold your horses, fellers, I'll be back in a jiff."

* * *

Not yet. Edith shook her head as she fell deeper into darkness. She couldn't die yet; she had to apologize to Winslow. She blinked and opened her eyes, but saw nothing but distant pinpricks of light.

Good grief, was she having a near-death experience? Surely not! She hadn't been stupid enough to really do damage . . . or had she?

Gradually the darkness faded. Edith rubbed her head—a miracle she hadn't hit it on the bathroom counter during her fall—and looked around. What she saw made her mouth go dry.

She was in a large room with white walls and gleaming stainless steel fixtures. A shriveled, blue human body lay on what looked like an operating table across the room, and her heart froze when she recognized the sleeping face—

Hers. The body was hers, but if not for the shrunken facial features she would never have recognized it. Someone had cleanly cut down the chest and opened it like a book, two walls of flesh lay neatly on the left and right, leaving the bloody chest cavity open and exposed.

An autopsy?

"I am dead!" The words flew off her tongue—if she still had one—then the sound of gentle laughter filled her ears. She looked up to see a tall man standing before her, a surgeon, from the look of him. He had long white hair, tied neatly in a ponytail, and he wore a spotless surgical gown and plastic gloves. The eyes above his mask were smiling down at her.

"Where am I?" she squeaked.

The man tugged on his mask, then smiled. "You're dreaming."

"I'm not dead?"

He shook his head. "It's not your time."

"Then what—" she pointed to the dissected body on the table—"is that?"

"Ah." He glanced toward the body and smiled. "That is a visual aid. A lesson the Father wants you to learn."

A lesson? Edith stared at the stranger in bewilderment, then bit back a scream as his hand approached, growing larger and larger. The hand kept coming until it loomed over her, as big as a house, then it closed around something and lifted, sending her off-balance.

"Look," the stranger said, moving to a mirror. "Look at your true self, Edith."

She looked. And in the mirror she saw the

surgeon reflected, shining and bright, and in his hand he carried a lidded glass jar in which a tiny light gleamed.

Shock caused words to wedge in her throat. She was . . . Tinkerbell?

"No," he said, apparently reading her thoughts. "You're looking at your soul, through which the light of Christ shines. This is the eternal part of you, the part that can travel from an earthly plane to the spiritual."

"I *am* dead," she whispered, "and you're taking me to heaven."

The man laughed. "I would not lie to you, Edith. The Father does not deceive his children."

Instantly, a dart of guilt pierced her soul, and the light in the glass jar dimmed slightly. She had deceived Winslow . . . oh, may God forgive her!

"He will and he has," the surgeon continued, returning her to the shelf or whatever her bottle had been resting upon when she awakened. "He forgives you because he loves you. And now he wants you to walk with knowledge."

In a weak voice she barely recognized as her own, Edith whispered, "I want to."

"Good." The surgeon nodded, then tugged

his mask into place like a thousand doctors she'd seen on TV. He moved to a stainless steel tray on a stand and lifted out a pinkish organ the size of his fist. Edith remembered enough biology to recognize it immediately— a human heart.

He held it up. "Do you know what this is?"

Edith nodded.

"Would you like me to place it in your body?"

Stunned by the question, she looked at him. "Well, of course."

"Then I will. But tell me first—do you trust the Father to care for it? Or would you rather regulate its beating yourself?"

Regulate it? What good would that do? Was this man implying that a heart attack lay in her near future and maybe she should take control to keep it beating . . . no, surely not.

"How can I control it? I have to sleep, and I couldn't possibly regulate my heart while I'm sleeping."

"So you'll let the Father be responsible for your heart?"

She squirmed, feeling vaguely uncomfortable with this line of questioning. "Sure."

The surgeon turned, then lowered the heart into the body. She couldn't see the working of his hands, but after a minute the limbs had plumped with life. They were still blue, but they no longer had that shrunken look.

The surgeon swiveled toward the tray and lifted out two shapes Edith immediately recognized as lungs.

"Would you like your body to have these?"

"Of course," she muttered.

"Would you like to control them, or will you yield their control to the Father?"

Edith released a sour laugh. "He designed them, didn't he? I'd be a fool to try to work them myself."

"You are a quick learner." The surgeon dropped the lungs into the body cavity, fiddled a moment, then stepped back and nodded in satisfaction when the body pinkened with oxygen-rich blood.

Edith smiled in relief. The body looked healthier now, rosy and pink. Surely this was the end—

But no. The surgeon turned to the tray once again, and lifted out another fleshy object, this one shaped vaguely like a half-moon.

"Recognize this?"

Understanding flashed through Edith like a thunderbolt. "Ayuh."

"Good. Do you want it?"

"I'd be dead without it."

"True. Now—do you want to control it, or do you want to trust the Creator's design?"

Indignation flashed through her. "That's easier said than done! It's not easy to control your stomach when you're at a party, or a buffet, or traveling—"

"The stomach does not go out of control during those times—on those occasions I suggest you address the hands that wield the fork, or the tongue that lusts after flavor." He held up the stomach again, lifting it higher. "I ask you—do you want to control it, or do you trust the One who designed it?"

Edith closed her eyes. "I don't know how to control it. But I don't know how to let God take charge, either."

"Do you worry about your lungs?"

"No."

"If you are holding your breath, what happens after a while?"

She thought a moment. "Your lungs burn."

He nodded. "Even so, if you neglect your stomach, after a while it will tell you it is empty. If you eat too much, it will complain because it is overfull." The surgeon's dark eyes softened. "The Father's way is simple. His yoke is easy, and his burden is light."

Edith remained silent as his words froze in her brain. He was right—God's ways were always simple, always the best, always liberating. For the last month she had been following one set of man-made rules after the other, stuffing her stomach with things it did not want, much less need . . . and she'd remained unsatisfied.

"I'm so stupid," she said.

"No." The surgeon lowered the stomach. "You have been swayed by the wisdom of the world, the lust of the eyes, the lust of the flesh, and the pride of life. Repent of those things, and all will be well."

She closed her eyes as the truth resonated in her spirit. The lust of the eyes—hadn't that peach dress enticed her? The lust of the flesh—she had eaten because she wanted food; she had drunk thousands of calories of diet shakes because she craved flavor. The pride of life—she had wanted to look good for Winslow, yes, but mostly she had wanted to look good.

She had coveted praise and attention. And she had wanted to accomplish her goals on her own.

Such independent pride wounded the heart of God.

Again the gleaming surgeon held up the stomach. "Do you want this?"

She nodded.

"And do you want to control it?"

"No," she whispered. "But I want to be healthy."

"The creator designed your body to be self-regulating. Trust him."

He held the stomach aloft, his brows silently lifting the unanswered question, and finally Edith nodded. "I'll trust him."

And with that promise, the stainless steel table upon which her body rested began to glow. Edith bowed her head as the truth struck her—that was no table, but an altar. She had wrested control of her body from God, preferring to rule it herself, when all she was and possessed rightfully belong to God.

As she wept, beloved and familiar phrases filled her head:

And so, dear brothers and sisters, I plead with you to give your bodies to God. Let them be a living and holy sacrifice. . . .

Don't worry about everyday life—whether you have enough food to eat or clothes to wear. And don't worry about food—what to eat and drink. Don't worry whether God will provide it for you. These things dominate the thoughts of most people, but your Father already knows your needs. He will give you all you need from day to day if you make the Kingdom of God your primary concern.

"I will," she whispered, lifting her gaze to the brightness hovering above her. "I will trust you, Father, body and soul."

* * *

Cleta stepped to the parsonage door and knocked. No sound from within the small house, but Edith had to be home.

She walked to the living room window and peered inside. Nothing moved, but a light shone from the bedroom. Edith was home, then, probably running the hair dryer and hadn't heard the knock. Might as well go on in and do a bit of neighborin' while she fetched Winslow's tie.

"Edith!" she called cheerily, half-hoping she'd get the scoop about the couple's spat while she was running her errand. She walked into the house, crossed the living room, and moved down the hall, noticing the rumpled bed in the guest room.

She rapped on the open bedroom door. "Edith? You taking a shower?"

Silence from the bedroom and no sign of Edith, but the bathroom light was on, too. Stepping around the corner, Cleta opened the bathroom door wider—and gasped when she saw Edith Wickam lying unconscious on the bathroom floor, wet-haired and wearing nothing but a gaping bathrobe.

"Oh, spit!"

She lunged inside the room and placed two fingertips on Edith's throat. She knew less than nothing about such things, but this is what they always did on TV.

She felt nothing but cold and clammy skin. Cleta leapt to her feet and sprinted through the house, yelling as she ran past the church. Rounding the corner, she nearly tangled with Tallulah, out on her afternoon walk.

Yip!

"Sorry, Tallulah. Emergency!" she panted as her Nikes pelted the sidewalk.

Yipping in excitement, Tallulah raced by Cleta's side, keeping pace as the woman ran toward the medical clinic at Frenchman's Fairest.

Cleta and Tallulah flew around the corner to find Dr. Marc talking to Annie at the gate.

"Come quick!" Cleta bellowed. "Edith Wickam just dropped dead."

"What?"

Cleta waved her hands helplessly. "She's cold and wet and on the floor. Hurry!"

The doctor raced inside for his medical bag, then ran ahead of her toward the parsonage. Cleta followed, then halted at the church, bending low to clasp her knees as her lungs burned for air.

"You . . . go . . . on," she panted, knowing he couldn't hear her. "I'll . . . get Winslow."

* * *

An hour later, Winslow paced his living room floor as Dr. Marc examined Edith in the bedroom. Birdie, Salt, Floyd, Annie, and Cleta sat on the long sofa, all of them silently keeping vigil with pinched faces.

Dr. Marc stepped out of the bedroom and pulled the door closed behind him. Smiling at Winslow, he closed his medical bag. "She's fine, Pastor. She fainted. Probably the result of her dieting and fasting today."

Winslow slumped into the only empty chair. "She was *fasting*?"

Dr. Marc nodded. "Fasting, done properly,

isn't harmful, but Edith wasn't doing anything by the book. But she's seen the error of her ways, and she'd like to talk to you."

Winslow sprang out of his chair, gave the doctor a grateful hug, then ran into the bedroom.

* * *

The wintry shadows of late afternoon had settled across the bed when Winslow stepped into the room. He had expected to find Edith resting, but she was sitting on the edge of the mattress, mascara wand in hand. She halted when she saw him, then lowered the mascara brush.

"Win." Tears leaked from the corners of her eyes. "I feel like such a fool. You won't believe what I've learned today."

He sank onto the bed next to her. "What?"

She swiped at her eyes with the cuff of her robe. "I had this crazy vision—but it wasn't crazy, if you know what I mean. I was in this strange hospital, but I wasn't in my body."

Concerned, Winslow pressed his palm to her forehead.

"Win!" Laughing, she caught his hand and held it. "I'm fine, I'm not delirious. I won't bore you with the details, but I learned this—I'm not going to diet anymore, ever. I'm going to trust God with my body and stop trying to micromanage it. I may never wear the size I wore as a young girl, but that's okay—I'm not a young girl anymore."

Winslow slipped his free hand around her shoulder and brought her close. "I was hard on you this morning, honey. I'm sorry."

"I was a fool, Win—hardheaded and proud. I'm the one who should be apologizing."

She lifted her watery eyes to meet his. "How are our anxious bride and groom? I feel terrible causing all this commotion on their wedding day."

Winslow checked his watch. "Everything's still on schedule—or it will be when I step into the living room and tell them you're okay."

He smiled at his bride, and the peaceful look on her face moved something at the core of his soul. He reached out, tenderly grasping her chin, and was about to kiss her trembling eyelids when a wail from the living room chilled his blood.

Edith's eyes flew open. "What was that?"

"I don't know." Winslow stood. "But maybe we should check."

Holding hands, they moved into the living

room. Birdie and Salt had left to prepare for the ceremony, but Caleb had come up the road to join the gathering. Trouble was, apparently he hadn't brought good news. Annie was weeping, and Dr. Marc had his arm around her shoulder, trying his best to comfort her.

He threw Winslow a look of male helplessness.

"I'm so sorry, Annie," Caleb was saying. "She doesn't usually get into closets."

Winslow's gaze shifted to the old butler. He held a bit of purple fluff over his arm, and after a minute Winslow realized he was staring at the remains of a dress. An expensive one, if a man could judge by the amount of fluff and sequins attached.

"Tallulah," Caleb whispered, when Winslow caught his eye. "She got into the closet and started tugging on the chiffon. Next thing I knew, she'd pulled it off the hanger and had herself a rip-snorting time in all this fabric."

"It's my only nice dress," Annie wailed, burying her face in Dr. Marc's chest. "I don't have anything else with me."

Edith stepped forward and gently turned the weeping girl to face her. "Wait here," she said, the sweetness of her smile making

Winslow's heart pound in a double beat. "Don't move."

She stepped into the bedroom, and when she came out a moment later, an elegant peach dress, lacy and sparkling, hung over her arm.

"I think this is just your size," she said, placing the garment on Annie's arm.

A look of sheer wonder bloomed on the girl's face. "Oh, Edith! I couldn't! This is so pretty, you should wear it—"

Edith stepped back and slipped her arm around Winslow's waist. "It's for you, Annie. I think it's been meant for you all along."

* * *

At three o'clock, with an hour until the wedding of the year, Annie checked her reflection in the mirror one final time. The peach dress did wonders for her complexion, and the dress fit like a glove. She had promised Edith that she'd serve at the reception table; it seemed only right that she'd be doing a favor for the woman who'd stepped in and given so generously to her.

The day had been a busy one, and she and Marc had not had a chance to speak about personal things since their meeting in the kitchen. Though Marc had seemed to welcome her news about staying in Heavenly Daze, Annie feared she had said too much, too soon. But words were like feathers flung into the wind; once spoken, they could not be called back. Marc now knew how she felt . . . the next move would have to be his.

She heard a creak outside her door and glanced up to see Caleb walking down the hall, a cordless telephone in his hand. She frowned at the phone, "Does that thing work? I thought the batteries were dead."

A guilty look flitted over the butler's face as he halted in mid-step. "I replaced them."

"Why?"

"Well—"

The word had scarcely left his lips when the phone rang. Annie stared at it, her mind whirling, as Caleb smiled. "I brought it so you wouldn't miss this call."

He handed her the phone, then paused. "Annie?"

"Hmm?"

"The Lord will not leave you comfortless."

She shook her head as the phone rang again. It could wait, the important thing was

Caleb slipping into bizarre mode again. "What do you mean?"

"I plan to see Olympia very soon. And I will give her your love."

An eel of fear wriggled in Annie's belly. What was he talking about? He was elderly, but healthy. Surely he wasn't thinking about death.

She forced a light laugh. "Caleb, you're going to live thirty more years."

"I'm going to live forever, Annie. But before I leave, I want to tell you something."

The phone rang; she ignored it. "What?"

"Don't worry about Olympia's body. The Lord has heard your prayers, and he knows the intent of your heart. I can assure you of this—Missy no longer cares about such trivial things. Now—" he nodded toward the phone. "Aren't you going to answer that?"

Staring at him in bewilderment, Annie pressed the talk button. "Hello?"

The caller identified herself as Nancy Lipps, from the Nu-Skin Beauty Company.

"I'm sorry," Annie said, watching Caleb in the mirror as she reached for a tube of lipstick. "I really don't have time to hear a sales pitch."

Nancy Lipps laughed. "I'm not a telephone solicitor, Ms. Cuvier. I'm the vice president in charge of product development."

Annie's hand froze in midair. "And why are you calling me?"

"You may have heard about a new line of cosmetics that use foods as principal ingredients. All-natural makeup is very hot right now—cucumber eye soothers, banana fade creams, lemon hair rinses."

Annie glanced at the mirror. She could use the cucumber eye soother right now; her eyes were still bleary from weeping over the destruction of her favorite dress.

"I've read something about them."

"Good. Since you're in a hurry, I'll get right to the point. We read about your new hybrid in *Tomato Monthly,* and one of our researchers obtained one of the plants from your college lab."

Annie snorted. "I'm sorry, Ms. Lipps, but those tomatoes were a colossal failure. They're inedible."

"We don't want to eat them, Ms. Cuvier. They have an unusually high acid content, high enough to exfoliate the skin but not so high as to be harmful. Your tomato will be the perfect primary ingredient for our new all-natural facial peel."

Annie's jaw dropped. "You want to use my plants—"

"We want to buy the patent from you so we can have exclusive use of your hybrid. No one else will be able to grow them, of course, but we'll mass-produce them in our greenhouses and manufacture the peel in our laboratories. I'm sure you're not ready to discuss details at this moment, but have your lawyer contact ours. I believe negotiations will begin with a number in the high six-figure category."

Annie clutched the edge of the antique vanity. Six figures? Why . . . that was hundreds of thousands of dollars!

"My lawyer," she whispered, thinking of Edmund Junior. "Certainly, I'll have him contact you Monday morning, if that's okay."

"Excellent. Thank you, Ms. Cuvier. We're very excited about this product."

Annie hung up the phone, then braced herself against the edge of the vanity. Money . . . from one of her experiments! Why, she'd be able to repair the house, live in it, even restore it to its former grandeur! With that kind of money in the bank, she could live on the island and conduct other experiments on Heavenly Daze. Marc could keep his clinic in the guesthouse, and she could use the barn for her greenhouse. And Caleb could stay—

She looked up, eager to share her news, but the butler had slipped away.

"Caleb?" She stood and ran to the door, then took the stairs two at a time. She checked the kitchen, the parlor, the dining room, but the butler had vanished. His bedroom was as neat as a pin, the sheets stripped from the mattress and the closet . . . empty.

"Caleb!"

Running through the foyer, Annie threw open the front door and scanned the porch. No sign of the butler anywhere, not in the yard, on the street, or even at the dock. He might be in town, but Annie had a sinking feeling he had kept his word and left the island.

Caleb had never broken a promise.

* * *

Annie tucked the last silk flower into her hair and smoothed her peach dress, then descended the stairs . . . and saw Marc standing in the foyer.

"I wondered," he turned at the sound of

her steps, "if you would allow me to escort you to the wedding."

Her heart in her throat, she nodded. "If you really want to."

He smiled up at her. "I do."

Her heart warming, she went to the bottom of the stairs, then reached for her coat on the hook by the door.

"Allow me." Marc pulled the coat down, then held it open for Annie. "You look beautiful. Peach is your color."

"Thank you."

"But you also look a little sad."

"I am. Caleb's gone—he slipped out this afternoon, without even saying good-bye." Her voice wavered, and she drew a deep breath to steady it. "I can't believe he'd leave like that."

"Annie." Marc's voice was gentle. "He's been saying good-bye for weeks. You just didn't want to listen."

Pressing her lips together, she nodded. "People have been telling me things all my life. . . . I'm not the best listener."

"Then hear this." He turned her to face him, his hands resting squarely on her shoulders. "Are you quite sure you wouldn't rather have me as a father figure in your life? We are quite a few years apart, you know. We are at different places in life, and as dear as you are to me . . . well, I want what's best for you."

Lifting her chin, she met his gaze head-on. "I've had three fathers, Marc—my dad, Uncle Edmund, and Caleb, in his way. I don't need a father now—I need a partner, a companion, and a friend. I need someone who loves Heavenly Daze as much as I do, someone who will be happy to make a life here." She stepped closer to whisper in his ear. "I think you might be that man. Is that wrong?"

With a suddenness that surprised her, he drew her into his arms. When they kissed, it seemed to her as if she had finally and completely come home.

After a long moment, their lips parted. Still they stood together, foreheads barely touching, breathing each other's breath.

"Is that wrong?" His voice went hoarse. "Let's proceed carefully, and see where the Lord leads."

* * *

With Marc trailing behind her, Annie slipped into a row and found herself sitting next to Babette Graham. "The church looks lovely," she said, gazing at the orchid-studded ferns around the platform. Floral sprays, sprinkled with ribbon roses, adorned the end of each pew.

Babette nodded. "Yes, it is beautiful . . . and I'm pregnant."

Annie blinked. "Wow! Congratulations!"

Babette nodded slowly, not taking her eyes from the flower-strewn altar. "I'm still adjusting to the idea." A blush brightened her cheeks. "You're the first person I've told, besides Charles, of course. I guess I'm testing the water, trying to get folks' reactions."

Annie folded her arms, not sure how to respond. "Well—change isn't easy. But all in all—" she glanced at Marc—"I think change is a good thing."

At four o'clock, the lights in the church dimmed. Sniffling conspicuously, Bea began to play the introduction to the old song, "Because."

Wearing an orchid the size of New Jersey, Vernie clumped to the front and began to sing in a warbling alto:

"Because you come to me,
With naught save love.
And hold my hand and lift mine eyes above,

A wider world of hope and joy I see—
Because . . . you come to me."

Leaning forward in the pew, Annie caught sight of Stanley on the other side of the church. His gaze was fixed upon Vernie, and a wide smile lit his face.

Annie smothered a grin. Not every man would be proud of a rectangular woman singing in a purple dress and Army boots, but Stanley obviously was. Such was the power of love.

As Vernie sang, Pastor Winslow and Salt Gribbon walked out of the small room behind the piano. Stiffly, somberly, they moved to the front of the church and stood before the communion table. Salt kept his eyes fixed upon the swinging doors of the vestibule, but Annie saw the pastor cast a fond glance at Edith, who sat in her customary place on the second pew.

After two verses and a grand finale complete with high note and uplifted hand, Vernie sat next to Stanley, then threw a strong arm around his shoulders. Annie covered her mouth to suppress a giggle as Bea began to play the "Wedding March."

Annie snuggled into the curve of Marc's

arm as Cleta came down the aisle, followed almost immediately by Salt's grandchildren, Bobby and Brittany. The little girl grinned as she sprinkled orchid petals over the wooden floor, but Bobby marched with grave solemnity, his attention riveted on a pair of gold rings gleaming on his pillow.

"They let Bobby carry the rings?" Annie whispered.

"Those are gold plastic rings. Birdie glued 'em to the satin." Marc's breath tickled her ear. "The real rings are in Winslow's pocket."

Annie smiled. Weddings had always delighted her—there was something mysterious about the love that drew two people together.

Something mysterious and wonderful.

* * *

Edith felt her pulse quicken when Bea thundered out the dah da-ta-da that signaled the entrance of the bride. With the other guests, she stood and turned toward the back of the church, noticing for the first time that Patrick Gribbon had made it home just in time for his father's wedding. Still wearing his overcoat, he stood near the entrance with Floyd, who carried his captain's cap.

Bless Floyd's heart, he had taken time out of this frantic afternoon to make one last ferry run. Edith caught the mayor's eye and winked to show she bore him no hard feelings for sharing her secret with Winslow.

Floyd Lansdown was a good man and a true friend, while her husband—she turned to admire the man she had married—well, just thinking of Win set warm kernels of happiness a-popping in the center of her heart.

She smiled as Abner Smith came forward with Birdie on his arm. Before them, trotting like two well-behaved ponies, Tallulah and Butch pranced down the aisle, their necks adorned with floppy purple ribbons.

* * *

While everyone else automatically turned to look at the bride, Marc couldn't resist facing forward to study Salt Gribbon. The old fellow had lived the life of a recluse until only a few weeks ago, then God had sent a woman to enrich his life.

Birdie Wester had done Salt a world of good. His eyes sparkled with health, his outlook had greatly improved, and he carried himself with more vigor than Marc had noted in months. Furthermore, he couldn't remember the last time Salt had threatened visitors to the lighthouse with blasts of lima beans and rock salt.

Yes, love could be good for body and soul . . . even an aging body and a weary soul. He still found it difficult to believe that God might intend for him to find love with a young woman nearly half his age, but, as Caleb would say, the Lord worked in mysterious ways. . . .

Feeling Annie nudge his ribs, he obediently turned to look at Birdie.

* * *

In years of ministry, Winslow had seen his fair share of brides, but none could match the degree of radiance shining from Birdie Wester's face. That good woman had spent her life serving the Lord and her fellow man, and God had been pleased to bless her with a man who would treasure her throughout life and into eternity.

Could any woman ask for more?

Well, perhaps Edith could. She could ask for more patience from him, more understanding.

He looked to his wife, then felt his mouth go dry. Even in an ordinary church dress, she shone with an aura of peace and contentment.

He was a blessed man.

Knowing that a minister ought to pay some attention to the bride, Winslow shifted his gaze from Edith to Birdie. Wearing a knee-length ivory dress with a full skirt, she came down the aisle carrying her mother's Bible beneath a spray of delicate purple flowers. Wisps of white hair framed her face, and as Abner tenderly placed her small hand in Salt's rough palm, Winslow couldn't help but think of a delicate flower growing in the shade of a weathered oak.

When every eye turned to him, he lifted his little black book. "Dearly beloved," he began, "we are gathered here today in the presence of God and these witnesses to join this man and this woman in holy matrimony. If there be anyone here who would object to these proceedings, let him speak now or forever hold his peace."

"Heavens, Preacher, don't stop now!" Vernie called from the third row. "Time's a wastin'!"

Winslow bit his lip as the congregation

roared in laughter, then he winked at the bride and smiled at the groom. If he didn't hurry, Salt might pass out. The old gentleman had gone as white as a sheet.

"Marriage is an honorable estate," Winslow continued, quickening his pace, "instituted by God and blessed by our Savior by his presence at the wedding in Galilee."

* * *

Marriage! Salt felt a shiver go up his spine as the word echoed in the sanctuary. The seamen under his command would have laughed at the notion of Captain Gribbon marrying at age seventy, but no one could deny the simple truth—he loved Birdie Wester. He wanted to spend the rest of his days, no matter how many or how few, in the light of her smile.

God had been good to show him that man was not meant to be alone. God had been merciful to send a partner as strong and loving as Birdie.

* * *

Birdie felt her stomach sway when Pastor Winslow looked at her. She'd been doing fine by concentrating on her slow steps and thinking about the significance of the Bible in her hand, but now the pastor was talking right to her, personally.

"Do you, Birdie Wester, take Captain Salt Gribbon to be your lawfully wedded husband?"

Birdie felt the pressure of dozens of eyes as she turned to meet Salt's blue-eyed gaze. From her place at the piano, Bea blew her nose with a honking sound.

Birdie couldn't resist a grin. *Welcome, Salt,* she told her groom with her eyes, *to my family, to my work, to my bed, to my heart.*

"I do," she whispered.

The pastor turned to her groom. "Do you, Salt, take Birdie to be your lawfully wedded wife?"

His love's eyes shone bright with tears. "I do."

Winslow Wickam beamed a mega-watt smile over the congregation. "Then by the power vested in me by the State of Maine, I am thrilled to pronounce you husband and wife."

Then, while the people of Heavenly Daze rose to their feet in applause, the man she had always known as ol' Captain Gribbon drew her into his arms and kissed her thoroughly in front of God, her fellow residents, and who knew what else? Maybe even a smattering of angels.

* * *

After the wedding, the entire town celebrated in the church basement. Patrick Gribbon stood with his father, his children, and his father's beautiful new bride as Dana Klackenbush snapped pictures.

Annie noticed that Georgie Graham had been diverted from swiping icing off the wedding cake by special candy-sprinkled cupcakes Abner had baked just for the children. Georgie sat at a small table with Bobby, Brittany, and Zuriel, who was entertaining the children with stories of Daniel in the lion's den.

"He tells that story with so much detail," Marc said, leading Annie toward the punch bowl, "you would think he'd been there himself."

Bea, who carried a box of tissues and still occasionally blew her nose, ate cake under Abner's protective gaze. Across the table from them, Barbara and Russell Higgs were busy telling Mike Klackenbush and Buddy Franklin about the apartment they'd found in Ogun-quit. "The rent's really reasonable," Barbara was saying. "And there's room for growth . . . if and when the Lord decides to bless us."

Annie clapped with the others when, right after Birdie cut the wedding cake, Babette Graham admitted that yes, she was preg-nant. Cleta immediately threw an arm around her daughter, Barbara, and then, with tear-bright eyes, she congratulated Ba-bette and wished her well.

"And I hear," Edith said, whirling around to face Annie, "that you're not selling French-man's Fairest after all. You're staying with us?"

Annie felt her cheeks warm as she faced the townspeople she had loved for so many years. "Yes, I'm coming home," she said, accepting the glass of punch Marc placed in her hand. "Where else could I possibly find neighbors like you?"

After Annie and Marc had toasted the happy bride and groom with Vernie's cran-berry punch, Abner brought over a thin young man with sandy hair.

"Annie," Abner said, "I'd like to present Lionel Smith, fresh from service in England."

Smiling, Annie extended her hand. "What sort of service are you in, Lionel?"

"Whatever needs to be done," he said, clicking his heels together in an old-fashioned bow.

Annie stared at him thoughtfully. She wasn't sure when the fellow had arrived, but he could have come on the ferry with Patrick Gribbon. "What brings you to Heavenly Daze? Friend of the bride or groom?"

"Friend of Abner Smith," he said, glancing at Birdie's assistant. "I'm looking for a place of service, and I understand you might have a position open. I've had experience as a butler, and I hear yours has just accepted a new post."

Annie glanced at Marc. She'd never thought about employing another butler. Caleb had been a part of the family, but butlers were more a part of Olympia's generation than hers.

"I'm not sure I'll need a butler." She shrugged slightly. "I'd like to think I can handle my own cooking and cleaning."

The young man gave her a broad smile. "Did I mention I'm also handy with a hammer, caulking gun, and paintbrush? I've also a gift with plants." He pressed one hand to his chest. "I hope that doesn't seem immodest, but the Lord has given me a unique gift with growing things. I don't really expect wages, but if you'll allow me to putter in your soil, I'd appreciate the opportunity to serve. I've a particular fondness for growing zucchini—"

"You're hired." Grinning, Annie lifted her glass. "First house off the dock, your room will be on the first floor, next to the kitchen. Welcome to Heavenly Daze."

The young man lifted his glass, too. "Thank you. Such a blessed place . . . already I feel at home."

"I know what you mean." Annie let her gaze rove over the dear faces of all those who called the island home. "I know this isn't heaven, but sometimes I think this town is the next-best thing."

Epilogue

Olympia arrived two days after the wedding. Salt and Birdie were the first to spot her; the newlyweds had been walking hand-in-hand on the beach when Salt spied the box washed up on the southwestern shore, in near-perfect condition.

They hurried the news to Frenchman's Fairest, whose occupants spilled out at once to set things right. While Annie blustered in confusion, Lionel Smith arranged to have the casket brought safely ashore. With Captain Stroble back on the job, Dr. Marc sent for a backhoe, and within twenty-four hours, Olympia's mortal shell rested beside Edmund's in the Heavenly Daze cemetery.

At our angel meeting the next Sunday night, Lionel told me that Annie struggled to make sense of the odd situation. Why had

God allowed Olympia to take that bizarre journey when it would have been so much simpler to bury her properly the first time?

Lionel answered her with heaven-sent wisdom: Who are we to question the mind of the Almighty? For through the ordeal of Olympia's mishap, Annie learned lessons in faith and patience . . . and from the portals of heaven, Olympia had learned about eternal priorities. We do not stop learning at the threshold of heaven, after all.

Annie was right—the one constant in Heavenly Daze is change. We have said farewells to several people over the last few months, but we've also made new friends. And those from whom we've parted are not truly gone—most of them are watching from the balconies of heaven, cheering as we run the course and endure till the end.

Those of us who remain live and learn and grow more like the Savior. Through love, we experience joy and sorrow. We weep when our hearts grow too full for words and we celebrate with those who rejoice. We bid reluctant farewells, entrusting much-loved souls to the Father's care, and we extend our hands to new members of the family.

And with every rising sun, we know that

the Father is faithful. As the Master said, "If God cares so wonderfully for flowers that are here today and gone tomorrow, won't he more surely care for you? . . . Don't worry about food—what to eat and drink. Don't worry whether God will provide it for you. . . . He will give you all you need from day to day if you make the Kingdom of God your primary concern."

My angelic brothers and I have been given the task of making Heavenly Daze our concern . . . but others of our angelic brotherhood have been charged to watch over *you*. Tread carefully, with eyes and ears tuned for the eternal, because the rustle you hear on the wind may be the sound of your immortal guardians winging their way to the Lord of all.

It is my prayer—mine, and all my brethren's—that you would richly dwell in the wondrous grace of Christ Jesus and look forward to the real joys of heaven.

Until we meet again, in this world or the next, I wish you restful nights and heavenly days.

—Gavriel

Edith's Chocolate Chess Pie

$1^3/_4$ cup sugar
$^1/_3$ cup cocoa
$1^1/_4$ cup butter, melted
4 beaten eggs
$^1/_4$ cup evaporated milk
1 teaspoon vanilla extract
2 unbaked pie shells

Thoroughly combine the sugar, cocoa, and butter, mixing well. Add eggs, evaporated milk, and vanilla extract. Mix thoroughly, then pour into unbaked pie shells and bake at 350 degrees for 35 minutes or until done.

This is *some* rich and delicious! Enjoy!

If You Want to Know More About . . .

- The angels' song of praise: Psalm 89:1–15

- Angels having their own language: 1 Corinthians 13:1

- Angels as servants and messengers: Genesis 24:7, Exodus 23:20, Hebrews 1:14

- Angels are as "swift as the wind" and "servants made of flaming fire": Hebrews 1:7

- Angels' special care for children: Matthew 18:10

- Angels as protectors: Psalm 91:11–12

- Angels eating manna, the heavenly food: Psalm 78:24, 25

- The marriage supper of the Lamb: Revelation 19:7; Luke 12:35–38

- Souls of children in heaven: Matthew 19:14

- Animals in heaven: Revelation 19:14

- The heavenly throne room: 2 Chronicles 18:18, Psalm 89:14, Psalm 11:4, Revelation 4:1–6

- Angels' limited knowledge: Matthew 24:36

- Angels eagerly watching humans: 1 Peter 1:12

- The third, or highest, heaven: 2 Corinthians 12:2, Deuteronomy 10:14, 1 Kings 8:27, Psalm 115:16

- A man should leave his father and mother and cleave to his wife: Ephesians 5:31

- Those who have died watching us: Hebrews 12:1

- What happens when we die: 2 Corinthians 5:8; Philippians 1:23, 1 Thessalonians 4:13–18